THE REVENGE

GENOSKWA
BOOK TWO

HEATH STALLCUP

Edited by Sheila Shed

Cover by Jeffrey Kosh Graphics

AUTHOR'S NOTE

Every once in a while, I'll create something that I'm really proud of. Almost like it was near perfect right out the bag. I'm not saying that *Genoskwa* was perfect by any means, but I liked the ending. It felt like it left doors open, but still had a certain finality to it.

The Beta readers loved it and asked for more. They wanted it to be a series, or at least a trilogy. I couldn't see creating a series without it getting really weird. I would have to assume too much from the creatures' POV for it to work, and I just wasn't ready to dip into that pool.

With that said, here's the sequel to the first, and hopefully it will lead me to a place where a third, unique story can be created. I hope you enjoy the journey.

1

FBI Field Office, Albany, NY

Division Director Mike Davidson rummaged through the stack of papers on his desk and cursed under his breath. “Mitch!”

Agent Mitch Webber rolled his chair to the Director’s door. “Yeah, boss?”

“The tactical teams are standing by for the briefing and I can’t find the—”

“The shelf behind you, sir.” Mitch nodded to the files laying haphazardly amidst the clutter on the bookshelf.

Director Davidson sighed heavily as he snatched the files from behind him. “This is going to be a Grade A clusterfuck.”

Mitch slowly stood from his chair and pushed it back towards his cubicle. “Uh, sir?” He nodded towards the elevators. “Archer just got here.”

Davidson hid the smile that threatened to cross his lips. "I knew he'd have a change of heart." He scooped up the files and pushed his chair out of the way. "Make sure the coffee's hot and the copies are standing by for each team leader."

"Yes, sir." Mitch turned and trotted towards the break room as Director Davidson stepped out of his office and towards the conference room.

He pushed the door open with his shoulder and was happy to see the number of team leaders scattered around the room. Each man had brought his second along for the briefing. "Sorry I'm running behind." Director Davidson walked to the front of the conference room and set down the stack of files. "I know that those of you who were given the inside scoop probably have a lot of questions—"

"Tell me it's not really Bigfoot," Chad Wilkins interrupted.

Director Davidson tapped the top of the files gently and glanced across the room. When his eyes met Archer's, he noted the man had raised a brow at him, waiting for the explanation to come.

Director Davidson cleared his throat and stood at his full height. "I don't know that the threat is actually the creature known as 'Bigfoot,' but—"

"That's lawyer speak, Director," David Ford interrupted. "I'd prefer you give it to us straight."

Davidson nodded slightly as he reached for the clicker on the table. He pressed the button to lower the white screen and powered on the slide projector. "In short, yes. It *is* Bigfoot." He clicked to the first slide and a slightly blurry, large, hairy hominid stood in a clearing, holding a long stick in its hand. "They have rudimentary weapons, like this spear."

"For fuck sake," Terry Walker groaned. "This is not what we were trained for." He pushed up from his chair and nodded to his second. "Next you'll have us out looking for Santa Claus or the Easter Bunny gone wild."

Dale Archer stepped to the side and cut off Walker's exit. "You might want to sit down and listen."

Walker cracked a slow grin and cocked his head to the side, measuring the man before him. "Don't tell me you believe this bullshit."

Archer crossed his arms and raised a brow at him. "Sit down," he replied softly, "and listen."

"Take your seat, Walker," Steve Barlow stated firmly. "We all have orders to respond, and this is your intel briefing. You have no other choice."

Walker closed his eyes and leaned his head back, taking a deep breath. "I can't believe you're buying into this horse shit."

Jason Corbit, Walker's second, gripped his team commander's shoulder. "Let's hear them out."

Walker sat down heavily and made a waving motion with his hand. "By all means, carry on."

Director Davidson forcibly unclenched his jaw and turned back to the slideshow. "As I was saying, they use rudimentary tools, like this spear."

"It's a man in a ghili suit with a walking stick," Chad Wilkins stated plainly. "There's nothing near the subject to use for correlating size."

Archer ground his teeth and clenched his fists. He turned abruptly and marched to the front of the room. "If I may?"

Director Davidson stepped aside and Archer gripped the sides of the podium. "I'm the sole survivor of an encounter with these…devils" He took a deep breath and let it out slowly. "I honestly don't give two shits what you call them, what you think of them, or if you believe they're real. I saw what they did to Gamboa's JTTF team and to both squads of my tactical team." He scanned each of the men's faces before carrying on. "Director Davidson offered me a tac-team to go back out there and get our pound of flesh—"

"And I'm glad you've reconsidered," Davidson cut in.

Archer glanced at him and sighed. "I didn't. I'm not going back out there." He turned back to the team leaders before him. "I only came here today to do two things. One, to give you what little information I have so that you might be better prepared to survive what's about to happen." He cleared his throat nervously. "And two, to say goodbye to those of you that I know personally, because you are *not* returning from this op."

"That was highly unprofessional," Director Davidson whispered as he stirred his coffee. He made a quick glance around the room then lowered his voice again to Archer. "Why did you even bother to come in if you aren't going to lead a team out there?"

Archer blew across the top of the coffee mug before taking a sip. "I told you why. I'd never be able to live with myself if I didn't do everything in my power to prepare those guys for what they're about to face." He turned and locked eyes with Davidson. "So far, I don't think any of them believe a word I say."

"I'm about to pull up the government studies on these creatures."

Archer turned and stared with wide eyes. "Did you say 'studies'? As in plural?"

Davidson squared his shoulders and took a deep breath. "Apparently there was more than one." He turned and leaned on the counter and stared across the room at the different team leaders speaking amongst themselves. "Teddy Roosevelt ordered the first one." He took a sip of coffee and let the pronouncement set in. "There were a series of others performed over the years. They were even able to tag one of the creatures and map its migrating—"

"Wait a damn second." Archer gripped his arm and turned Davidson to face him. "They *tagged* one of those things? And they never bothered to go public with any of the information? How many people have gone missing in the woods over the decades that might have been prevented with this knowledge?"

Davidson took a deep breath and let it out slowly. "None of this was my decision, Dale. You're barking up the wrong tree."

Dale let the man's arm go and stepped back. "I can't believe they've known about this for…" he trailed off.

"Only a handful of upper echelon in the agency ever knew about this, and they were told to keep it hushed." He looked back at the team leaders assembled and shrugged. "I guess whatever secret they were wanting to keep is about to get made public."

"These are trained agents. If they're ordered to keep it quiet, it will remain that way." Dale's voice held more than a tinge of anger. "We both know that."

"Agreed." Mike Davidson adjusted his coat then

picked up his coffee. "And I don't disagree with you that the public has a right to know."

Dale watched him walk back to the head of the conference room and settle in behind the podium. With a slight nod of his head, the team leaders all took their seats again and Archer stood at the rear of the room, unsure if he wanted to know the whole truth.

The rest of the day was spent going over the previous studies of the creatures and their migrating habits. Had it been known to the government researchers that they were capable of making and using tools, their study summaries might have been different, and its priority bumped up. Every study seemed to end with the same conclusion: the creatures are highly intelligent, extremely shy, and do everything in their power to avoid human contact.

Archer listened quietly until the conclusions were announced then stepped forward. "That's not right."

All eyes turned to him as he approached the front of the conference room. "I spoke at length with Agent Red Moon, and he told me what he could remember from his grandmother's stories."

"Please, enlighten us, Agent Archer," Terry Walker said loudly.

Dale had to swallowed back an acerbic remark as he turned to the group. "There are different tribes of these...Sasquatch, these animals, and each group has unique characteristics." He picked up the printed copies of the studies and held them up. "Every one of these studies was performed in the Pacific Northwest. There's an entire continent separating these creatures from the ones we encountered."

"Your point?" Walker grinned, egging him on.

Dale set the study reports down gently and stepped back. "Never mind. You're all chomping at the bit to get out there and either bag yourself a Bigfoot or prove me a liar." He shot Walker a sardonic grin. "Maybe the next group—well, the one on deck, anyway, will be a little more eager to actually listen."

"Okay, that's enough." Davidson stepped closer and gripped Archer's arm. "I think you've accomplished what you set out to do. You're free to leave."

Dale spun on him and held a finger in his face. "We were warned." He pointed to the men seated around the table. "You're sending them into a meat grinder."

"Have a good day, Special Agent Archer." Davidson's eyes made it clear that he was excused.

Dale spun and exited the conference room to a round or murmurs from the team leaders and one slow clap from the back of the room.

As the briefing came to a close, Director Davidson handed out redacted copies of Archer's After Action Report. "Believe him or not, take heed of what both his tactical team and Gamboa's JTTF teams reported."

Walker scoffed as he tossed the AAR to the table. "If Gamboa's people are all dead, how was he able to report any of this?"

Director Davidson slid the report back to him. "Field notes, recordings, photographs, all were uploaded to a ruggedized computer in the field. That computer was recovered and verified Archer's report."

Walker slid the AAR into his file and stood. "I think

we've got enough information to formulate a plan." He glanced at the other team leaders. "Anyone disagree?" The other team leaders either shrugged or shook their heads.

Davidson stood tall and squared his shoulders. "Fine." He flipped to a page in his notepad. "Walker and Corbit, your team is Alpha. Wilkins and Langford, your team is Bravo. Barlow, Kilmore, your team is Charlie. Ford and Murphy, your team is Delta. McCoy and Palmer, your team is Echo." He flipped the notepad closed and eyed the last two men. "You'll be setting up the FOB, and since Palmer is rotary wing qualified, he'll be piloting the chopper."

Palmer grinned and whispered, "Yes!"

McCoy offered a fist bump. "It's about damned time."

Palmer stood quickly, "Director, I have to ask. Why did they decide to allow me to—"

Davidson held a hand up, cutting him off. "Normally, I'd say don't look a gift horse in the mouth, but the truth is, I wasn't told. I can only guess to the why, and that guess would be that they want to keep the number of people who could be potentially exposed to these…things…as low as possible."

"Understood, sir."

"We roll out at 0600."

Special Agent David Ford parked his Expedition in the underground parking structure and removed both of his tactical bags. He nearly jumped when Dale Archer appeared beside him.

"Don't sneak up on a guy like that. Especially when he's armed to the teeth."

Archer glanced around and quickly slid between the parked SUVs. "You were the only one to actually listen yesterday."

"Yeah, well we've known each other how long?"

Archer nodded quickly and lowered his voice. "Dave, you have *got* to have your head on a swivel out there."

Ford reached up and closed the rear door of the Expedition. "I plan to." He dropped the bags near the rear bumper and stepped between the vehicles. "Listen, I went through your AAR last night and I have questions. Did you ever figure out what was wrong with the drone?"

Dale shook his head. "We never even recovered it. Why?"

"I did a deep dive on the internet last night." He gave him a knowing look. "I mean, like, deep into the rabbit hole."

Archer's brows knit. "Okay…and?"

"There's all kinds of reports of electronics going screwy, batteries being drained almost instantly…all kinds of goofy shit when people get too close to these Bigfoots."

Archer felt his chest tighten. "And?"

"That got me to thinking. They tracked the migration patterns in the past, so I used that and did another deep dive. Turns out, there's a metric shit ton of lodestone along those migration paths."

Archer shrugged. "I'm not following."

"Natural magnets." Ford chuckled. "Some of those rocks are so magnetic that it can throw off radio signals, like the drone remote. It can cause all kinds of issues with other electronics, too." He offered a smirk and a knowing look. "I'd bet money that whatever these things are, they're sensitive to the magnetic fields, like a lot of other animals, and they use them to guide migration along the same paths."

Archer nodded as he processed the information. "Okay, well, that makes more sense than them being magic."

Ford gave him a questioning look. "Magic?"

Archer waved him off. "Something Red Moon said, about how things go screwy around them. His grandmother thought they were magical." He leaned against the SUV and sucked at his teeth as his mind rolled the information around. "Maybe you should say something to the others. Give them a heads up."

Ford scoffed. "They already think I'm not right in the head. I stood by your report. Told them I'd never known you to exaggerate, and I vouched for you."

Archer grinned. "Don't tell them it comes from me. Just tell them you studied the migration paths from the other studies and noticed there was a lot of magnetic fields that they travelled." He clapped the man's shoulder. "And you found the same thing in the Catskills."

Ford nodded slowly. "I doubt they'll listen. As far as they're concerned, this is a three day camping session for them."

Archer offered a sad smile. "Unfortunately, once they get there, they'll find out that isn't the case." He pulled the man closer and gripped his shoulder.

"Promise me you'll keep your wits. Stay vigilant. Stay *alive*."

Ford pulled him into a quick bro-hug. "Always, bruh. Always."

2

Deep in the Catskills

Walker barked orders as the sixty odd men set up the Forward Operations Base in a level clearing between the main paved road and the abandoned camp where Gamboa's team had initially made contact with the creatures. Tents were quickly erected and trees and shrubs were cleared along the periphery of the FOB to increase the line of sight in any direction to over a hundred yards.

Two dozen support personnel arrived via two ton military trucks and supplies were off loaded. A mess tent was quickly created and a logistics building was erected complete with long range communications and short range repeaters.

Special Agent Terry Walker made his rounds and gave each project a quick inspection as the men continued creating what was affectionately being called "Dog Town."

The chop-chop-chop of blades slicing the air caught his attention and he stepped towards the middle of the camp to watch as the support helicopter approached low and slow. He began making exaggerated arm movements, directing the Huey past the tents and to a makeshift landing pad.

As the craft's skids hit the deck and the engine began to power down, Walker was taken aback by the passenger that disembarked. A mixture of emotions flashed through his alpha male brain and he made a quick march towards the helicopter.

Director Davidson adjusted his BDU blouse and pulled a field cap onto his head. "Director? What are you doing out here?"

Director Davidson approached Walker and offered a wan smile. "It seems the main office insisted I oversee this operation." He sighed heavily and shrugged. "I tried to tell them that we had enough leaders out here, but they insisted." He glanced to the side then lowered his voice. "I think losing Bishop and Ostini out here has them all on edge."

"So they sent you?" Walker did a horrible job of keeping the disdain from his voice.

"We aren't born into admin, Walker. We work our way up from the front lines, just like you." Davidson clapped the man's shoulder as he walked past him. "Don't worry. I'm no micromanager."

"Son of a bitch." Walker groaned as he fell into step behind him. "As you can see, we've about finished Dog Town."

Davidson paused and turned to him. "Dog Town?"

Walker shrugged. "In the CAT skills, so…it just sort of happened."

Davidson chuckled. "Whatever keeps the men happy." He walked down a slight incline to the mess tent. "Tell me they have the coffee brewing."

"They do, but it just started, Director. We can offer instant."

"I'd rather wait." He turned and took in the collection of tents and hard-sided logistics center. "Coms are up?"

"They are, sir." Walker pointed to the array of antennas and dishes mounted to the top. "We'll even have satellite TV for downtime."

"Well." Davidson nodded to himself. "Isn't that special." He turned and began inspecting the array of tents. "And these are?"

"Five are team bunkrooms. Two are for support personnel. One is being used as a makeshift armory for storing ammunition and explosives."

The director turned to him. "Explosives?"

Walker nodded. "Yes, sir. In the event that this isn't just some fairytale, we intend to go in heavy and not let up until every last one of them is removed from the mountain."

"Explosives." Davidson slowly shook his head. "This is being lauded as a training exercise to the press."

"Don't worry sir. The state police have sealed off the highway ten miles in either direction of the road that cuts in here. The press will only know what we tell them, sir."

Davidson gave him a curt nod. "I want every able body that's weapons qualified armed at all times. Sidearms, if nothing else." He turned and squinted at the thick woods surrounding the FOB. "I also want perimeter watches set every fifty meters with regular check-ins."

Walker stepped in front of him and raised a brow. "I thought you weren't a micromanager, sir?"

"That isn't micromanaging. That's just taking the threat seriously and preparing for it, Agent Walker." Davidson turned and walked towards the logistics building. "Keep me updated, if you would."

Terry Walker watched the director disappear into the building and took a deep breath. "This is so fucking stupid."

Jason Corbit appeared at his side. "That's a kick in the head. You should be calling the shots, Terry."

Walker shook his head. "Actually, no. This is perfect." He turned to Corbit and grinned. "Now if somebody gets hurt out here chasing shadows, the blame rests fully on his shoulders."

Corbit returned the smile. "I like that." Suddenly his face fell. "But that doesn't mean we're actually going to let something happen, right?"

Walker held his hands up. "We're not going to *let* anything," he turned back to the logistics building, "but when you put this many alpha males in the woods with live ammo?" He scoffed. "Shit's inevitable."

"McCoy!" Walker barked from across the camp. "Echo is up for perimeter watch."

Les Palmer, second in command for Echo Team, stepped forward. "We just came off perimeter watch."

Walker offered a slow shrug. "Echo is assigned to the

FOB. Perimeter watch is part of those duties." He formed a slow smile. "So get to it."

McCoy gripped Palmer by the rear plate carrier and held him back. "I got this," he said softly. Randol McCoy stepped towards Walker and locked eyes with him. "The Director said we were responsible for setting up the FOB, not assigned to it."

"Yeah, well, now you are." Walker crossed his arms and smiled down at the shorter man.

"By whose order?"

Walker scoffed. "Mine."

He turned to leave when McCoy shot back, "Stand the watch yourself. We have more important things to do."

Walker spun on him, his face a mask of anger. "What did you say?"

McCoy smiled up at him, his hands balling into fists at his side. "I'm pretty sure I said it clear enough. But in case you're hard of hearing, 'Go. Fuck. Yourself.' Is that clear enough for ya?"

"What the hell is going on here?" Davidson shouted as he stepped out of the logistics building.

Walker continued to glare at the man in front of him with McCoy glaring back every bit as intently. "It seems that Echo leader here is ignoring a direct order."

"This isn't the Army, Terry," Davidson fired back. "Who gave the order?"

McCoy turned to him and hooked a thumb towards Walker. "He thinks he's in charge. He's placed my team on unending perimeter watch, and I won't have it."

Davidson towered over the pair and locked eyes with Walker. "Is this true?"

"Let me guess. This isn't micromanaging either?"

"Answer the goddamned question, Walker." Davidson kept his voice low as he stared at him. "Why are you making assignments?"

He spun and faced the director. "You told me to. You wanted perimeter watches every fifty meters, remember?"

"I remember. I don't remember specifying that it be only one team."

"You stated in Albany that Echo was responsible for the FOB." He gave him a knowing look. "That means that Echo gets to stay back and drink coffee while the rest of us march through the woods getting eaten alive by ticks."

Davidson rolled his eyes. "I told Echo that they were responsible for setting up the FOB, which they have overseen and accomplished." He turned to McCoy. "Your men have already stood watch?"

"Four-hour shift. It took all twelve men to stage fifty yards apart." He glanced at Walker and scoffed. "I'll be damned if we end up standing twenty-four hour—"

"No need to elaborate." Davidson turned back to Walker. "Let me be clear. Designating your team as Alpha does not give you rank over any other team leader, nor does it give you command over their teams. If you can't handle a simple thing like maintaining a watch rotation, then perhaps I chose wrong when I requested your assistance here." He turned back to McCoy. "Create a watch rotation and disseminate it to the other team leaders. Make sure you split the rotations up so everyone gets the maximum time for the main objective."

He turned back to Walker and stepped closer, lowering his voice. "What in the nine Hells has come over you? Do yourself a fucking favor and try to put yourself in other people's shoes. How do you think you'd react if Ford came over and started throwing his weight around, ordering your people to shit duty?"

Walker ground his teeth. "This was supposed to be my operation."

"And now I see exactly why HQ wanted an administrative person overseeing this." He stepped back and gave Walker a warning glare. "The bullshit stops now. Either you're a team player or you and your guys pack your stuff and leave now. Those are the only two options."

Walker's jaw flexed as he struggled to keep calm. "This is a fuckin'—" His words were cut off by a scream along the perimeter, and all heads turned to the noise.

One of the support personnel staggered towards the tents, both hands covering his face as blood oozed from between his fingers. Davidson and Walker ran to the man's side and gripped his arms. "What happened?" Davidson yelled.

"The trees!" The man tried to point and blood poured from his hands.

Walker gripped the man's arms and pulled them from his face before letting go. "Christ…" he muttered. "Medic!"

"What happened?" Davidson asked again.

"I dunno!" The man spat thick blood from his mouth and bent over as medics appeared at his side with first aid kits. "There was this horrible smell—it nearly curled my stomach. I turned to see what it was and something hit me in the face. If I didn't know any better, I'd swear it was a brick." He spat again and Davidson could have sworn there were teeth in the spittle.

He stood up and pointed along the trail of blood. "I want a team in there, NOW!"

Chad Wilkins called in Bravo Team and the twelve men geared up for insertion into the woods. "Load for bear," Wilkins stated, then paused. "Like, literally. Load as if you're hunting grizzlies. If these things are real, they're bigger, faster and stronger than any of us."

"And smarter," Rob Langford added. He stuffed the last of the magazines into his vest carrier then came to his feet. "Standing by."

"Let's do this." Chad tugged the tent flap open and ushered his team back out into the midday sun. "Stay tight, heads on a swivel."

Davidson stepped back into the logistics building and ordered the helmet cams brought up. The technician tapped at a keyboard and for a brief moment, twelve different helmet cams appeared on the large monitors. One by one, they began to go out, their images replaced with black and static.

"What the hell is going on?" Davidson quickly came to his feet. "Where's the feeds?"

"I don't...I don't know, sir." The tech tapped furiously at the keyboard but the camera feeds remained black. "They should be working."

"Get them back." He reached for his radio and keyed the mic. "Bravo Team, be advised, we have lost all signals from the helmet cams."

He stood to the side and awaited a response. "Bravo, this is Command, do you read?" Davidson shot an angry glare at the logistics team. "Tell me these were keyed in before we sent twelve men into the woods."

"They were, sir. We tested them this morning as soon as the building was erected." The technician wheeled to another computer and began tapping quickly at the keyboard. "I don't…I don't understand."

"Dammit!" Davidson threw the handheld radio to the ground and threw open the door. "Barlow! Prepare Charlie Team!"

Kilmore jumped to his feet and stepped inside the team tent. A moment later, both he and Barlow exited, speaking into their local coms. "We'll be geared out in five, sir," Barlow replied.

As the men disappeared into the armory tent, muffled gunshots echoed across the FOB. Davidson spun and stared in the direction the team had inserted into the woods and waited. A moment later it sounded like a war had erupted in the shadows of the forest with muffled gunfire and high-pitched screams that ended too abruptly.

Davidson felt his skin go cold as the sounds died down to an eerie and sickening silence. "Somebody tell me they have coms with Bravo," he said in a shaky voice.

A round of softly spoken negatives sounded far too loud as the entire forest had grown quiet. Even the insects refused to break the silence and the breeze refused to blow. He glanced at the tops of the surrounding trees and wasn't surprised they stood completely still.

"Ready, sir."

Davidson turned slowly to face Barlow and his team.

He nodded slightly then reached out and gripped the man by his plate carrier. "Find them. Bring them back."

"Yes, sir." Barlow gave him a curt nod, then had to physically reach up and pull the director's hand from his plate carrier. "We'll get them, sir."

Davidson watched in horrid silence as Charlie Team disappeared into the shadows of the woods. He hadn't realized he was holding his breath until the first shot was fired.

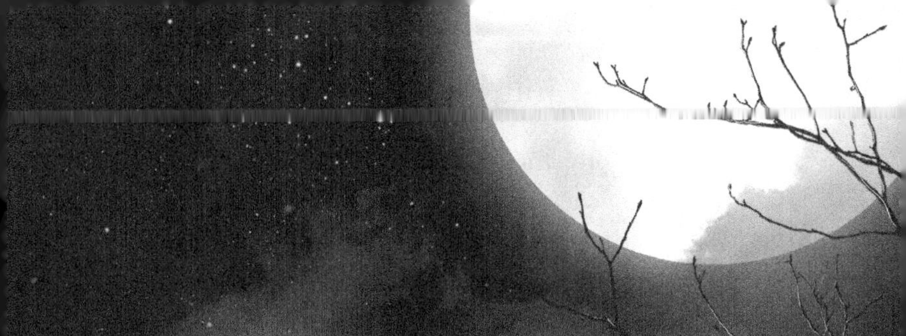

3

Agent Max Kilmore led Charlie Team into the woods, following the trail left by Bravo as he pushed through the thick underbrush. "This is crazy." He spat to the side after a small, leafy tendril dragged across his mouth. "It's too thick to—" His words were cut off as his feet slipped out from under him, landing him flat on his back. "What the hell?"

"Oh, shit," one of Charlie Team murmured as Max struggled to stand, his hands and feet sliding in a mysterious warm, wet, and slippery substance. "Fuck, dude, that's blood."

Max stopped struggling and brought his hand to his face. Blood mixed with rich, dark earth and pine needles coated his skin and most of his uniform. "Son of a…" his words trailed off as the realization struck him that he'd likely been break dancing in human remains. "Jeezus Christ!" He immediately spun to his side and struggled to stand.

"Don't just stand there," Agent Barlow barked. "Help him up!"

Max gripped the man's hand and pulled himself to a standing position as clumps of bloody mud fell from his uniform. "Goddammit!" He slung his hands to the sides, trying to dislodge the larger bits. "Tell me that's a fuckin' deer."

Steve Barlow knelt close to the ground and shook his head. "I think this was Langford." He used the tip of his knife to lift a torn fragment of uniform. The letters L-A-N were still visible.

Max felt bile rise in his throat and he swallowed hard to keep it inside. He quickly glanced deeper into the darkness of the woods and squinted at the shadows. "I think I see movement—"

With a low grumble, a thick, hairy arm gripped him by his chest plate and pulled him into the thicket as the startled agents behind him opened fire. Shooting blindly into the woods, the agents peppered Max's prone form as it hovered feet above the ground, his body absorbing the rounds that would have cut through the trees.

"Cease fire!" Steve Barlow yelled into his non-functioning coms. He pulled the mic aside and held his fist aloft. "Cease fire!"

As the shooting slowly rolled to a stop, Barlow pushed forward, stepping around the agent in front of him. He glanced up at the sunny sky then peered into the darkness, wondering to himself how shadows could be so inky during the midday. Instinctively he swept aside a small branch and tried to step over the gore that Max had fallen into, delving deeper into the thickness.

As his eyes adjusted to the interior of the forest jungle, his heart sank and he stepped forward without thinking. "Medic!" He slid in next to Max's still form and gently touched the man's neck, praying for a pulse. "I need a goddamned medic in here!"

Steve could hear the hurried rustle of boots across the littered floor and the snap of small limbs behind him and leaned to the side as one of his agents appeared, unzipping a portable medkit. "I couldn't feel a pulse." His words were barely whispered as he stepped back, wiping the blood absently on his trousers. "I couldn't..."

He turned away, certain that his friend was gone. The man's eyes were glazed over and staring up into the tree canopy, his body resting in an unnatural pose.

"Holy shit, boss. What happened to him?"

Steve turned and stared at his agent for a moment while a whirlwind of thoughts raced through his mind. "Maybe the fact that every last one of you opened fire without even zeroing your intended target?" He stepped closer and his jaw trembled with anger as he leaned in toward the younger man. "Range safety 101, O'Malley. Know what's beyond your target." He could feel the adrenaline surging through his system and had to take a step back. "How about just *seeing* your goddam target before squeezing the fuckin' trigger?"

"He's gone." The medic leaned back and reached for the medkit. "Never stood a chance." He zipped the bag closed and came to his feet.

"Something pulled him into the woods, boss." The agent nervously shifted his eyes over Barlow's shoulder. "I heard a growl just before—"

"We'll never know exactly what happened," Steve interrupted.

The medic appeared at his side and lowered his voice. "He was peppered with shots to his backside."

Barlow gave the man a curious look. "Shot in the ass?"

"Negative. He had GSW's all over his back side. From head to toe." The medic raised a brow at him. "Like something used him as a human shield."

"A shield?" Steve Barlow narrowed his gaze at the man. "Max was over two hundred pounds."

"Yo, boss," another agent nodded to him. "We have multiple trails through here."

Steve felt his chest tighten at the words and pulled the medic closer. "Assign two agents to take Kilmore's remains back to the FOB. Tell them to get their asses back rikki-fuckin'-tik." He turned and pushed deeper into the woods. "Show me these trails."

The agent hunkered low and peered across the ground. "At least two sets of tracks going east. More going southeast and something large broke through that row of brambles." The man pointed to snapped and crushed thorny vines. He reached forward and plucked a tuft of long reddish-brown hair from one of the vines. "If we're really out here hunting down bigfoots..." He let the sentence trail off.

Barlow stood to his full height and made a motion with his hand, converging his team. He broke them into three, three man groups and assigned them each a trail. "You saw what happened with Max." His eyes hardened as he spoke. "Coms are for shit, so keep your eyes on your team. No cowboy crap out here. Remember the mission, find Bravo...or whatever is left of them, and return to base." He gave them all a stern stare. "And for the love of god, watch your fuckin' fields of fire!"

"Stupid question, boss," O'Malley raised his hand

nervously. "If we find Bravo, radios are out. How do we notify any of the other teams?"

Barlow sighed heavily. "Three rapid shots." He locked eyes with the men and nodded slowly. "Locate Bravo or any evidence of them, three shots. The rest of us converge on the location." He looked up at O'Malley and raised his brows. "Good enough?" O'Malley fought the urge to smart off and chose to simply nod. Barlow made a circle with his finger. "Oscar Mike."

The three teams broke off and followed the broken trails into the forest as silently as they could. Each man could smell the fear radiating from their teammates and it only added to the apprehension. Each rustle of a leaf, snap of a twig or call from a bird had their adrenaline spiking.

"Hold up." O'Malley held his hand in the air and slowly bent low, peering across the leaf and pine needle litter on the ground. "I've lost the trail."

The two agents with him slid forward and peered over his shoulder. One pointed to the left and was about to respond when he was unceremoniously lifted from the ground by the neck. As he kicked and thrashed, his hands gripping the large hairy wrist at the back of his neck, he noticed his partner rising alongside him, a crushed gurgling sound coming from his throat as they both rose higher into the air.

O'Malley spun and stared at two large, thick, hair covered legs and slowly rose to a standing position, his eyes darting between his two teammates. In shock and unable to react, he suddenly snapped out of it and raised the barrel of his weapon.

The creature lifted a leg as thick as an oak and planted a kicking foot directly into O'Malley's chest, sending him reeling back and into the nearest pine. O'Malley slid to the floor of the forest, sucking forcefully, trying to pull air back into his crushed lungs. He barely noticed the two prone bodies thrown at his feet, their necks snapped.

He rolled over onto all fours and sucked harder to refill his burning lungs and would have screamed when he was lifted from the ground if he'd been able. His head snapped up and he was face to face with something that should not exist. For the briefest of moments, he'd forgotten that he couldn't breathe and held his breath.

The rough hand that covered his entire face was the last thing he saw before the sides of his head were compressed. He actually heard the bones of his skull crack under the pressure and an electric current coursed through his spine, jarring his senses before the burning sensation of torn flesh registered with his mind.

Just before everything went black, O'Malley had a simple realization as his head was effortlessly torn from his neck...he no longer felt panicked to breathe.

Agent James Dearborn paused every ten or fifteen feet and strained to listen to the surrounding woods. After the fourth time that he'd stopped the team, one of the other agents angrily cleared his throat. "We have a mission, Jim. We're never going to find Bravo if you stop us every two minutes." Dearborn shot Connor an angry look then motioned them forward again.

The forest felt alive around the three men. The wind

rustled tree limbs high above them in the canopy and insects buzzed them as they sweated in the warm, still air along the forest floor. Birds called out, searching for a mate or claiming their territory. Every sound was a warning that Dearborn was not prepared for.

He raised his fist in the air a fifth time and both of his teammates groaned quietly behind him. He spun and shot them hateful looks. "An entire tactical team disappeared in these woods just minutes ago and Kilmore was…" he trailed off, unable to repeat the carnage. Saying it aloud would make it real.

"Do you want me to take point?"

Dearborn had opened his mouth, a blistering retort ready, when the woods fell deadly silent. He held his mouth open as his eyes slowly scanned the shadows and he felt his tongue go dry. Fear-fueled sweat popped out on his forehead and he slowly turned back, his eyes scanning the trees for the cause.

"What the actual fuck?" Santiago whispered.

A low guttural grunt sounded to their right and all three men stiffened, their weapons coming to bear. "Tell me that was a wild pig," Dearborn whispered.

"Yeah. Sure," Connor replied. "Let's go with that."

Dearborn felt pressure build in his head to the point that he had to squint to keep his eyes open. He instinctively reached up and pressed a hand to his temple. "What the hell?"

The two agents with him were also feeling the pain, slowly lowering themselves to one knee, hands pressed to the sides of their heads. "I'm gonna puke—" Santiago bent over and began spitting as his mouth watered uncontrollably.

Connor suddenly stood and leaned against a small

tree, bending over and clutching his middle. The bile and spew that erupted was matched only by the liquid waste that filled his BDU pants.

Dearborn peered past his men and could have sworn he saw eyes staring at them in the shadows. He raised his rifle and pointed it in the general direction of the creature and squeezed the trigger. As the rifle spewed bullets into the shadows, Jim screamed, praying that the pain and pressure in his head would stop. He emptied half a magazine into the darkness and nearly dropped to the ground when the source of their discomfort ended.

Dearborn fell to his knees and sat on his heels as the marbles in his head reset and the waves of pressure that had formed in his gut subsided. He heard a crackle in his earpiece and instinctively touched the plastic mic. "Charlie actual, come in."

After a short static burst, Barlow's voice echoed in his ear. "Tell me you found Bravo."

"Negative, actual." Dearborn bent over and spit bile from his mouth. "We've had an encounter." He spat again.

"Say again? You're breaking up."

Jim keyed his radio again, "I repeat, we've made contact with the creatures." He turned and spat again then added, "I think I shot it."

Dearborn strained to listen but nothing came over the radio but static. He sighed heavily and plucked the earpiece out. "Coms are down again." He glanced at his men and realized that Connor had shit his pants. "Really?"

Connor's face flushed and he glared at his team leader. "Like I had any fuckin' control over that."

Santiago spat small bits of matter from his mouth then took a long breath. "What the fuck was that?"

Dearborn pushed up and onto one knee. "I read in Gamboa's report something about infrasound." He eyed the other men cautiously. "I think we just got our first taste."

"I can't do this." Connor pushed away from the tree and pulled his pack from his back. "I can't tromp through these fucking woods with…this." He motioned to the lower half of his body.

"Try to be quick." Dearborn turned and scanned the woods surrounding them. "You don't want to get caught out here with your pants down. Literally."

"You're not funny." Connor tugged his boots off then cursed. "It's in my fucking socks."

Santiago took up position to Connor's rear so that both men had him covered as he tried to wipe away the evidence and change into something cleaner. "Just try to hurry. I have a very bad feeling about this."

Dearborn brought his rifle to his eye and scanned through the scope. "Switching to IR." He flipped the switch on his optics and the forest lit up with various colors.

"IR won't work during the day, Jim." Santiago grumbled. "Too much heat from above."

"Actually," Jim replied quietly, "I'm picking up something." He lowered the gun and sighed. "And it's gone."

"Probably a squirrel," Connor stated as he tugged a fresh pair of pants on and buttoned them. "The bushy tailed rats are thick out here." He bent to retrieve his boots then screamed abruptly.

Both men spun in time to see his hands disappear under a thick stand of brush as he was dragged away, fingers clawing at the earth until they were out of view.

"What the hell!?" Santiago yelled as he ran to the bushes and tried to peer through them.

A short scream by Connor was quickly ended with a gurgling sound and Dearborn felt bile rise in his throat again. "Come on." He pulled a machete and tried to hack at the brush, attempting to follow Connor's trail.

Santiago gripped his arm and pulled him back, his eyes rising up and behind the thicket. "Holy mother of…"

Dearborn followed Santiago's eyes and strained to look up at a creature that he couldn't even imagine. The beast as at least ten feet tall with thick, hair-covered arms and a chest that looked like rock. "What the hell?" He raised his rifle and found himself falling hard to the ground as his feet were pulled back and out from under him.

As his face impacted the forest floor, he saw Santiago being lifted from the ground by another creature and slammed into the nearest tree. A moment later and Dearborn felt his body being dragged over the litter-covered floor of the forest, jagged rocks tearing at his stomach as he was yanked at a rapid pace.

He tried his best to twist in the rock-hard grip, his hand struggling to pull his sidearm from his drop leg holster, but the jerking motion of the creature dragging him made it nearly impossible.

When the monster stopped dragging him, Jim slapped at his holster and had just gripped the weapon when the beast grabbed an ankle in each hand and lifted him from the ground as easily as one might a water hose, snapping it hard and beating the agent mercilessly against a rock outcrop.

Jim had nearly blacked out the first time his body impacted the immovable stone but fought to remain conscious. He could see the darkness forming along the edges of his vision as he tried to raise the pistol to his intended target but lost his grip when the creature lifted him a second time and whipped his body against the rock again.

Jim's head lulled to the side and his vision went black as he was lifted a third time. Luckily, he didn't feel the back of his head give in when it came into contact with the outcropping.

4

Deep in the Catskills

Charlie Team Leader Steve Barlow cursed under his breath when rapid fire echoed through the woods. He turned to try to pinpoint the direction of the source and instinctively keyed his coms. "This is Charlie Actual. Report!"

"Charlie actual, come in." Dearborn's voice was static-laced in his ear.

Barlow felt hope rise in his chest. "Tell me you found Bravo."

"Negative, actual." Dearborn's reply was barely understandable with the static. "We've had >shhhkt< an encounter."

Barlow cursed under his breath. "Say again? You're breaking up."

The broken reply was barely coherent. "I repeat, >shhhkt< contact with >shhhkt< creatures."

"Dearborn, say again. You're breaking up!" Barlow

held his breath and strained to listen. "Say again your last!"

The three men stood silently in a small clearing, straining to listen to their broken coms. Steve Barlow looked up at the other two for verification but both men shook their heads. "Negative read, boss." Jake Bigelow shrugged slightly. "I couldn't even tell it was Dearborn until you said his name."

"Same here," Hank Johansen added. "All I got was static."

Steve Barlow hung his head and clenched his jaw. "It sounded like they'd made contact with something out here." He stood to his full height and scanned the area. "Anybody catch which direction that came from?"

Hank turned and pointed to the east. "Out that way, but the trees redirected a lot of the sound."

Jake nodded slowly. "My best guess as well." He slung his rifle up onto his shoulder and raised a brow. "We're coming up a big goose egg out here, boss. Do you want to go and see what the hubbub was about?"

Barlow sighed and stretched his neck. "I have a feeling I already know what we'll find." He spat to the side and wiped his brow with the back of his sleeve. "But we may as well check since we're in the neighborhood."

He turned and began to trudge in the general direction of the gunfire. Jake trotted up beside him. "What do you think we'll find?"

Barlow raised a brow at him. "Come again?"

"You said you felt like you knew what we'd find. I'm curious what that is."

Steve took a deep breath and let it out slowly. "Let's

just say my gut tells me that this is now a recovery mission."

"Recovery?" Hank interjected. "For Bravo or Dearborn?"

Steve thought for a moment then tightened his grip on the rifle. "Yep."

HANK bent low and poked at the discarded trousers with the tip of his knife. "Somebody shit their pants."

Barlow scratched at the side of his head absently. "Something scares the shit out of them, literally, and in the middle of being scared—"

"Or fighting," Jake interrupted.

Barlow nodded. "Or fighting, they had the time to pull their pants and boots off?"

Hank held the pants up and peered at the inner waist band. "Connor." He let the pants slide off the tip of his knife and land with a wet splat. He wiped the blade on the nearest tree and shoved the knife back into its scabbard. "Something doesn't look right."

"None of this looks 'right.' It's hokey as shit." Barlow bent low and tilted his head, trying to read the trail. "There. Somebody was dragged that way, under the bushes."

Jake squatted and studied the disturbed ground. "Whoever it was, they clawed like hell." He leaned forward and planted his fingertips into the trails left behind. "That's one."

Hank leaned close and pulled a shred of black material from a nearby tree. "I think somebody impacted here."

Barlow narrowed his gaze. "Impacted?"

Hank nodded, holding up the shred of black material. "Part of our BDU uniform was caught on this small limb." He pointed to the height. "Nobody on the teams is tall enough for it to be from brushing past." He pointed to a small, broken branch facing them. "This one has blood on the tip, and if you look behind the tree, none of the other branches were disturbed."

"I'm not seeing it." Barlow slowly came to his feet. "Show me what you're thinking."

Hank used two hands and gripped an imaginary person by the chest, lifted and slammed into the tree. "Like so." He cocked his head to the side and peered further up the tree then behind it. "Ah. Over here."

Hank slid part way down a shallow embankment and bent low. When he stood again he held a government issue M4 in his hand. "My guess is that whoever was beaten against the tree, lost this."

"We can track the serial number." Barlow extended a hand and gripped the weapon. He pulled his camera and took a picture of the serial number before slinging the weapon over his shoulder. "Just in case I don't make it back with the weapon itself."

"What now, boss?" Jake asked as he nodded towards the thick bushes. "Do we follow the fingertracks?"

Barlow took a deep breath again and slowly nodded. "We've got nothing else to go on." He spun a slow circle and strained his eyes to find movement in the shadows. "We haven't seen hide nor hair of Bravo. Most of our team is MIA. The only clue we've found so far is this."

"Follow the yellow brick road," Jake whispered as he

came to his feet. He leaned closer and stared at the thicket. "Somebody hacked at this. Recently." He plucked a thorny vine and held it out. "That's a fresh cut."

Barlow studied it for a moment then dropped it. "Copy that." He nodded towards the thicket. "Shall we?"

FOB Dog Town

Director Davidson paced nervously in the logistics building, pausing from time to time to stare over the shoulder of a tech as they worked tirelessly to try to restore coms or helmet cams.

"Sir, you're making them nervous." Randol McCoy, Echo Team Leader gently gripped the man's arm and pulled him back. "They're working as fast as they can."

Director Davidson sighed heavily and stepped away. "There hasn't been any more gunfire reported out there, has there?"

"Negative." McCoy looked around nervously and pulled the director aside. "After Barlow's men brought back Kilmore's body, I ordered the other two men to stand down. Until we can reestablish coms or get some idea of what's going on out there, I felt it necessary to protect every asset we had. I didn't want two men tromping aimlessly through the woods alone."

Davidson stared at the man a moment then slowly nodded. "That makes sense, but I can't help but wonder if Barlow is out there, right now, waiting on those men to return to fill in a fire team."

McCoy shrugged slightly. "Understood, sir. But the last they heard before they left the woods was Barlow breaking the team into three, three-man groups. I don't think he's waiting on these two to return."

Davidson turned and pushed the door of the logistics building open with McCoy on his heels. "Where are these two men?"

McCoy pointed to the mess tent. "Coffee, sir."

Davidson stepped into the mess tent and was immediately greeted with the sounds and smells of food cooking. Barlow's two agents stood when they saw him approaching. "Tell me what you saw."

The two glanced at each other then shrugged. "I didn't actually *see* anything."

"How did your 2IC get killed?"

The two men seemed to deflate. "Gunfire, sir."

Davidson raised a brow. "The wood apes have guns now?" The sarcasm wasn't missed.

One of the men stepped forward. "Kilmore was on point. He heard something and broke away, going deeper into the woods when something picked him up and pulled him in." He cleared his throat nervously. "The team panicked and opened fire."

The second man stepped forward. "Everyone was on edge like you wouldn't believe. Bravo had just disappeared and there was this smell and..." he trailed off.

"We fucked up." The first man squared his shoulders and stood at attention. "We fired without knowing the location of our target, or what might lay beyond it."

Davidson sighed heavily and wiped a calloused hand

across his worried face. "So, Kilmore was killed by friendly fire."

"If he wasn't dead already, sir," the second man replied quietly. "Whatever it was that grabbed him, lifted him with one arm and held him aloft like he weighed nothing."

"Did you see what grabbed him?" McCoy asked.

Both men shook their heads. The second man finally met his gaze. "I thought I saw a hairy arm, but it was so fast that I can't be sure what I saw."

"You realize that there will be disciplinary actions taken for your conduct?" Davidson stated more than asked.

Both men nodded, their eyes averted.

McCoy turned and faced the director. "Let's worry about that bridge when we come to it. We need Steve to return and file his AAR."

Davidson nodded absently. "You're not wrong." He glanced again at the two men then turned for the opening in the tent. "But even if Barlow doesn't return, they've hung themselves by their own admission."

"When we come to it, sir," McCoy repeated.

Deep in the Catskills

Hank held a fist in the air and bent low, scanning the surrounding area. "I hear something."

Barlow sidled in next to him. "What are you hearing?"

Hank slowly turned his head, allowing both ears to listen. "I think it's the FOB."

Jake pulled his topomap and compass. "Fuck." He clipped the cover back on the compass. "Needle is spinning like a fan blade."

Barlow held a hand out, stopping him. "Hold on." He stood slowly and tried to scan beyond the short incline ahead of him. "I hear something too."

Jake folded his map and shoved it back into his vest pocket then did a double take when something dark and wet dripped onto his arm. "What the…" He craned his neck to look up and gasped. "Yo, boss."

"Not now." Steve Barlow placed a booted foot on the edge of the incline and reached for a small sapling to help pull himself up.

"No, boss," Jake's voice cracked. "Look up."

Steve Barlow turned and stared up into the tree canopy. It took his eyes a moment to adjust and another moment for his brain to register what he was looking at. "Oh, dear god."

Hank shifted and craned his neck to look then lost his footing and slid to his back. "Holy shitrocks!"

Hanging from tree limbs high above the three men were the missing members of Bravo and possibly some of their own team; it was difficult to say. Human bodies hung upside down, many tied to the branches by their own entrails, like human wind chimes.

"I think I'm gonna be sick," Hank groaned as he slowly pushed back over.

Steve Barlow reached for his phone and quickly snapped off a handful of pictures. "Okay, okay, let's go. It sounds like the FOB is just beyond this hill. We gotta to report this."

Jake glanced around the area and slowly shook his head. "The FOB should be the opposite direction. I know my compass is fucked, but my internal compass tells me that we—"

"Move!" Barlow's anger was manifest in his voice. "If your internal compass is right then we'll backtrack."

"And pray we don't run into whatever did that to the teams." Hank spat to the ground.

"Right." Barlow reached for the sapling again and pulled himself toward the top of the small hill. "If that is the FOB, somebody try the short range coms again."

Jake keyed his mic, "Charlie Team to Command, come in Command." A blast a static filled his earpiece but no voices were mixed with the white noise. "Nothing, boss."

Barlow reached the summit of the short hill and peered through the leafy foliage. He could just make out people milling about near tents and sighed heavily. "Hank, you were right." He stepped forward and used his arms to push through the dense vegetation.

As he erupted from the thick overgrowth, he dragged his boot in the loose soil, marking the entry to where the bodies were hanging.

"Halt and be recognized!"

Steve Barlow turned slowly and faced the sentry now pointing a rifle in his direction. "Really? Do I look like a fucking bigfoot to you?" He unsnapped his helmet and plucked it from his head. "Where is Davidson?"

The sentry stiffened, then turned and pointed to the logistics building. "Last I saw him, he was in there."

Hank and Jake brushed past him as they trudged towards the tent, their ordeal temporarily over. The weight of losing so many comrades wore heavily on their shoulders.

The sentry stepped closer and cradled his weapon. "Any sign of Bravo?"

Barlow hung his head a moment and took a deep breath. He slowly began to nod. "Yeah." He glanced back at the thick woods and hooked his chin toward the shadows. "We'll need a recovery team."

5

FOB Dog Town

"We're going to need a morgue." Davidson raised a brow to McCoy, hoping the man could figure out where they could store the bodies.

"Use Bravo's tent," Terry Walker scoffed. "It's still theirs, after all."

Director Davidson felt his temper flare but McCoy quickly tamped down the flame. "No, that's actually a good idea." He stepped between the two men and met Davidson's glare. "It works. It's on the far end so the smell shouldn't bother too many as long as the wind cooperates." He nodded understandably. "It works."

Davidson took a deep breath and let it out slowly. "We're going to need more body bags."

Walker made a show of checking his fingernails. "So maybe ol' Archer was right." He kicked off from his chair and came to his feet. "These critters are going to separate the wheat from the chaff. Only the best are gonna be able to take down these cavemen." He smiled broadly and held his arms aloft. "My team is ready."

McCoy couldn't keep his own anger in check and spun on the man. "Maybe you should just go ahead and gear up then you sorry—"

"That's enough!" Davidson interrupted. He reached out and pulled McCoy back. "Now isn't the time to go off halfcocked. We need a plan here."

"I already got you a plan, director." Walker sneered at McCoy as he walked past him. "Let me and my team gear up and insert." He paused long enough to smile up at the director. "Tonight. While it's dark. We can use thermals to lock onto these sons of bitches and eradicate them."

David Ford scoffed as he leaned back in the folding chair. "You didn't bother to read either of the previous AAR's, did you?" He leaned forward, bringing the front legs back down firmly. "They're nocturnal."

"Well, they sure as shit did enough daytime damage, didn't they?" Walker turned his back on Ford and eyed the director. "What say you, director? You ready to put the varsity squad in and get this over with?"

Davidson glanced at McCoy who gave him a barely perceptible shrug. Slowly the director began to nod. "Very well." He turned and faced Walker. "Have your men standing by and ready. As soon as the sun sets, you have your go."

Walker grinned so big, it threatened to split his face. "It's about goddam time." He spun and marched out of the logistics center.

Ford came to his feet with a grunt and raised a brow at the director. "Did that really just happen?"

Davidson shrugged. "That son of a bitch has been

crawling around under my skin from the moment I got here." He returned the raised brow to Ford. "Either he'll get the job done—"

"And we'll never hear the end of it," McCoy interjected.

"True." Davidson turned back to Ford. "Or he'll show what an incompetent ass he truly is and he's out of our hair."

"Yeah, permanently," Ford added. "Why do I get the feeling you just green lighted his death?"

Davidson shrugged. "Sometimes you gotta let the big dog off the chain for a while. If it bites him in the ass then I guess he wasn't as big a dog as he thought."

"Just like that?" Ford scoffed. "There's no maybe to it. Yes, the man is an asshat. But he has no idea what's waiting for him in those woods."

"I guess he'll find out." McCoy grabbed the transcript of Barlow's verbal AAR and shoved it into a folder. "Either way, one of our problems will be solved."

As the sun made its descent and the last licks of crimson light stretched over the purple sky, Delta and Echo teams stood at the ready as Terry Walker and Alpha Team prepared to make entry.

Steve Barlow stood at the entrance of Charlie Team's tent with his two surviving team members as Walker strutted by. "Time to show you boys how real operators get shit done."

Steve took a deep breath to prevent saying something he might regret. He noticed Hank stepping forward, his mouth open with a flaming hot retort and he quickly pulled the man back beside him. “Let him figure it out on his own.”

Hank’s jaw flexed in time with his hands making fists. “He has no idea what he’s walking into.”

“Exactly. And nothing you or I say or do will educate him. You can’t teach the unwilling.”

“Or the stupid,” Jake added.

The three men watched as Terry escorted his team to the edge of the camp and made a big show of readying their weapons and dropping the IR goggles.

David Ford nudged Randol McCoy. “Care to lay odds on how quick they call for reinforcements?”

McCoy shook his head. “Moot. They’ll lose coms the moment they step inside.” He watched as Alpha Team disappeared into the thick then turned to face Ford. “The only way we’ll hear from them again is if there are survivors.”

“Dammit!” The tech kicked at a box of gear and threw a remote across the table. “I’m standing right over this thing and it still won’t respond.”

Barlow squeezed the shoulders of his men as he stepped past them and approached the tech mid-meltdown. “What’s going on?”

The tech sighed heavily and rubbed at his temples. “Nothing is working. The coms won’t stay connected, the long range radios are all wonky and now the drones won’t even pick up the remote signals.”

Barlow squatted next to the oversized drone and gave it the once over. “And you’re sure the thing is turned on?”

The tech gave him a go-to-hell look. “Do you really

think I'd waste this much time without first making sure it was turned on?"

Barlow fought the grin tugging at the corners of his mouth. "Just checking." He bent low again and wiggled a dangling wire. "Is this the antennae?"

"Yeah." The tech picked up the remote again and turned it on. "For whatever reason the signal isn't—" His words were cut off as the six electric motors came to life, their fans spinning up and preparing for flight. "What did you do?"

"I think you have a bad connection on this wire." Barlow flipped the switch, turning the unit off then whistled to Jake. "You feel like some soldering?"

"Hell yeah." Jake trotted over and studied the drone as Barlow flipped it upside down and placed it gently on the fold out table.

"That wire is the antennae, and it's got a loose connection." Barlow stood back as Jake rummaged through the boxes of supplies.

"I'm going to need some silver solder." He glanced at the tech. "It makes for a better conductor."

The tech grinned and disappeared into the logistics building. When he returned, he held his hand out. "Low temp silver solder."

"Perfect." Jake began removing the thousand tiny screws holding the bottom on and placed it aside as the soldering pen heated up. He flashed the LED torch on the circuit board and nodded. "Yeah, it's got maybe three strands actually soldered on."

Barlow clapped the man's back as he stepped away and allowed him to work. He watched from a distance as Hank approached. "I thought the lodestones around here prevented anything electronic from working right?"

Barlow shrugged. “Even a small win would be gladly accepted right about now.” He turned and stared at the spot where Alpha Team had made entry. “If the damned thing will fly, we might be able to use the drones as a relay for the coms.”

“Screw that.” Jake set down the soldering pen and began buttoning up the bottom of the drone. “I want to use the thermal and see what the hell is going on out there.”

The tech flipped the power switch on as Jake flipped the drone back upright and set it on the ground. “Here’s hoping that’s the only problem.”

“How many more drones do you have?” Jake asked as he stepped away from the machine.

“Two more, but this is the only one with thermal imaging.” The tech stepped back and flipped on the remote. “Here’s goes nothing.”

The men had to resist the desire to cheer as the drone came to life and began to hover a few feet from the ground. “Get after it,” Barlow said as he swept his arms towards the woods. “Show us what we can’t see with our naked eyes.”

The tech nodded to another man who began tapping at a keyboard. A moment later and a large screen came to life, displaying the men milling about Dog Town. A moment later and the drone was buzzing toward the trees, rising in height as it approached the canopy.

“Cross your fingers that it keeps working,” the tech adjusted the controls and the thermal camera zoomed in. As the machine buzzed over the canopy, thermal images of Alpha Team appeared on the large view screen, slowly advancing through the forest.

The tech nodded to Director Davidson. "Coms relay is up if you want to test it."

Davidson grabbed the nearest mic. "Alpha Team, this is command, do you copy?"

The lead heat signature paused and the drone relayed the movement as he reached upward and keyed his coms. "Five by five, director. Your boys finally figure out how to make it work?"

"We're bouncing signal off an overhead drone. Fingers crossed the patch works."

"Copy that. Alpha Actual going dark."

The men of Delta and Echo team gathered loosely around the big screen TV as Alpha Team slowly advanced deeper into the woods. Movement was picked up by the drone camera and the tech zoomed out, broadening the picture. "I've got movement, Director."

"Show me." Davidson moved closer and crossed his arms, his eyes taking in the quickly moving heat signatures. "Wait...zoom in on this one." He pointed to the TV screen and the tech adjusted the controls. A moment later and the picture enlarged.

A huge bipedal creature was seen moving quickly through the woods, the brush and limbs obscuring a large portion of its wide body. Davidson reached for the mic again. "Alpha Actual, we're picking up numerous heat signatures at your twelve o'clock."

"And here, sir." McCoy pointed out.

"And your three o'clock."

McCoy nodded to the tech. "Zoom out again. I want a wide angle view of those woods."

The tech adjusted the camera, then sent the drone into a higher orbit. Heat signatures made a near perfect circle around the tactical team and the foliage made it nearly impossible to get an accurate head count.

"Dear lord…there's dozens of them," McCoy whispered. He turned suddenly to Davidson, "Pull them out, sir. There's too many"

Davidson keyed his mic again. "Alpha Actual, retreat! Withdraw now! Thermal imaging shows dozens of hostiles in your immediate area!" He stared at the slowly advancing heat signatures and cursed under his breath. "Is this already broken?" He tossed the mic aside and fought the urge to scream.

"He said he was going dark, director," Barlow replied as he sidled in next to him. "I'd bet money he turned his coms off."

"How the hell do we get their attention?" Davidson barked as he turned a slow circle. "What if we fired off rounds?"

"Sir." Barlow nodded toward the TV screen.

The crowd watched in horror as the larger heat signatures slowly advanced on the team, picking off those who were at the rear first. The attacks must have been silent as the other heat signatures ahead never paused or turned to see what happened behind them.

The first heat signature "abducted" was soon scattered about the forest floor in quickly cooling pieces as the attackers slowly closed the circle around the team.

"Good god…they're tearing them apart." Davidson felt bile rise in his throat and he turned away from the screen.

"Let me gear up my men. Those things won't expect a second team to come up their rear." McCoy's voice was quiet but stern. "I know we can catch them off guard."

Davidson turned back to the TV and winced as more of the Alpha Team signatures quickly cooled in the night air. "I…I don't think…" Davidson's mind reeled as he watched the carnage in real time.

When the first gunshots echoed through the trees, the thermal readout indicated that Walker and his 2IC, Jason Corbit, were the ones pulling the triggers. The whole camp watched in horrid fascination as a large heat signature appeared to superimpose over Corbit and a moment later, Jason's outline was splayed across the ground with the larger heat signature viciously ripping pieces away and throwing them.

"What the actual hell?" John Murphy muttered.

David Ford clapped the man on the shoulder. "Monkey boy used the damned trees. Dropped down on top of him and crushed him before…" He trailed off, unable to say out loud the sickening parts.

"Why in the seven bloody hells didn't they keep their coms active?" Davidson shook his fists in the air and screamed.

A moment later and full auto fire echoed through the woods and the men watched as dozens of creatures surrounded Terry Walker before he was bludgeoned to death. From the number of blows directed to his heat signature, they were fairly certain he was pounded into a paste.

After the systematic murder of Alpha Team, a very large, lone heat signature was followed to the edge of the trees and a quick arm movement was captured. The sentry closest to the tree edge loosed a scream as Walker's head bounced twice before rolling to a stop at the man's feet.

Barlow sighed heavily and fell into a fold out chair.

"Somebody help me devise a tactic that will work with these *monsters*."

David Ford appeared at his side and squeezed his shoulder. "I'll work it with you."

McCoy nodded to the pair. "Count me in." He turned to the tech and pointed. "Get me a copy of this. Every second of recording you have, we need."

"Yes sir. Give me five minutes."

McCoy crossed his arms and stared out at the pitch black of the woods. "Short of air-to-ground missiles… we might have bitten off more than we can chew."

6

FOB Dog Town

Steve Barlow threw the coffee cup across the tent with a clatter. "All we have is a couple of minutes of *one* attack. This doesn't tell us their tactics."

David Ford stroked the edges of his goatee and stared at the screen. "They pulled a classic pincer movement. Circled their prey and closed the gaps."

McCoy stood and cleared his throat. "As big an asshat as Walker was, he didn't deserve to go out like that." He stepped to where Barlow's coffee cup crashed and picked it up, blowing dirt from the inside. He stood in front of the coffee pot and slowly filled the cup as he thought. "We need somebody with actual face time with these things."

"Forget it." Ford came to his feet and shook his finger at the others. "Archer refuses to come back to these woods."

"So we don't bring him to the woods." Barlow stood

and pointed to the screen. "We pull him here, onscreen."

McCoy chuckled. "They can barely get the local coms to work, there's no way—"

"Satellite." Steve crossed his arms and raised a brow at him. "There's a reason they send sat phones out with deployed teams. They work anywhere on the planet."

McCoy looked at Ford who barely shrugged. "You can try, but I don't think Dale is going to be much help." Ford stepped over to the makeshift box of files and rifled through the tabs. "His AAR was very detailed. And if you knew Archer the way I do, the guy is anal when it comes to detailing everything." He tossed the AAR to the table. "Look through his summary."

Barlow scooped the file up and flipped to the last section. He scanned the paragraphs then gave both men a discerning look. "He actually wrote that?"

"What?" McCoy reached for the folder. "I barely made it halfway through Gamboa's notes. I don't think I even looked at Archer's account."

Barlow crossed his arms and waited. "I can't believe he actually wrote that."

"Wait a second…" McCoy stepped closer to the light. "He actually said this?"

David Ford nodded. "He wouldn't have added it unless he believed it."

"That they're intelligent creatures—possibly as intelligent as humans?" McCoy scoffed and held the report aloft. "That their tactics were not unlike guerilla fighters of third world countries?"

Ford nodded again. "With hit and run tactics, psychological attacks and—"

"Wait," McCoy held his hands up. "Psychological attacks?"

Ford stepped closer and took the file, reading from it. "'The 'war whoops,' while remaining hidden, were classic fear tactics.'" He scanned the document and came to the next lines. "'The debilitating symptoms of infrasound coupled with the creature's ability to remain hidden from even infrared goggles added to the 'psyops' utilized by the creatures.'"

"Bullshit." McCoy stood and paced the tent. "They're just some kind of mountain primate. They don't have the cognizance to—"

"Randy," Barlow interrupted. "Humans are primates, too." He raised a brow at him. "Look, I'm not saying that Archer is right and I'm not saying that he's wrong. All I'm saying is these things live in large units, isolated in the mountains, and they have developed—possibly over centuries—the ability to stun their prey with this infrasound crap. It's a lot easier to kill a deer if the damned thing is too confused to know where to run."

Ford held his hands up to quiet them both. "All I'm saying is that Archer already gave us everything he had. He won't come back to these woods, and even if we piped him in through a remote, I seriously doubt he could tell us much more than we already know."

McCoy hung his head and sighed. "And I'm just saying, it couldn't hurt to have him on standby as an advisor."

Ford gave an animated shrug. "You can try, but I can tell you exactly what he'll say."

"What's that?" Barlow asked.

Ford gave him a serious look. "Cut your losses and get the hell out of these woods."

DIRECTOR DAVIDSON HOVERED over the techs as they continued their work. "I think we're about ready, sir."

"Put him on the big screen." Davidson stepped back and smiled as Dale Archer's face appeared on the screen. His eyes were still swollen like he'd just been rolled out of bed and his hair was mussy.

"What's so important you need to talk to me at 3A.M.?" He sniffed hard and wiped at his eyes. It was obvious he was using his cell phone to complete the face to face.

"I really wish you were here with us, son," Davidson began.

"Sir, we've hashed this out so many times—"

"We need your input." Barlow stepped forward and stared into the camera mounted about the TV. "We've lost three teams already and—"

"Jeezus! *Three teams?*" Dale's face pixelated as he came to his feet and flipped on another light. "What the hell were you guys thinking?"

"That's just it, Archer." McCoy stepped closer to the camera and sighed heavily. "We don't know what to think. We've gone over the data sets that we have available and to be completely honest, we're drawing a blank here."

Ford cleared his throat loudly and stared solemnly into the camera. "We need to pick your brain. And since you refuse to come here, we thought we'd bring the mountain to Mohammed."

"Fuck me..." Archer groaned as he stood and pulled a shirt on. "I need coffee, so you'll have to bear with me."

The man trudged through his apartment and flipped on the coffee maker then sat down heavily at the counter. "Okay, talk to me."

Barlow went over the basics and explained how Bravo inserted to investigate an incident and didn't return. His team inserted shortly after to provide support or to be a retrieval team. He glossed over the details of how the men were found.

Ford told of Alpha Team's demise as Archer drank coffee and listened. He explained how the creatures acted and the speed and ferocity utilized to dispatch Walker's team.

Dale had his phone propped on the counter and listened intently as the men spoke. When they finished he stared at the screen with red eyes. "Director, I don't want to say 'I told ya so,' but—"

"Then don't!" Davidson replied loudly. "Just tell these boys what they need to know to get the job done."

Archer hung his head and sighed. He closed his eyes and sat silently for a long time. For a brief moment, Davidson feared he'd fallen asleep. When he sat up again he took a deep breath and let it out slowly. "I watched these things use stick and stones as weapons. Hell, one of them threw a fucking trailer tire like a Frisbee and took out one of Gamboa's people. Crushed him like a beer can." He sat back in his chair and pinched his eyes closed. "I don't think there's a tactic that we can employ that they can't counter."

"What are you saying?" Davidson asked.

Dale sat forward and gripped his phone. "I'm saying, you're all tromping through their backyard. They know those woods like you know your own house. You can't sneak up on them. They'll either hear you or smell you. You can't use overwhelming force because…" he paused and sat back, his mind going to a place he hadn't even considered before.

"I know that look." Ford pushed forward and stared at the screen. "Talk to me buddy. What are you thinking?"

Dale downed a quick gulp of coffee then set his phone back down. "I can't even guarantee this would work."

"Talk!" Davidson barked.

Dale held a hand up while his mind tried to put the pieces of the puzzle together. "You'll need to find a way to bring them together. Set a trap, of sorts."

"What kind of trap?" McCoy asked cautiously.

Dale leaned closer until his face filled the screen. "Did you bring any armaments with that chopper?"

"CHRIST," McCoy whispered. "Air-to-ground missiles?"

Ford sat back and rubbed at his eyes. "I mean…it doesn't sound like he's wrong."

"Isn't that like using a cannon to swat a mosquito?" Barlow asked.

Ford scoffed. "If it's a thousand pound skeeter that can rip your own arm off and beat you to death with it, then I'm all for using a fucking canon."

McCoy paced the tent, his mind racing. "How can we lure them all to a central place?"

Barlow scoffed. "Walker did it."

"Just before they killed his entire team," McCoy replied back. "I'd prefer to walk away alive, thank you."

"With the terrain we're talking about, there can't be any strikes that are danger close." Ford began pacing opposite of McCoy.

Barlow sat on the edge of the table and watched the other two pace. "I'd bet even money that if we put that bird in the air, the apes will beat feet. They'd be in the next county before the chopper could even get in position."

Ford snapped his fingers. "Then we don't use the chopper."

"I'm not going to carry an air-to-ground missile into those woods." McCoy raised a brow at him. "That's suicide."

"We have explosives." Ford smirked at the men and crossed his arms. "We have Claymores. We have mines. We have grenades."

McCoy chuckled to himself. "I'd love to see what a bouncing Betty could do to those things."

Barlow pushed off the table. "Do we have shrapnel mines?"

Ford shrugged. "If we don't, I bet we could come up with some."

"YOU WANT TO DO WHAT?" Davidson narrowed his eyes as the three team leaders laid out their plan.

Ford stepped forward, "I think Steve is right. If we put the chopper into the air, the creatures are going to scatter."

"Then we start using it for daily operations." Davidson shrugged. "We put it up for a bit every day until they get used to it and—"

"But we don't need it." McCoy cut him off. "We can use the drone to ensure that there's nothing in the woods waiting for us or watching us and we use their existing trails to set Claymores and shrapnel mines. If these things try to get close, boom. No more monkey man."

Davidson sighed heavily. "And if it doesn't work?"

Barlow shrugged. "Then we fall back on the chopper."

Davidson paced the logistics building slowly. "I've got two air-to-ground missiles coming in this afternoon." He glanced at his watch then the tiny window showing him that the sun was up. "Use the early daylight hours to get your munitions set." He turned and gave them a serious glare. "And for fuck's sake, go deep to set your explosives then work your way back to the middle."

The three team leaders gave him a duh look simultaneously. "Sir, this ain't our first rodeo," McCoy replied.

"I'm just saying," Davidson held his hands up. "You boys are working on no sleep and tensions are high after losing three teams."

"We got this, sir." Ford stepped back and nodded to the other two. "We'll get the drone up now and start as soon as we've verified the area as clear."

The three men exited the logistics building and headed straight for the armory tent. Barlow waved Hank and Jake over and ordered them to round up Delta and Echo teams and meet back at the armory.

Once all of the men were assembled, Ford and McCoy laid out the plans. "Davidson has the techs prepping the drone now. Once we've verified the area clear, we head out. Remember to GPS every charge you set."

Hank raised a hand, a questioning look on his face. "If nothing electronic works out here, how will we be able to GPS anything?"

McCoy tossed him the unit. "Links directly to the satellites. Uses lasers or some such."

"You'll need some kind of opening in the canopy," Ford added. "Any size will work. If you can see daylight, the signal can get out."

Hank flipped the device over and nodded approvingly. "I'll take it."

Barlow took the device and held it up. "Just in case, take your topo maps and mark it. Be as accurate as you can. When we leave here, we have to ensure that all unexpended charges are accounted for."

Ford raised his voice to be heard over the murmur of the teams, "We can't have some hiker coming through years from now and losing a leg or worse because we screwed the pooch."

The tech approached quietly and gave the teams a solemn look. "As much as I want to make this work, there's just too much reflected heat from the top of the canopy. It's washing out the filters."

Barlow's shoulders slumped. "So we're going in blind?"

The tech shrugged. "Maybe not?" He held out a pair of IR goggles. "You'll be under the canopy and even though it's daylight out here, it's pretty damned dark in there." He turned and pointed to the sentries. "There's no way I could get an accurate read on all of you anyway. I just can't get enough height from this thing and I'd lose your heat signature under all that foliage." He sighed heavily and turned to Ford. "If you guys could do one section at a time, I could try to insert under the canopy and attempt to keep—"

"No." Ford stepped back and stared at the men assembled. "We're going in without overwatch. Heads on a swivel and watch the man to your left and right."

"Dave," Barlow whispered, pulling him aside. "I like the idea of doing sections at a time. We could bunch the men tighter and be better able to keep an eye on each other."

Ford considered the option and slowly nodded. "Agreed." He stepped away from Barlow and relayed the change in plans. "We're breaking the project up into four quadrants. We'll be better able to keep tabs on each other." He made a circle in the air with his hand. "Saddle up, boys and girls."

7

DEEP IN THE CATSKILLS

"I'M CALLING IT." David Ford marked off on his digital map the outer boundary. "This is two hundred fifty yards to the edge of the clearing. They'll have to come through this gauntlet to even get close."

His 2IC, John Murphy marked the topomap then shifted the heavy canvas bag to the ground. "What do you want to start with?" He reached into the bag and withdrew a Claymore. "I say we go with a classic."

Ford glanced up and saw a glint of sunlight off the small drone acting as a coms relay. "All units, mark the boundary at two five zero and begin." A series of acknowledgements chirped in his ear as he tucked the ruggedized tablet away. "Can't go wrong with a Claymore." He nodded to the base of a tree next to the trail. "Wire or laser for the trigger?"

Murphy's mouth scrunched up as he considered.

"Both have pros and cons. I say laser and mount it high enough that a stray bunny won't set it off."

"Done." David handed him the laser trigger and watched as he pushed it into the bark of the tree and aligned it before attaching the detonator. "I have a strange feeling out here."

"Who wouldn't?" Murphy carefully inserted the detonator then stepped back carefully. "We've lost enough people in these woods; time for a bit of payback."

David shouldered the canvas bag and stepped back about five meters. "This looks good for secondary."

Murphy pulled out a pressure mine and set it aside. With the folding shovel he carefully cut through the thin grass and dirt, hollowing out a perfect circle in the ground. "You really think they're as smart as Archer said?"

Ford handed him the Allen key to remove the plate lock. "Dale Archer is many things, but stupid isn't one of them. If he thinks they're smart, then he's probably right."

Once the mine was set in place and a thin layer of topsoil, grass and leaves were strategically placed along the top, Murphy pulled the lock plate to the side and slipped it back into the bag. "Set." He looked up at Ford and raised a brow. "If they're smart, then we need to be more creative."

Ford narrowed his gaze at the man. "How so?"

Murphy looked up into the canopy. "We need to figure out a way to set some charges up high. Didn't one of the bigfoots use the limbs to drop down on Corbit?"

Ford nodded. "Granted, but how do we choose the right place? There's a lot of trees in these woods."

Murphy slowly stood and gazed into the thick shadows of the forest. "We know these things are big. Heavy."

"Close to a thousand pounds, if rumors are to be believed."

Murphy scoffed. "I don't see how anything weighing that much can be quick or stealthy in these woods, but…" he trailed off, his eyes scanning the area. "There."

Ford turned and stared in the direction that Murphy pointed. A large pine with thick limbs stood out amongst its neighbors. "Hmm." Ford stroked his goatee as he slowly moved in closer. "I think you're right. Look at the bark along the trunk. It's like something rubbed it smooth in spots."

"Something like big feet trying to gain traction?" Murphy chuckled to himself as the moved closer, setting charges and trip wires along the way.

Ford verified the men to his left and right as they continued working their way into the shadows. "Bag's getting lighter."

"Maybe we planted them a little too thick out here?" Murphy twisted his neck to each side with a welcoming crack. "Hand me some of that moss."

David bent and scooped a double handful of moss and Murphy tossed it into a smaller canvas bag. "I'm guessing another Claymore set where the limb comes out of the main trunk?"

"And covered with moss so the cave monkeys don't see it." Murphy hopped up and grabbed the lowest branch, pulling himself into the limbs of the tree.

Ford stood in the shadows and watched as Murphy scrambled up the tree like a professional. When he reached one of the larger branches he swung himself around and planted both feet on the limb.

Ford watched him duck low and peer along the length of the limb. "Oh yeah. Something has been using this spot." He extended his hand and plucked a small tuft of long, reddish brown hair. Holding it close to his nose he winced. "Yeah. This is our hairy friends, alright."

He spun around and sat on the limb. Pulling the Claymore from the bag, he pushed as hard as he could to set the prongs into the softer outer bark of the pine then placed the moss over the top and around the exposed metal of the prongs.

Ford watched him sit back and scratch at the side of his head. "What's wrong?"

"For the life of me, I can't figure out how to rig the trigger. There's no place to attach wire, and a laser is out of the question."

David stared at the bottom of the limb and slowly shook his head. "Maybe we use it on the trail instead of the canopy?" He shrugged. "I mean, it was a helluva idea, but if it can't work, it can't work."

Murphy continued to study the problem. "I think I can do this."

"Echo actual, come in." A voice crackled over their coms and everyone stiffened, listening to the traffic.

"Echo actual, go ahead."

"Sir, we're picking up a helluva stench over here. North edge of the line."

"I'm calling it!" McCoy's voice was firm. "Everybody out of the woods. Finish what you're doing and we evac, now!"

Ford looked up at Murphy. "You heard the man. Climb your happy ass down and let's beat feet."

Murphy tugged at the Claymore trying to get the set prongs loose from the bark. "It's not giving up."

"Then leave it." Ford's head swing side to side, looking for any kind of movement in the shadows. "Come on, John. Now!"

Murphy cursed under his breath and quickly attached a wire to the trigger and let it dangle. Maybe they'd get lucky and the beast would trigger it on the climb up.

He shifted his weight and began to drop down to the lower branches, letting the limb bounce under his weight before he dropped to the next one. When his boots impacted the pine needle covered floor, Ford all but dragged him towards the exit points. "Where's the Claymore?"

"Couldn't get it." Murphy smiled at him. "I attached a wire to the trigger and left it. Maybe they'll pull it out of curiosity."

"Right." Ford pulled a limb aside and held it for Murphy to step back into the sunlight. As he exited from the thick he saw the other team members emerge from the forest and did a quick count in his head. "I think they're all clear." He reached for his coms and activated the mic, "Echo Actual, Delta, come in."

"Go for Echo."

"I suggest we flip 180 and continue on the other side of Dog Town. Let the locals sniff around on this side while we continue leaving surprises for them."

"Copy that, Delta. All units form up on Delta and prepare to resupply."

Ford turned and walked backward, away from the

forest edge, while studying the shadows. "They're watching us. I can feel it."

FOB Dog Town

Director Davidson studied the overheard drone footage. "I'm not seeing anything under there."

"The drone is primarily for com relay, sir."

"I know, but you'd think you'd see *something*." He huffed and pushed away from the table. "How are we on time?"

"Sun sets in two hours, sir."

Davidson sighed heavily and reached for the mic. "Gentlemen, we won't have time to complete all four quadrants before the sun goes down."

Ford's voice nearly boomed over the overhead speakers. "I think we should at least start it, director. I don't like the idea of having a full sector unaccounted for."

"Understood, but we have less than two hours and how are you on Sector Three?"

McCoy's voice shot back over the coms, "Recommend we split part of the team off to cover the last sector, sir. They won't finish, but at least we'll have some coverage."

Davidson mulled the idea for a moment then reached for the mic again. "Very well. McCoy, assemble your men and converge on the last sector. I'll have techs standing by in the staging area with the remaining munitions to speed your departure."

"Copy that, sir." McCoy switched to local coms. "You got this, Ford?"

"Yeah, take off and I'll leapfrog my men to cover your gaps."

"Copy that. Good luck." McCoy keyed off as Ford began redirecting his people.

"All units, be advised, sentries from Sector One are reporting a strong, pungent odor wafting out from the woods. I think our nocturnal friends are getting an early start. Echo Team, remain vigilant."

"Understood Command." McCoy raised a brow at his 2IC, Les Palmer. "Bet you're wishing you were flying that Huey right about now, aintcha?"

Les chuckled as he repacked his munitions bag. "And miss out on all this fun? Please." He hefted the bag over his shoulder and pushed past the techs. "Keep supper warm for us, boys. We'll be back before you know it."

Randol McCoy hefted his own bag and fell in line behind Les. "Stay alert, bud. This sector butts to Sector One, and I do not want to have to train somebody else to be my second."

"Like anybody else could compare to me!" Les joked as he pushed his way into the woods. "Crap. I'll never get used to how dark it is under this canopy."

"I'd say you get used to it, but you don't." McCoy waited until the last of his men entered the trees then nodded. "Just like the last three times, go to two-fifty, mark and GPS your plants. Allow at least fifteen to retreat once the sun starts to set. These things won't wait until full dark to start their shenanigans so stay alert. Head on a swivel. Know where your buddies are, and for the love of Pete, I want everyone walking out of this unscathed." He nodded curtly then stepped deeper into the forest. "And, go."

Echo Team worked diligently, quietly and quickly placing charges at the most tactical locations, doing their best to camouflage each one as they worked their way back to the clearing. Every few seconds, McCoy would look up and verify the man to his left and right before diverting his attention back to the task at hand.

"Remember people, slow is smooth, smooth is fast, but let's step it up a hair. I do not want to get caught out here with my dick in my hand."

"You're leaving yourself wide open there, boss," Palmer smirked. "You're fortunate that we're all professionals here."

"Cut the chatter and plant more posies. The better the coverage, the better the odds—" His words were cut short by an explosion to the north and all members of Echo company froze and turned in that direction. "Echo Team, sound off!"

As each member responded, McCoy allowed himself to breathe. He slowly stood and stared on the direction of the explosion then checked his watch. "I'm calling it, fellas. Set and mark your last and let's clear the woods. Something tells me these things aren't going to be happy."

"Echo Actual, Command, come in."

"Copy, Command. I take it you heard that as well?"

"Sentries report it was about one five zero yards north of your sector. Recommend immediate evac."

"Copy Command. We're already on it. Echo departure in five mikes."

"Five mikes, copy you." The coms fell silent and

McCoy felt his chest tighten. He quickly set the trip wire for his last munition then turned for the clearing.

"Echo Team, sound off." McCoy pushed through the limbs making the border of the tree line east of Dog Town and stepped into a quickly darkening scene.

One by one his members reported in and he watched as they exited the woods and stood just yards from the ever darkening shadows, watching and waiting for some form of retaliation.

Randy McCoy made a circular motion with his hand. "Converge on me."

He watched as his team approached, vigilantly turning to check their six as they closed the distance. Once they were together he nodded to the north. "Sentries reported the explosion to command but we have no idea if there are any casualties. It will probably be a minute before—" His words were cut off as the thermal drone buzzed by overhead, its camera light blinking in the darkening sky. McCoy chuckled as it zipped by. "I stand corrected. We should know shortly if our efforts were successful."

He slowly began to back away from the edge, urging his team to fall back along with him. "If Archer is correct, these things can be deadly even at a distance. Best if we put as much room as we can between us and them."

McCoy turned and trudged up the slight incline until he and his team were in the middle of Dog Town. "What's the verdict?"

The tech tapped at his tablet then spun the large screen around. "Successful."

"Holy cow..." Les leaned closer and stared at the image. "That thing is huge."

Barlow appeared beside him and cocked his head to the side. "Is that just *one*? It looks like there might be an extra arm…or is that a leg?"

"Looks like Claymore damage." Murphy set his jaw as he stared at the image. "But I think Steve's right. That looks like more than one."

Ford nodded to the tech. "Can you give us the thermal feed? I want to see if there are any others in the area."

The tech tapped at the tablet and the feed switched to a live feed with the drone slowly rising in the sky, its image widening. "That's more like it."

Barlow loosed a low whistle as more and more heat signatures began to pop up. Some would come and go from the screen as the canopy covered them. "How many is that?"

Ford bent low and shook his head. "A helluva lot more than I thought we were dealing with."

"There's got to be dozens." Murphy's voice was barely a whisper. "Where the fuck are they all coming from?"

Davidsons' voice seemed to boom as he spoke. "These mountains are littered with caves and it's believed that most are linked with a tunnel system not unlike lava tubes. Not to mention all of the abandoned mines, not all of which were legal or even mapped." He planted his hands on his hips and stared at the screen. "Our ploy to set booby traps might have backfired."

Barlow turned and gave him a curious look. "How's that?"

Davidson nodded towards the screen. "I think they've called in other clans to help them deal with us."

8

FOB Dog Town

Steve Barlow paced slowly in front of the large screen, watching as more heat signatures popped into existence. "The tunnels must be scattered throughout the woods."

David Ford stood watching, his eyes casting furtive glances towards the chopper. "Somebody tell me the guns on that thing have ammunition."

Randol McCoy shrugged. "That's Davidson's department." He leaned closer and watched as the heat signatures formed another pincer maneuver on Dog Town, slowly encircling the perimeter. "How far out are they?"

The drone tech checked his data. "They're closing on the outer perimeter of the charges." He leaned forward and plucked a laser pointer from the table. Circling a particular heat signature, he stated, "This one is closest and moving the quickest. He should be inside the zone in moments."

The three team leaders watched the screen with anticipation, praying that the munitions would deter any others. At least for the night.

"That was my area." Ford nodded to Murphy. "Does the terrain on that screen look familiar?"

Murphy shook his head. "Not from above." He crossed his arms and breathed slowly, praying that their hard work wasn't for nothing.

On the opposite side of the screen a munition exploded, splattering the heat signature closest to it. All of the heat signatures appeared to halt their advance and the men could almost see the gears in their heads turning as they considered moving closer.

"I really thought this big one over here would be the first to go," Ford moved closer and studied the now still heat signature. "What the hell is he doing?"

"Considering his mortality?" Murphy chimed in. "I know I would be if I were him."

"That's assuming they understand what happened." The men turned to see Director Davidson watching the screen from behind them. "I'm thinking they probably have some idea what that noise was."

"Sir?"

Davidson turned to the tech standing next to him. "What is it?"

"The sentry closest to the tree line is reporting sounds that..." he glanced away then lowered his voice. "He said it sounds like language. Just no language he's familiar with."

Davidson's brows hiked. "Is that so?"

Ford nodded slowly. "Gamboa's data had a snippet

in there, I think it was Red Moon, reported that he overheard the creatures 'talking' to each other in a guttural language."

"Then I guess they suspect what the big booms were." Barlow sighed heavily and fished out Tylenol to battle the sleep deprivation headache.

Another blast echoed through the trees and they all turned to see where it occurred. Ford sighed when he realized it was the large heat signature he'd been watching. "Looks like he found the Claymore."

"Why aren't they running for the hills?" Murphy asked.

McCoy shot him a sideways look. "This is war for them. This is their home." He pushed away from the television and reached for more coffee. "They aren't going to turn tail and run for the hills."

Les Palmer stood and got Davidson's attention. "I can have the chopper warmed up in a matter of minutes, sir."

Davidson held a hand up, stopping him. "Not yet. Let's see how they react once more of their kind is lost to the booby traps."

The drone tech cleared his throat and slowly came to his feet. "Sir, the drone is running low on battery. I have to have it return to base for a recharge."

Davidson felt his stomach tighten. "Can you just replace the battery and send it back out? We need to know how close to the tree line they get."

The tech shook his head. "Internal power, sir. It's actually a major surgery to replace the batteries on these units."

"What about the camera? Could we swap it with another drone?" Barlow asked.

"Negative, sir. The cameras are proprietary to that unit."

"Useless piece of.... Fine. Bring it back." Davidson sighed heavily. "How long to recharge it?"

"About two hours, sir."

"Two..." Davidson trailed off.

"If they figure out how to detect our traps, sir, they could break the tree line in a matter of moments," Ford stated quietly.

"I am fully aware." Davidson nodded to the tech. "Hurry up. I want that thing back in operation as soon as possible."

"Sir, I recommend stationing the team members not already on sentry duty between the active watch stations." McCoy was already reaching for a rifle. "If they break the tree line, we're going to need as many trigger pullers as possible."

"Make it happen." Davidson sat down heavily and rubbed at his eyes. "Something tells me this is going to be a long night."

As another explosion rocked the forest, Ford scanned the area with thermal goggles. "How sad is it that I no longer jump when they go off?"

Murphy chuckled as he scanned the opposite direction. "It's not sad for us. Every time one goes off I hope there's a dozen of the hairy bastards hunkered over it." He lowered his goggles and sighed. "That many fewer for us to deal with."

Ford stretched his neck and stared up into the night sky. "I want to find these tunnels."

Murphy chuckled as he continued to scan the area. "You got a death wish or something?"

Ford shrugged. "If I could set a charge near the opening, we could collapse the exit."

"And judging by what we watched earlier, there are dozens more tunnels they can use in its place."

Ford nodded. "Possibly. Or we scare them into thinking that they're all rigged and they stay underground."

"Right because they have plenty to eat underground." Murphy dropped the goggles and gave him a knowing look. "They'll risk setting off charges if they're hungry enough."

"Yeah, you're right." He brought the goggles back up and continued searching. "But I'd still like to find one."

"Just so you could say you did?"

Ford shrugged. "I want to know as much about them as I can."

"The better to kill them, gotcha."

Ford sighed and stared out into the darkness. "Do you think they could be reasoned with?"

Murphy spun and stared at him. "You're not serious."

Ford shrugged. "Why not?" He turned to Murphy and lowered his voice. "Did you read Archer's report?"

"No." He turned his attention back to the tree line.

"Archer is convinced that the leader of the clan allowed him to leave. To spread the word to the rest of us to stay out."

"And yet, here we are."

"What if we'd listened?"

"To what? Archer?" Murphy lowered the goggles and stepped closer to Ford. "The guy lost his shit in the woods and started thinking that a bunch of dumb animals can be reasoned with. He got the shit scared out of him to the point he won't even come back here and he's trying to convince you that he's right." He scoffed as he turned his attention back to the tree line. "Dude is done. He'll never work in the teams again."

Ford stared at his silhouette in the darkness. "What do you mean?"

Murphy lowered the goggles and hung his head. "I shouldn't have said anything."

"No, you done opened this can of worms, spill it."

Murphy took a deep breath and let it out slowly. "I may have overheard Davidson talking with HRT leadership." He turned and gave Ford a tight-lipped smile. "Davidson recommended that Archer be benched."

"He doesn't have the say in—"

"They *asked* him his opinion and he gave it." Murphy gave him an exaggerated shrug. "Dude is done."

Ford felt the goggles slip from his grip and fall to his chest, the lanyard keeping it from falling to the ground. "He's my friend," he whispered.

"We know, Dave. That's why I'm sorry to be the one to tell you."

"They can't know what he went through out here."

Murphy rolled his eyes. "He went through the same shit we're going through now."

"No, he didn't. He didn't know what was out here when he came to these woods. He thought he was bailing out a JTTF team that ran into trouble, not some Neolithic hairy hominid that wasn't supposed to exist."

"And?" Murphy turned and closed the short distance between them. "Dude was given a chance to come back out here and exact a bit of revenge and he turned it down flat." He stepped closer and nearly got in Ford's face. "He's lost his nerve and the upper echelon knows it now. I'm telling you, the dude is shellshocked. He's done."

Ford stiffened and squared his shoulders. "Back off, John. Or you won't like what happens next."

Murphy stared at him wide eyed then backed away. "My bad, boss. I shouldn't have..." He trailed off, searching for the right words. "I just have a hard spot with cowards."

It was Ford's turn to scoff. "Dale Archer is no coward. In fact, he's one of the bravest sons of bitches I've ever known." He turned his attention back to the tree line. "They'll see soon enough."

"Yeah, sorry, boss. I don't agree with ya on that one. But if you want to fight to keep the guy around, that's on you. I don't think I could stick my neck out for him after this."

Ford sighed heavily as he turned away from him. Under his breath he murmured, "The funny thing is, I would have done the same for you—before all this."

McCoy paced slowly, his eyes peeled to the tree line. "I can almost feel them out there, ya know?"

Steve Barlow hefted the rifle with the thermal scope

and peered through it again. "I know what you mean, but there is nothing showing on IR."

"They're out there. Trust me." He held his arm out. "See? The hair is standing on end. We're being watched."

A tech approached from behind. "The director sent coffee."

"Hell yeah." McCoy snatched one of the cups and handed it to Barlow before taking the other one. "Thanks man."

"You guys seeing anything out here?"

McCoy shook his head as he sipped the bitter brew. "No, but they're out there. Watching. Probably waiting for us to lower our guard."

Barlow chuckled as he sipped the coffee. "I think McCoy has already had too much caffeine. He's seeing things."

"Trust me, bro." McCoy turned back to the tech, "Keep them coming, bud. It's already been a long night."

"Yes, sir. Will do." The tech shot him a big smile then backed away, glancing at the tree line behind him.

"So what's the deal with Palmer?"

McCoy shot him a curious look. "What do you mean?"

"Just that he seemed really eager to put the chopper into play."

McCoy broke into a toothy grin. "Oh, hell yeah. He's the designated pilot for the Huey. He's itching to prove himself on it."

"Ah, okay. Now it makes sense." Barlow tossed back the last of the coffee and hung the stainless steel cup from his vest. "I guess I can't blame the guy then."

"Did you not hear Davidson during the briefing?"

"I didn't hear a lot of that briefing." He tapped the side of his head. "Tinnitus."

"Ah, okay." McCoy stepped closer and said loudly, "Do I need to shout?"

Barlow laughed and pushed him away. "Get the fuck out of here with that. I'm not a grandpa yet."

"Woah, hold up." McCoy grabbed the rifle and brought the scope up to his eye. "Movement."

"What is it?"

McCoy steadied the rifle and took off the safety as a raccoon lazily jumped to a lower branch. "Shit." He clicked the safety back on and handed Steve the rifle. "Fucking raccoon."

Barlow chuckled as he shouldered the weapon and scanned the tree line with it. "I guess you could make yourself a coon skin cap like Davey Crockett."

McCoy laughed as he finished his coffee. "You think he really wore a coon skin hat?"

Barlow shrugged. "Who knows? I wouldn't put it past him. I seem to recall reading that he was a real jokester."

"Wasn't he in Congress for a while?"

Before Barlow could respond, something large and heavy thudded to the ground in front of them. Both men spun and Steve brought the rifle up again, scanning the area.

"Holy shit, bro..." McCoy stepped forward and toed a huge rock just feet from them. "That wasn't there a moment ago."

Barlow continued to scan the area and barely caught a flash of color slide between two trees. "I got something."

"Tell me it's a clear shot."

"Negative." He continued to scan the area, sweeping the rifle side to side. "There's…*something*, but it's behind the trees and—" His words were cut off by another large rock landing feet from them once again.

"Fuck me!" McCoy racked a round into the shotgun he held and swept it side to side. "Tell me where to point it, Steve. Just tell me where to point it."

Barlow continued to scan the area with the thermal scope and slowly shook his head. "I'm not seeing jack shit out there."

A series of heavy footsteps thumped near them and McCoy felt panic rise in his chest. "Where the fuck is it?!"

Barlow continued to scan the trees and didn't see the dark blur that came in from their blind side and plucked McCoy from the ground. A muffled scream behind him had Steve spinning but losing his cheekweld on the buttstock. As the heat signature began to show in the scope, something large tugged the rifle from his hands and lifted him from the ground.

Without thinking, Steve yelled and the closest sentry spun and leveled his rifle on the huge retreating dark form.

Steve Barlow never heard the rifle round that went through his chest. Nor did he hear McCoy's gurgling scream as the other creature twisted his head from his neck.

9

FOB Dog Town

"Goddammit!" Davidson swore and threw the coffee carafe against the side of the logistics building. "How in the fuck do *two* of those goddam things get inside our perimeter…into our damned camp, and just cart off two of our best team leaders?!"

Les Palmer did his best to contain his emotions but finally stepped up. "Sir, I was stationed two men down from them and I assure you, we didn't see anything."

"*Didn't see anything?*" Davidson repeated, glaring at the man. "We had a fucking line cook standing sentry with you out there. There was a…a data entry something or other out there as well." He clenched his fists to keep from swinging at an inanimate object. He lowered his voice considerably and stepped closer to Les. "I could accept that excuse from one of them, Palmer. But not from a bureau trained SWAT officer."

Palmer felt his chest tighten and he looked up,

meeting Davidson's gaze. "Let me take up the bird, sir. The Vulcan is fully armed. I may not be able to get them all, but I can knock a fuckin' dent in 'em."

Davidson cocked his head to the side and studied the man standing before him. "It's daylight now. But once the sun goes down and these things are feeling brave, you're a go." His voice was so soft he could barely be heard. "The air-to-surface missiles should be here this morning. Once they're prepped and ready, you are clear to send 'em all to Hell."

As Palmer practically ran from the lineup, Davidson turned to Ford and Murphy. "You two are the last of my leadership around here."

"What would you have of us, sir?" Ford asked.

Davidson's jaw trembled as he paced the small building. "Gather the men that are left and split them." He pointed at Murphy. "You're now in charge of what's left of Echo. Incorporate Barlow's remaining agents and find a goddam way to make everyone work together."

"They'll blend seamlessly, sir," Murphy stated without thinking. "They're trained officers and—"

"And we've lost three dozen 'highly trained officers' in the last two fucking days!" Davidson yelled over him. He stopped himself and took a deep breath. "I'm requesting backup for this operation."

Ford stiffened. "Sir?"

Davidson held a hand up to stop him. "Since this clusterfuck has fallen to shit, I'm certain my career with the Bureau is over, but I'll be damned if a bunch of goddam monkey-faced, ten foot tall hairballs are going to kill my men and get away with it!" He gripped the back of a chair so tightly that his knuckles turned white. After another deep breath, he pushed off the chair and turned to face the two men. "I'm calling in backup. I don't know if they'll send SWAT from the city or fly in HRT, but I've requested the full gambit."

Murphy glanced at Ford then turned back to Davidson. "The 'full gambit,' sir?"

"Everything from dogs to EOD robots. I want a fully stocked mobile command center instead of this..." he kicked at the folding table and sent binders and paperwork sliding across the room. "This piece of shit Port-O-John turned office!" He turned back to face them and had to control his breathing.

"EOD robots, sir?" Ford asked, not considering the man's state of mind.

"I know it sounds crazy, but they have thermal cameras and a wide angle view. Why put men at sentry and risk their lives when a damned robot will work just as well."

Ford shook his head slowly. "Sir, with all due respect, those robots are slow as hell to react and they're not armed. If the tangos—"

"I'll not have another man dragged from Dog Town, Agent Ford!"

Ford nodded curtly and lowered his eyes. "Of course not, sir."

Davidson took another deep breath and turned to glance at the techs still trying to work in the room, their heads bowed far too low as they tried to disappear from view. Davidson sighed as he turned back to the men. "Try to eat something, get some rest and..." he glanced at his watch. "If support is coming like I hope, they won't be here for at least six hours. Consider the daylight hours as down time to recharge your batteries.

Once our support personnel arrive, we'll readdress the situation."

"Yes, sir." Ford nodded and backed away towards the door.

Murphy fell into step behind him and once they were far enough away from the logistics building, he pulled Ford aside. "What the fuck did we just witness?"

Ford glanced back at the building and sighed. "The end of an illustrious career."

LES PALMER CLIMBED through the combat converted Bell 407 and ran through his preflight inspections, paying particular attention to the state of the batteries.

"What are you doing?" Hank asked, a cold breakfast burrito in his hand.

"Making sure the bird is prepped and ready for when the missiles arrive." He paused long enough to crack a grin. "Davidson finally cleared me to take the fight to the monsters."

Hank nodded slowly. "Give 'em hell, Les." He took a deep breath and glanced towards Charlie Team's tent. "I get to go wake up Jake and let him know that the boss was…" he trailed off, unable to continue. He turned back to Les and handed him the burrito. "Here. Keep your strength up. I think I've lost my appetite."

Les accepted the offering and watched as Hank sauntered away. In a soft voice he vowed, "No worries, bud. I'll avenge them all."

David Ford jerked awake and found Murphy standing at his feet with a stick in his hand, poking him. "Hey, transport trucks are on their way." Ford grunted and rolled over, pulling the military issue wool blanket up over his shoulder. Murphy rolled his eyes and jabbed him with the stick again. "C'mon, man. Davidson expects us out there."

"Davidson can kiss my ass."

"Oh, shit. Uhh, he didn't mean that, sir," Murphy softly replied.

Ford sat up and looked around the tent, peering through puffy eyes. "Fucker. He ain't here." He slowly fell back to his side and pulled the blanket up again.

"Dude, come on." Murphy grabbed the blanket and pulled it off, dropping it to the floor.

"You're a bastard." Ford sat up and rocked slightly as he tried to get his bearings. "Why do we need to be there?"

"Fresh meat for the grinder is coming in behind the transport trucks." He kicked at the leg of his cot. "You up?"

Ford turned a sleepy eye to him. "Do I look up?"

"Hustle it. You're burning daylight."

As Murphy exited the tent Ford grumbled, "We're supposed to be sleeping *through* the daylight." Slowly he leaned to the side and fell back onto the cot, curling into a fetal position.

Outside, Murphy cracked the can of another energy drink and sucked it down, squeezing the can as he swallowed. He tossed it to a trash barrel and had to step aside as the transport trucks pulled into Dog Town, air brakes hissing as they came to a stop.

"Somebody order some missiles?" The driver shot Murphy a confused smile.

Murphy gave him a curt nod then waved Davidson over. "Director, where do you want the missiles?"

Davidson turned and pointed to the chopper. "Offload them beside the helicopter." The driver raised his brows in surprise then put the truck into gear.

As he drove the truck away, Davidson glanced around at the men hurrying with the supply offload. "Ford still asleep?"

Murphy glanced at the tent then shrugged. "Probably. I tried twice to wake him but it didn't stick."

"Leave him to rest. I'm sure he needs it." Davidson watched as support personnel offloaded the supplies and smiled at the tech's excitement with the new drones. "Those have longer flight times and better cameras."

"We can definitely use that." Murphy checked his watch then asked, "Any word on the backup?"

Davidson nodded solemnly. "We have one team coming in from the city." He raised a brow at him. "HRT, not SWAT."

Murphy rolled his eyes. "Should we get our kneepads out now so we can start kissing their ass as soon as they arrive?"

Davidson scoffed. "I think we might have gotten lucky this time. I happen to know their commander."

"I'll not hold my breath."

Davidson sighed heavily and rubbed at his eyes. "We've got a few more hours until they arrive. I'm going to try to get a little sleep. Something tells me it's going to be a long night."

Murphy chuckled at the comment. "Not if Palmer has any say in it. He's determined to use every round that Vulcan has to eradicate these things."

Both Murphy and Davidson sobered as the bodies of the fallen were carried on litters to the now empty supply truck. Body bag after body bag was carried out and Murphy bowed his head, offering a silent prayer.

Director Davidson stood vigil as the bodies were loaded and once the last had been cleared from the tent, he approached the driver. "Get 'em chilled as soon as you can. Make sure the ME is read in on the project."

"Copy that, director."

Davidson instinctively slapped the side of the truck as it pulled away. He watched it disappear along the bumpy, makeshift road, a trail of dust following it.

He glanced at Murphy standing beside him. "Nothing like tallying up your dead to put everything back into perspective."

Murphy lowered his eyes and clenched his jaw. "There has got to be a way to level the playing field." He glanced toward the tree line and sighed. "Bastards have the home field advantage."

Davidson scoffed. "Not for long." He turned and checked out the techs assembling the new drones. "Tonight, if all goes according to plan, we'll have a half dozen drones in the air with thermal cameras, a fully loaded combat attack helicopter and three elite tactical teams ready to bring these things down."

Murphy could feel eyes on him as they spoke. "Sir, you said something last night that stuck with me."

"What's that?"

"You felt like they called in other 'clans' to fight with

them." He raised a brow at him. "What made you think that?"

Davidson sighed and glanced around to ensure nobody was within hearing range. "Something Archer told us during his AAR. He said he only saw maybe a fifteen to twenty subjects when he was being held."

"Okay. And?"

"And there were dozens...probably close to seventy five of them registering as heat signatures." He shrugged. "It just seemed to me that they must have called in reinforcements."

Murphy scratched at his neck absently. "Maybe they had some of their people on watch, like we do. Or maybe a hunting party had returned. There's any number of possibilities why he didn't see them all."

Davidson nodded. "Yeah, you're right." He turned to leave then paused. "Or maybe they called for help with neighboring clans and there's a whole shitload more of these things than we ever expected."

Murphy watched him trudge towards his tent and made a mental note. *The old man thinks outside the box.*

FORD WINCED as he swallowed the energy drink. "You ingest this crap on purpose?"

"It's not so bad." Murphy waved him on. "Come on, tilt it back and down it. There's enough natural stimulants in that to equal three cups of coffee."

"Tastes like ass." Ford tilted the can back and swallowed, doing his level best to not actually taste the vile concoction as it went down. As he crushed the can, Ford's face twisted in revulsion. "Oh, that's nasty."

"You get accustomed to it."

"Not me." He came to his feet and tossed the can in the bin. "When this op is over, I'm going back to coffee." He loosed a belch and gagged. "Oh, god…it's worse the second time around."

"Quit being such a baby." Murphy clapped his shoulder and pulled back the tent flap. "I hear the trucks."

"Yay," Ford deadpanned. "I've yet to meet an HRT operator that I could stand."

"Davidson says he's buddies with their commander, so maybe it won't be horrible." Murphy escorted Ford to the center of Dog Town and the pair waited for the trucks.

Davidson exited the logistics building all smiles. "It's nearly here."

"It?" Ford asked.

"The new command center." Davidson craned his neck and smiled as the huge RV bounced over the rough dirt road. "And there she is."

"Dude. It's a Winnebago." Murphy shrugged. "I'm sure you—"

"It's a state of the art, MCC. A mobile command center," Davidson corrected. "They just happened to shove it all inside an RV."

"Well, boss, if you're happy, then I'm happy." Murphy patted the man's back but shook his head "no" at Ford.

The techs directed the RV beside the logistics building in order to network their computers with the MCC. Director Davidson had to stop himself from heading straight to his newest toy as two black SUVs pulled in behind the MCC.

"I'm guessing this is them," Ford murmured.

Davidson searched the faces of the men exiting the SUVs and had to do a double take when the side door of the MCC opened and ten men piled out. The last man out was unmistakable, and Director Davidson broke into a toothy grin when he saw the grizzled old man.

Walking directly to him, Davidson draped an arm over the man's shoulders and escorted him toward Ford and Murphy. "Gentlemen, I'd like you to meet Simon Locke. The toughest son of a bitch you'll ever meet."

When the man looked up and met their gaze, they were both taken aback.

10

FOB Dog Town

Simon Locke wasn't a large man. In fact, he was short and slight of build. Seen from the back, he could be mistaken for an average, adolescent male. From the front, however, he was rather intimidating, despite his size. His most distinguishing characteristic was a deep, ugly scar that ran from his right eyebrow to his chin. He sported a three day beard and wore a black knit cap over his short cropped salt and pepper hair. Once you got past the scar, his silver-blue eyes proved piercing. In fact, it was said that Simon Locke didn't look at you, he looked *through* you…and he saw everything.

Locke extended a hand and Ford accepted it. "Nice to meet you, sir."

"Don't 'sir' me, son. This ain't the fucking Army." Simon's eyes narrowed and he leaned closer studying the man before him. "You're Ford, aintcha?"

David grinned at the much shorter man. "Guilty as charged."

"I considered poaching you more than once for HRT." He narrowed his gaze and a slight grin formed. "You'd have told me to go to Hell, but I still think you'da made a good choice."

"Oh, I'm not so sure I'd—"

"Yeah you would." Simon turned to Murphy and extended his hand. "I don't know you."

"John Murphy, sir." Murphy smiled as he shook his hand.

Simon's face went slack as he let go of Murphy's hand. "Cannon fodder." He stepped back and turned to face Davidson. "Alright, Mike. You dragged my sorry ass out here. Tell me what the fuck has your panties in a bunch."

Davidson swept his arm to the side. "If you'll allow me. I've got the whole thing—"

"Just tell me who it is we're hunting. Turkistan Islamic, al-Qa'ida, Boko Haram, Hamas, Segunda Marquetalia?"

Davidson cleared his throat and glanced to the side. "Uh…sasquatch."

Locke stared at him blankly for a moment then glanced at Ford. "You brought me out here to hunt bigfeets?"

"These things have killed a JTTF team and five tactical teams," Ford answered quietly. "They're big, strong, silent, and know these woods like the back of their hands."

"Got that right," Locke replied. "The 'squatches in the Catskills are some of the most aggressive goddam critters on the planet."

Davidson's face showed instant relief. "So you know about them."

"Of course." Locke pulled a can of snuff from his vest pocket and tucked a pinch of tobacco in his lip. "Mean sumbitches." He spat to the side and slid the can back into his vest. "The males use this homemade concrete and smear it all over their chests. It's a ritual path to adulthood. Also purported to be arrow proof, which is why the local Iroquois left them the fuck alone."

"Apparently that concrete is also impervious to small arms fire."

"I would think so." Locke spit again and wiped his chin on the back of his sleeve. "How many do you reckon are out there?"

"We counted dozens…maybe a hundred on the thermals last night," Murphy chimed in.

Locke's face finally displayed a modicum of emotion as he raised a brow. "They don't usually form clans that large. Too many to feed. Too big a drain on resources for any particular area." He thought for a moment then turned back to Davidson. "How long have you been interacting with them?"

"Us, as in our group here? Or from when the first group encountered them?"

Locke hung his head and exhaled forcefully. "The first time, recently, that they had to deal with humans." He glanced up at Davidson. "If that helps."

Davidson tried to do quick math. "Uh…"

"Two weeks," Ford stated. "Since Gamboa and his team first arrived out here. They were investigating a possible terrorist training camp. They'd been out here about three weeks prior to Gamboa arriving."

"So, near on a month and a half." Locke nodded as he spit again and shook his head. "They've called up their distant kin to come fuck with you. That's why you're facing so many."

"How do you know so much about these things?" Murphy asked.

Locke cracked a tight-lipped smile. "It's my job to know about any and all potential threats, son."

He turned a slow circle and took in Dog Town. "We're going to need to reinforce the borders of the camp. I'll have my guys install IR trip wires and connect them to the noise generators."

"Wait…noise generators?" Ford asked.

Locke nodded slightly. "Something I made up years ago. Trip wire sets it off. Shotgun shells, air horns, confetti, the works. Designed to startle the hell out of an interloper. To creatures as basic as the 'squatches, it should run them off PD-fuckin'-Q."

"Sir?" Palmer approached slowly. "Bird is almost ready to go. They're finishing up the main fire control in the cockpit now. She'll be ready to rain hell on 'em tonight."

"Who they fuck is this and what the fuck is he talking about?" Locke gave the man stinkeye.

"This is special agent Les Palmer," Davidson stated. "He's our Huey pilot and he's scheduled to rain hell on the monsters tonight."

Locke shook his head. "Not tonight you're not." He turned back to Davidson. "Tonight, me and my teams will be inserting into these woods and doing a little basic recon on these fuckin' things."

Palmer stiffened. "But…sir? They killed Randy and—"

"And I don't give a tinker's damn, boy!" Locke turned around and glared at him. "You can stay on fuckin' standby while we run our recon. Do you under-fuckin'-stand me?"

Palmer's head bounced from Davidson to Locke and back. "Sir?"

"I'm afraid that until further notice, Commander Locke is—"

"I'm the head muthafucker in charge." Locke squared his shoulders. "You'll fly when I tell you that you can fly." He turned back to Davidson and hitched his chin toward the MCC. "Follow me, Mike. I'll show you where you can push buttons, turn dials, watch screens, and listen in."

The two men disappeared into the MCC and it was only then that Ford realized Locke's men were already scampering about Dog Town doing things that only they knew about. He felt Murphy nudge him and it took a moment to get his attention. "What?"

"I don't think we're the varsity team anymore, bro."

"Yeah. Actually, I'm feeling more like a pawn."

"So it seems."

"Fuck those drones. We're setting up thermal cameras around the perimeter. That bank of screens will display their feeds." Locke checked his watch then turned back to Davidson. "I got another crew coming in. Tech wizards and the like, they'll be monitoring all of this crap."

"I've got techs in the logistics—"

"Have they been qualified on this equipment? Because I guaran-goddam-tee you that my people can fix this shit split lickety if there's any problems."

"I, uh…well, I don't know if—"

"Just keep your people on your gear and I'll keep mine on ours." He clapped Davidson's back as he reached for a satellite phone, "I've also got a crew of rapid response sentries coming. They'll put eyes on our perimeter so your people don't have to pull double duty."

"What the hell are rapid response sentries?"

Locke's smile broadened. "Highly trained security guards with alpha level clearance. Poached 'em from Wackenhut couple a years ago." He turned from Davidson slightly and lowered his voice. "ETA?" After a few nods he sighed. "We're setting up now. The moment your boots hit the fuckin' ground…" he trailed off, nodding. "Excellent."

Davidson watched him hang up the phone and take a deep breath. "Everything okay?"

Locke gave him a surprised look then nodded. "Yeah, my boys from G4S is—"

"Wait, who?"

"The Wackenhut crew. The ones I grabbed from S4 and Area 51. They'll be here inside the hour."

Davidson's eyes widened. "You requ'ed security teams from Area 51?"

Locke nodded slightly. "Wouldn't say there was much paperwork. Woulda been a lot cheaper to just contract with G4S, but I don't like beholding to lawyers." He shrugged. "I just kept throwing money at them until they signed with me."

"What the fuck are you up to? I thought you were

HRT."

Locke smiled again. "That was then. This is *now.*" He clapped Davidson on the shoulder and stared down at the man. "Now? I'm the guy you call when you need a big bad problem taken care of. Doesn't matter if you need it done slow and quiet, fast and loud or 'to hell with who finds out, just getterdone'. I'm the guy."

Davidson stared at him with a blank expression. "The FBI doesn't have—"

Locke's stifled laugh sounded almost menacing. "Who said I was *just* the Bureau?" Locke crossed his arms. "We've known each other for fuckin' years, Mike, so I'm gonna read you in just enough to remove those nagging questions from the back of your noggin." He pulled a rolling chair closer and sat across from him. "My team and I are tasked with taking on the nastiest of the nasty. You've heard of DEVGRU?"

"Yeah, uh…SEAL team six was—"

"Right," he interrupted. "So consider us the non-military version of DEVGRU. Every member of my team was an operator at some point in their career. They each have their own skills, whether it's weapons, electronic warfare, surveillance, guerilla insertion, you name it. I poached the best." He grabbed a paper coffee cup and spit in it, wiping his chin. "Even the guys who empty the bins were operators at one point, so maybe spread the word with your team not to fuck with 'em, eh?"

"That won't be a problem. My men are professionals."

"Good." Locke grinned broader and came to his feet. "Now let's see how many of those cameras are up and running."

"I CAN TELL by the way they move." Palmer stood in the shade of the armory tent, watching the newcomers scurry about Dog Town.

"I call bullshit," Murphy quietly objected.

Ford sighed and stretched his neck, peering through his sunglasses at the new men going about their business. "I don't guess it really matters who they are or what they've done. They're here now and they're Bureau, so…"

"I'm just saying." Palmer pulled a foldout chair closer and sat gingerly, his eyes cutting furtive glances towards the chopper. "I've worked with enough of those guys that I can tell." He glanced up at Ford and nodded. "Either these guys are Special Forces or they were trained by them."

Murphy craned his neck at the sound of engines roaring up the trail. "What now?"

Ford stepped out of the shadows and watched as three black, lifted, four wheel drive vans rolled to a stop behind the MCC. When the sliding doors opened, men in full tactical gear stepped out and immediately dispersed to the perimeter of Dog Town. "What the actual hell?" Ford slowly pulled his sunglasses off and stepped closer, watching as the men conversed in whispers through their coms.

"Either more meat for the grinder or more fingers for triggers." Murphy shrugged. "Either way, I'll take it."

"Wait a damned second." Palmer appeared at his side. "I know these assholes."

Ford crossed his arms and hiked a brow at him. "Go through the academy with them?"

"No." Palmer waved him off. "No, last year when I was on temporary assignment in Nicaragua, these guys showed up. A few days later and we were all packing our stuff to go home." He snapped his fingers and shot them both a wide grin. "I told you they looked like Special Forces."

"So who are they?" Murphy asked.

Palmer lowered his head and strained his brain to think. "I heard one of the contractors mention a name but I thought he was referencing the Navy…" he trailed off. "Haze Gray?"

Ford noted that one of the new guys carrying totes past them stiffened when Palmer spoke. He instinctively reached out and tapped Les' shoulder, shaking his head. "Not now."

The soldier barely glanced in their direction before resuming his assigned task.

"What was that about?" Murphy whispered.

Ford gently pulled them both back into the armory tent. "I have a feeling that Palmer wasn't supposed to know who they are." He gave him a cautionary look. "Maybe I'm wrong, and maybe you're wrong about them, but either way, I say we play this shit close to the vest."

Palmer gave him a confused look. "I don't get it. Who cares what they call themselves?"

Ford took a deep breath and glanced through the open flap of the tent. "Tell me something. Did the contractors talk in hushed tones? Did any of the guys they were talking about ever mention their unit?"

Palmer thought for a moment and slowly shook his

head. "Come to think of it, we never did know for sure who they were. But yeah, the contractors were whispering about them." He shrugged. "I guess they weren't being paid by the job, but daily. I don't really know. I just know they were pissed when these guys came in and fixed everything."

"Wait, 'fixed' it?" Murphy asked.

"I was barely off the plane myself so I'm not sure what the mission even was." He crossed his arms and sighed. "I was looking forward to flying and never even warmed up the engine."

Murphy glanced at Ford and raised a brow. "So who *are* these guys?"

Ford gave them a slow shrug. "I honestly don't know, but I say that until we have a better idea of who we're dealing with, we stay out of their way."

Palmer hung his head. "I'm never going to get to fly the chopper, am I?"

"Hey, Locke is in charge and until—" A loud commotion cut him off and Ford stepped toward the opening in the tent flap. Pulling it back, he watched as members of his own team and the new guys all ran towards the other side of Dog Town. "Something's up."

Exiting the tent, the three men were swept into a current and slowed near the tree line as people quickly formed a semi-circle. Not a word was spoken as they all took in the grotesque display.

In an exhibit that would make Vlad the Impaler proud, Steve Barlow and Randol McCoy were hung, stripped nude and impaled on small tree trunks, their limbs dangling like worn out rag dolls.

11

FOB Dog Town

Ford had to look away and nearly threw up as the reality of the scene struck home. He barely heard Locke yell as he stormed into the area.

"What the hell are you gawking at?! Get them down from there!"

Murphy grabbed Ford by the arm and pulled him from the assembled crowd. "That just recently happened," he whispered.

"No shit," Palmer stated as he fell into step with them. "Otherwise the sentry would have—"

"That's not what I meant." Murphy shot him a *shut the hell up* look. "The wounds were fresh. The blood hadn't even dried yet."

"Wait, you mean.... You don't mean they were kept alive this whole time?" Palmer felt his legs grow weak.

Ford glanced back and watched the men try to catch their bodies as the poles were tugged up from the ground. "Their arms and legs were broken," Ford whispered.

Murphy nodded. "Probably to keep them from trying to free themselves."

"Dude," Palmer shot him a flat stare. "They were *impaled*. McCoy's tore through the side of his neck and Barlow's stick was in his damned throat."

"Stop!" Murphy held a hand up. "We all saw what you saw."

"So they were dead the moment that thing pierced their livers."

Ford held his hands up, stopping the argument. "I saw the bruises on their arms and legs and the unnatural angles they were at. They were broken. Maybe so they couldn't escape until the 'squatches were ready to put them on display. I don't know. All I know is, they were definitely tortured."

Murphy hung his head and sighed, ignoring the crowd that marched past the trio. "They were sending a message."

"Of course they were," Ford whispered, glancing at the last of the crowd leaving the area. "Archer was right. They're smart as hell."

Murphy glanced at the bodies being carried back to Dog Town by stretcher, each with a lone man following, holding the end of the stake. "They're a lot more human than we give them credit for."

THE FIELD SURGEON held the x-ray up to the light and sighed. "This was exceptionally painful."

"No shit." Locke snatched the x-ray film from his hand and loosed it onto the floor. "Tell me a goddam way to impale somebody through the ass that *isn't* painful!"

The field surgeon glared at him as he reached for the next set of films. He purposely stepped away from Locke and held them up. "As suspected, both arms and both legs suffered multiple fractures." He sifted through the films and held one out to Davidson. "Director, as you can see, the femur in this film isn't just broken, it's shattered, and the femur is the strongest bone in the body. This could only have been caused by twisting and crushing." The surgeon stepped closer to Barlow's body and pulled the sheet away, exposing his thigh. "The skin had started to display the hematoma when the victim was…impaled. The bruise will continue to form with time, but what I wanted to show you was this." He pulled a marker from his shirt pocket and drew a crude outline on Barlow's thigh.

"What's that?" Davidson asked.

The field surgeon locked eyes with him. "Your assailant's hand." He stepped back and pushed the cap back on the marker. "Whoever did this had hands the size of…" He trailed off, shaking his head, giving them both a knowing look.

"We already knew the woodboogers did this. Who the hell else would?" Locke waved him off.

"I realize that." The doctor sighed. "I was merely trying to show you the size of the assailant's hand." He held his hands out about twelve to fourteen inches. "At least this wide. With fingers thicker than bratwurst sausages."

Davidson lowered the x-ray film. "How big would you guess this thing is?"

The surgeon shrugged. "I'm not familiar with Gigantopithecus Amercanus anatomy, so I couldn't really say."

Davidson gave him a questioning look. "Excuse me?"

"That's the fancy name the science types gave these things," Locke grumbled. "Like naming it gives us any more answers into how the goddam thing thinks."

Davidson glanced down at Barlow's thigh and held his open hand over the bruise. "Good heavens that is huge."

"That's what my ex-wife said on our wedding night." Locke grinned at him. "She meant my bank account though." He tugged at Davidson' arm. "Come on. We got work to do."

"Wait." He pulled away. "What did you mean when you first said it was such a painful way to go?"

The surgeon sifted through the x-rays and held one out. "The bark was intact and there are small spines where the branches were snapped away, but not smoothed." He looked away and shook his head. "It's bad enough what was done to these men, but this?"

"Fucking animals…" Davidson trailed off as he handed the films back.

"No shit, they're animals." Locke glared at him. "And we're going to return the favor in spades."

Locke checked his gear loadout once more then nodded to Davidson. "Send up your eye in the sky whenever you're ready."

Director Davidson gave him a thumb's up and watched as the teams departed Dog Town. He turned his attention to the screens then ordered the drones into the air. "I want a full 360 on them."

The drone buzzed slightly then shot into the air, displaying the people in the camp in brilliant colors over a dark background. As the machine maneuvered to the edge of the woods, multiple heat signatures appeared on the screen.

"Locke, we're picking up heat signatures about ten meters inside the tree line."

"Understood. Keep a fuckin' eye on 'em. If they start to move in or try to circle us, I want to know."

"Copy that." Davidson held the headset mic in his hand and continued to stare at the screen.

Ford stepped into the MCC and received a handful of hard stares from the technicians on either side of Davidson. "Are they inserting?"

"About to." Davidson shifted to the side to allow Ford to approach the monitors. "These are the cameras surrounding the perimeter." Davidson pointed to the array of small black and white screens overhead. "We're actually receiving their helmet cam feeds. These are them." He pointed to another row.

Ford made a quick count of the screens. "His team is only seven members?"

Davidson smirked and stepped back. "He's got the rest of his men on standby. If they make contact, they'll swarm the area."

"IFF active," a technician announced.

Ford glanced at the overhead feed from the drone and the seven heat signatures slowly advancing into the forest began flashing IFF signals. "Nice."

"If you're going to be in here, you'll need to maintain silence." Both Davidson and Ford turned to the closest tech, whose facial expression indicated it wasn't an option.

Ford held a hand up and leaned closer to Davidson. "It's okay. I'll go outside and watch the drone feed with the guys." He backed slowly out of the MMC and shut the door behind him.

"So?" Murphy asked.

"Like Cape Canaveral in there." Ford glanced back at the large windshield, now covered with reflective fabric. "And tense."

"Check it." Palmer nodded to the large screens set up outside the logistics building. "The 'squatches are watching but they aren't approaching."

Ford watched as the point man for Locke's team slowed to a stop. He could see the heat signature shimmer slightly, and a small burst of heat popped in and out of existence nearby. "Ho-boy," Palmer exclaimed. "They're running suppressed out there."

"Excuse me?" Ford leaned closer.

"No sound, but a muzzle flash of heat? Gotta be running suppressed."

Murphy nodded slowly. "Makes sense." He leaned closer and pointed. "Oh, man…I think they got one."

One of the large heat signatures closest to the insertion team was no longer moving and appeared to be slowly cooling as its color began to shift from red hot to orange to yellow.

"And so it begins." Ford sighed and rubbed a

calloused hand over his face. "Why aren't the others reacting?"

Murphy shrugged. "Maybe they aren't aware yet?"

"Hold on..." Palmer turned to them excitedly. "One shot, one kill?"

"Had to be a headshot," Murphy replied.

"Armor piercing rounds."

The three men turned to see a hulking, red-bearded man in full tactical gear standing behind them. He gripped the top of his vest with both hands and stared at the screen. "That was probably West. He likes taking point." He raised a brow at Ford. "Best opportunity to improve his kill score."

"Kill score?" Murphy asked.

The red-bearded man nodded slightly. "He and some of the others keep track."

Palmer glanced at Ford then turned to the man. "Hey, were you guys the ones that came to Nicaragua about a year and a half ago? In-and-out type of op?"

The man stared at him blankly, refusing to answer. It took a moment for Palmer to put two and two together, and soon he started nodding. "Good job. Maybe next time, don't be so good at it though. I never got a chance to take a bird up."

"You're welcome," the man replied stoically. "Eight out of ten birds were shot down in the first three minutes of flight." He nodded slightly as he stepped away. "Nice chatting with you fellas. Time to go to work."

Ford's eyes followed the large man as he met up with more of his team. In the low light of Dog Town's inner encampment, he could barely make out their faces, but their equipment was impressive. He noted a wide array of M4 variants, a SCAR heavy, HK MP7's and a few more obscure, but high end weapons. It appeared that all of them were suppressed.

"Yeah, these guys aren't HRT." Ford spun a slow circle and noted the men grouping into teams and readying for insertion. "I think things are about to get busy."

DEEP in the Catskills

"SAY AGAIN YOUR LAST," Locke whispered into the coms.

Davidson keyed the mic, "We have positive count of four more heat signatures to your north."

Locke keyed the coms, indicating "message received" then switched to local coms. "Give me a count."

His team responded with either a positive or negative target acquisition. Satisfied, Locke gave the order, "Initiate on three. One…two…three, initiate." He applied gentle pressure on the trigger and the spit hiss of the suppressed 300 blackout rifle was barely audible to his own ears. "Report."

Davidson watched the overhead drone feed and slowly nodded. "One tango remains."

"Good." Locke stood from his position and shouldered his weapon. "Let him run his hairy ass back and tell them that the humans aren't fuckin' around." He made a circle in the air with his finger. "Converge on me, prepare for strategic withdrawal."

As Locke and company exited the woods, they flipped up the thermal imagers and sauntered into the edge of camp. "I want all three companies on standby for the night." He glanced up at the drone still making lazy loops in the night sky. "Keep the thermals up for constant surveillance. If we pick up anything hotter than a squirrel fart, I want two teams minimum inserting and initiating. Understood?"

A round of soft "ooh-rahs" was his answer. "Stand down until needed." He squared his shoulders and sighed. "I need a drink."

Locke jerked open the door to the MCC and fell into the front passenger seat. Digging under the dash he withdrew a small flask and twisted the top.

"Is that it?" Davidson asked.

Locke took a long pull from the small silver flask then screwed the lid back on. "For now."

"Four out of a hundred?"

Locke scoffed and kicked his feet up onto the doghouse of the RV. "We can't kill what ain't out there, Mike." He sniffed hard then tucked the flask into his vest. "They sent five critters to keep an eye on us and we shot four of 'em in the fuckin' head." He turned slowly and met Davidson's gaze. "Eighty percent on a first encounter with zero casualties is a fuckin' win in my book."

Davidson hung his head and set the mic aside. "I thought we were taking the war to them?"

"We are." Locke kicked his feet off the doghouse and stood. "But we have no fuckin' clue where they hang their hats at night. Yeah, there's a metric shit ton of tunnels and caves out there, but I'll be damned if I'm sending my men underground without logistical support." He pulled the flask from his vest again and took another pull. "Trust me, they'll get the message. Kill two of ours, we kill four of yours. And we have a whole lot more people than they do." Davidson opened his mouth to argue but Locke stepped past him. "If they send any more out tonight to sniff around, I have teams on standby ready to shut 'em down. We'll neutralize them before they can make any more trouble."

"You left one standing."

Locke nodded, his hands on his hips. "I did." He offered a weak shrug. "Somebody has to run back and tell big daddy that their lookouts are all dead. If the leader is as smart as I think he is, he ain't gonna come near Dog Town so long as he has grunts he can send." Locke shrugged again. "And if he ain't as smart as I think he is, I'll blow his fuckin' head off myself.

12

FOB Dog Town

Ford struggled to keep his eyes open as he stared at the big screen mounted outside the logistics building. The techs had cycled drones throughout the night, maintaining a constant surveillance of the surrounding woods.

"You should get some rack time."

Ford looked up at Murphy standing over him. "I'll sleep when I'm dead."

"Yeah, yeah tough guy." Murphy pushed his boots off the edge of the table and Ford nearly fell forward in the fold out chair. "Go to bed. I'll wake you if anything starts to brew."

Ford glanced at the teams on standby, gathered in their clique-ish groups and speaking in low tones. "We won't go back out as long as those guys are around."

"Then why stand vigil over the monitor?" Murphy nudged him again. "Get some rest."

Ford looked up at him and squinted in the low light. "Why aren't you tired?"

"Took a power nap." Murphy grinned at him. "Then downed about three of these." He held up an energy drink.

"Those things are going to kill you. They'll make your heart explode or something."

Murphy shrugged again then took a long pull from the can, crushing it once he was done. "Better these than what those things can dream up."

"Movement." Both Ford and Murphy turned to the screen as the tech zoomed in on the incoming heat signatures. "Sure enough. Looks like our lone watcher went back and reported what happened to his buddies."

Ford stood and wiped at his eyes. "We should gear up."

"That won't be necessary," Davidson announced a bit too loudly. "Locke and his men are here."

"Then why the fuck are we still here?" Murphy asked aggressively.

Ford immediately stood between them and stared Murphy down. "Sir," he added quietly.

Murphy hung his head and sighed. "Then why are we still here, *sir*?"

"You're still the responding SWAT team. You're just on standby." Davidson gave the two men a hard stare.

Locke nearly bounced from the MCC and gave his men a knowing look. They immediately began to double check their gear as Locke sauntered through the bullpen outside of the logistics building. "We're going to assess the situation."

"You mean ambush, right?" Murphy gave him a tight-lipped smile.

Locke turned and pointed to the screen. "How many critters you see worming their way through the woods?"

Ford and Murphy both turned and did a quick tally. "A dozen?" Murphy replied.

"Fifteen," Ford corrected.

"We killed four last time and left one. We'll kill fourteen this time and leave another." Locke double checked the status of his HK then slapped the charging lever down. "I'll play this game until there's only one left standing." He winked at Murphy. "I'll leave him for you."

The pair watched him slowly walk through Dog Town, his teams falling into place behind him. Murphy took a deep breath and let it out slowly. "I really don't like that man."

DAVIDSON HOVERED behind the techs monitoring the situation inside MCC. He resisted the urge to report every movement of the targets once they had settled in.

"They're still clumped in groups of three and four," he practically whispered into the coms. "They seem to be standing in small units."

Locke eased tighter to the closest group and paused. He double clicked his mic, indicating he was in position. Bringing the scope to bear he stopped and stared at the scene. "Anybody else seeing what I'm seeing?" A soft round of affirmatives replied in his earbud.

"I've got a direct overhead view. I can't tell what they're doing." Davidson almost sounded left out as he spoke. A moment later and he excitedly keyed the mic again. “I got movement!”

“We see it.” Locke silently sucked at his teeth. “Initiate on three.” He glanced at the man beside him and nodded. The quiet understanding being that Locke had the two creatures on the left and his partner took the two on the right. “One…two…three, initiate.”

He gently squeezed the trigger of the suppressed 300 blackout and watched as all four animals fell. As he slowly came to his feet he keyed the coms and switched to the MP5 slung to his chest. “Verify.”

He stood over the pile of corpses and sighed as his grip tightened on the 9MM HK. His partner stood to the side, a suppressed pistol in his hand. “Were they praying over the dead?”

Locke gave him a long shrug then leveled the barrel of the MP5 on the closest animal and sent a single slug into its cranium. He popped his second target then raised a brow at the other man. “It looked like they were doing something.”

The man quickly verified his targets would stay down then holstered the pistol. “Somehow that didn’t feel, I don’t know, *right.*”

Locke spat at the closest primate before he turned to leave. “Tell that to Barlow and McCoy.”

“I don’t get it. Why did they just stand there?”

Ford stared at the monitor and slowly shook his head. “It’s like they were waiting to get shot.”

Davidson stepped out of the MCC, a wide smile painted across his face. "All targets down."

"Yeah, so much for leaving one alive to report to the others," Murphy scoffed.

Ford continued to stare at the rapidly cooling heat signatures. "Why would they just stand there?"

"They were paying homage to their fallen." Ford turned to see the large, red bearded man standing behind him. "They all stood there, surrounding the bodies we left and…" he trailed off, unable to find the right words.

"Wait." Ford held a hand up, his features twisting with confusion. "You're saying they were having some kind of 'service' over their dead?"

The red bearded man shrugged, his eyes locked on the heat signatures on the screen. "They all stood there silently, their heads bowed and their hands cupped in front of them." He glanced back at Ford and shrugged again. "Looked like prayers to me."

"No fuckin' way," Murphy shoved his chair away from him, toppling it. "These are *animals*, remember?"

The red bearded man chuckled. "I've fought enemies that acted worse than most animals." He locked eyes with Murphy. "And they prayed. A lot."

"I'm not buying it." Murphy turned and stormed away, his anger and disbelief palpable.

Ford slowly approached the larger man and lowered his voice. "You personally observed this?"

The man nodded slightly. "Just before I put their heads in my crosshairs and ventilated their skulls."

Ford sighed heavily and turned to stare at the screen again. "Do you believe they were praying?"

The larger man slowly shook his head. "I hope not."

He patted Ford's shoulder. "Because then they're no longer animals."

SIMON LOCKE actually laughed when the drone feed indicated two heat signatures creeping through the woods and dragging off their dead, one by one. "I think they figured out we ain't fuckin' playin'!"

"Sun will be up in half an hour," Davidson announced. "Should we send someone to extract a body for study?"

Locke turned and gave him a curious look. "Why? The government has studied these things up one side and down the other."

Davidson paused and glanced at the others gathered. "They…they have?"

Locke scoffed. "Of course. They've had bodies on ice for years. Decades even." He sat back in his chair and smiled again as the two creatures came back into view to retrieve another of their fallen. He sat upright suddenly and slowly turned to Davidson. "But it might not be a bad idea to have these fuckin' things followed. Find out if they're using a mass grave somewhere or if they're dragging them underground."

Davidson stammered a bit as he came up from his chair in the MCC. "Do you really think we should risk—"

"What risk?" Locke pulled his knit cap back on and stepped outside the RV. "I'll put my two best on it. They can laser point the grave or cave entrance, whichever they find." He clipped the MP5 back to his vest and stretched his neck. "At least we'll have the goddam spot marked."

Davidson held back while Locke marched towards the tents that his teams were using and disappeared inside. A moment later, two men came out and began rummaging through the many crates they had brought with them. Davidson watched as the men geared up and painted their faces with camo sticks. A moment later and the two men were inserting into the woods with pure confidence.

"How do they do that?"

"Do what?" Locke gave him a confused look.

"Just walk into the woods without a care in the world?"

"They're professionals. The only care they have is possible mission failure." Locke took a fresh dip of snuff and slid the can back into a vest pocket. "The difference between my men and yours? Yours came out with a defeated goddam attitude. They came to hunt the big bad monsters that kill people and suck the marrow from their fuckin' bones." He spat to the side and wiped his chin with the back of his glove. "My men came out here with the attitude that *they* are the goddam monsters and they intend to kill anything that might threaten to take that title away from 'em."

Davidson gave him a shocked look. "That isn't fair to my men, Simon. These are good operators and—"

Locke held a hand up. "I didn't say they weren't." He turned and locked eyes with Davidson. "I said their 'attitude' wasn't right. They came out here afraid. Mine didn't." He spat again, his eyes still locked with the directors. "That's how my men do what they do."

As Locke walked away, Davidson knew that he

wasn't far off the mark. The men who believed they were coming out to fight the legendary Sasquatch were reticent. Others thought it was all a wild goose chase and that they'd be pursuing shadows in the woods. Locke's team came locked and loaded, expecting a formidable enemy and prepared to outmatch them.

He glanced across the bullpen and saw Palmer wiping down the chopper like a rider would brush down a horse. Ford and Murphy were still camped in front of the large screen monitor outside the logistics building. He felt a short jab as he realized how people's expectations were falling short of their reality. Knowing that he was the cause only served to make it worse.

About midday, Davidson saw the activity level of Locke's men surge. He quickly trotted to the MCC and the place was abuzz with activity. "What's going on? What happened?"

Locke gave him a self-satisfied grin. "My boys located a cave entrance where the critters are coming and going."

"Are they going to insert?"

Locke's face fell. "Not alone they aren't." He turned his attention back to the screen and the pulsing indicator overlayed on a map. "I want two teams geared up and ready to go in five!"

Davidson was practically run over as the men rushed out of the RV and to their respective tents. Davidson had to wait until the operators were clear before he planted his ass in a chair and squeezed between two overly large techs. "So where is this place?"

One tech ignored him completely while the other barely raised his voice. "Two clicks east-northeast from Dog Town."

Davidson leaned forward and studied the map. "I don't think any of our people have been out that way."

"That's about to change, Director." The tech continued tapping on the keyboard in front of him and a series of helmet cams came to life on the overhead large screen. "Be advised, Charlie Team, you are active."

"Copy that," a disembodied voice replied.

As another series of helmet cams flickered to life, the tech announced, "Be advised, Delta Team, your cameras are active."

"Good thing I'm wearing pants then, eh?" The laughter and jovial tone of the Delta Team members cemented Locke's comment in Davidson's mind. They had no reason to be fearful. *My men believe they are the monsters…*

The teams quickly assembled, and a second drone was placed into duty as the teams inserted into the woods and quietly made their way towards the marked location. Locke suddenly appeared at Davidson's side and with a quick nod of his head, unseated the director and took his place.

"I thought you'd spearhead this one like you did the others."

Locke quietly scoffed. "I'm no tunnel rat." He leaned back in his chair and gave Davidson a knowing look. "I have men that are specialized in everything." He leaned closer and emphasized, "Every. Damned. Thing."

"Okay..." he trailed off.

"I'm not anybody's first choice for dark, confined spaces, but these men were born for it. That's why they'll be spelunking and I'll be monitoring."

Davidson nodded curtly and stood back, crossing his arms. "Makes sense, I suppose."

Locke glanced back at him then hooked his chin toward the door. "I've got this. Take a break." He grabbed a headset and pulled it on, adjusting his mic. "You can watch from outside. We're feeding the monitors you have set up out there."

Davidson didn't immediately catch on to the inflection. "Oh, I'm okay here. I'll just stand and watch and—"

Locke sighed heavily. "Your presence is neither required nor desired." He spun and raised a brow at him. "In other words, it wasn't a request, Director." He stared the man down until Davidson caught on and reached for the door.

He slowly shut the door and pressed it latched. "Good hunting."

13

FOB Dog Town

"Decided to join us nobodies, sir?" Murphy asked, his eyes still glued to the monitors.

"Getting some air, that's all." He stood behind the men and glanced to the edge of the camp as Locke's men disappeared into the thick. "They located one of the underground entrances." He crossed his arms and continued to stare at the screen. "Locke decided to send men to check it out."

Ford glanced up at him. "He does realize these mountains are eat up with tunnels and old mines, doesn't he?"

Davidson shrugged. "They followed the bodies; this hole is where they were taken."

Murphy scoffed. "He's going to sic his guys on a caveman morgue. What a maroon."

"Easy, Murph." Ford patted the man's shoulder. "At

least it's not us putting our necks on the line for something stupid."

Murphy came to his feet. "This time, anyway."

"Where ya going?"

Murphy waved him off. "Shake the dew off the lily. I'll be back."

"Bring popcorn," Ford chuckled as he rubbed at his eyes. "Think they'll all be asleep?"

"Not all of them." Davidson sat in Murphy's chair and lowered his voice. "What are your thoughts on Locke and his people?"

Ford raised a brow at him. "I don't know any of them well enough to say." He leaned back and gave the director a sidelong look. "I thought you and Locke were tight? It sounded like it when he first got here."

Davidson sighed and held his head in his hands for a moment. "He's not the same guy I knew." When he looked up, he suddenly looked tired and much older. "Simon used to be good people. Salt of the earth, but also one of the most effective operators I ever met."

"And?"

"And…now he's different. It's like he's on a power trip. His way is the only way, that sort of crap."

Ford shrugged. "Well, just to play Devil's advocate, the body count has changed sides significantly since they arrived." He held his hands up as he quickly qualified his statement. "I'm just saying, we were definitely on the losing side of these altercations until they entered the arena. That's how an outsider would see it."

Davidson took a deep breath and let it out slowly. "He had prior knowledge of the enemy. We were still learning from our mistakes."

"Again, from an outside perspective, you've got to admit, his numbers are impressive."

Davidson opened his mouth to argue then slowly closed it. "Yeah. I guess from an outside perspective, it looks that way."

Ford leaned forward and lowered his voice even more. "Look at this way. As long as Locke is here and doing what he does, our people aren't put at risk." He leaned back and smiled. "The mere fact that he's turned the hunters into prey? That's just icing on the cake."

"Approaching target zone," the disembodied voice was clear but tinny over the speakers. "Contact scouts."

"Understood. Proceed with caution." Locke sat back and stared at the screen as the techs switched the helmet cams from normal to night vision. A handful of the cams were thermal capable and brought color to the monitors.

As the teams went deeper into the darkness the signals from the helmet cams began to break up. Locke cursed under his breath as he keyed the coms. "Move one of the drones to the tunnel entrance. Let's use it as a repeater."

A moment later the helmet cam signals cleared and Locke sighed with relief. "Maintain coms. Break into their local coms if you need to. I want to hear what's going on."

The tech tapped at his keyboard and a constant static came over the headset. "You're in, Commander."

Locke stared at the screens and strained to listen as

the men advanced deeper into the ground. When the signal began to fade, he keyed in, "Delta Actual, set an RF repeater before moving on."

"Copy."

Locke could tell the moment the repeater was turned on. The tech closest to him leaned to the side and whispered, "That thing will only do so much the deeper they go."

"I'm aware." Locke continued to stare at the screen and his breath caught in his throat as the men entered a large underground chamber. "What in the fucking hell?"

The men scattered along the far wall of the chamber and multiple views of bodies laid out on ground displayed in NV green. Some had wildflowers scattered across them.

"Control, it would appear we've discovered where they lay their dead."

Locke sighed as he studied the images. "I guess that's one reason why we've never found the remains of these things." He keyed his coms again, "Try to GPS the location for reference then Oscar Mike."

"Copy. Marking location."

Locke found himself forgetting to breathe as the teams slowly advanced through the tunnel systems. He wasn't really surprised when the tunnel T'd out at an old mine, complete with rails and ceiling braces.

"Moving right," Charlie Actual whispered.

"Moving left," Delta announced.

Locke continued to monitor the screens and cursed to himself when the signals started breaking up again. "Charlie Actual, drop a repeater. Delta, you as well."

The camera signals improved significantly and Locke sat back with a sigh of relief. "Maintain coms."

"Copy."

As the teams advanced further into the old mine, local coms were kept to a minimum. The eerie silence only added to the creepiness, and Locke half expected something to jump out at them at any moment.

One of the thermal cams picked up Charlie Actual holding a fist in the air and lowering himself closer to the ground. "Movement," he whispered.

The entire MCC held their breath until a field rat came into view. Charlie Actual's voice sounded relieved as he stood again. "False alarm—"

As if from the rock itself, a giant arm shot out and gripped the man by his tactical vest, pulling him from view and into a natural vestibule. A muffled shout of surprise was all that was heard.

Charlie Team suddenly snapped to the ready and advanced on the position, weapons leveled and ready to fire, but the narrow craggy opening was empty. "What the actual fuck!?" The lead operator pushed into the stony crack and swept the small antechamber with his weapon. "They couldn't have just disappeared."

"Move."

The lead man stepped away and a smaller operator wedged into the opening and stepped into the antechamber. "There has to be another way out." One by one, Charlie Team entered the dim antechamber and ran their hands along the walls, searching for any kind of opening.

One of the men happened to look up, but before he could react, something huge dropped into the middle of the team, swinging the dead body of their team leader like a club.

LOCKE SAT on the edge of his seat, his eyes wide as he tried to watch every helmet cam feed at the same time. He nearly jumped out of his skin when the room erupted.

One of the thermal cameras picked up a wall of heat simply appearing behind the rest of the team and one by one the helmet cameras blinked out, their feed replaced by static.

"No!" He came out of his seat so abruptly that he upended the chair. "Kill that fuckin' thing!" His voice cracked as he screamed into the coms. "Do you hear me?"

He felt his knees go weak as the realization struck. "Charlie Actual, do you copy?" He leaned heavily against the counter behind him and continued to stare at the dead feeds. "Charlie Team, does anybody copy?"

"Control, Delta Actual. Request permission to backtrack and—"

"Granted!" Locke cut him off. "Seventy yards from the entrance, on your right. There's a small chamber through a narrow opening."

"Copy."

Locke watched Delta's helmet cam screens as the men raced back along the mine. Delta Actual began counting as his team passed the entrance. As he closed in on sixty, he slowed and moved to the far side of the mine, his weapon at the ready as he advanced.

When the narrow opening came into view, he hunkered low and scanned upward before moving closer. His breath caught in his chest and suddenly his camera went black as he flipped the NV goggles up and switched on the LED torch mounted to his rifle. "Oh my god."

"Report!" Locke leaned forward and stared at the other helmet cam feeds. "What's the status of Charlie Team?"

"KIA, commander." Delta flipped off the light and lowered his NV goggles again, allowing the camera to display the carnage as his eyes readjusted to NV. "No sign of the tango."

Locke felt his legs shake and he reached for something to steady him. "Delta, can you retrieve the bodies?"

A long pause almost had Locke yelling into the coms. When Delta Actual replied, it was very quiet. "Negative, commander. We'll need multiple body bags and assistance to cart the…pieces…out."

Locke sat on the floor and lowered his head, his jaw clenching in anger. "Copy that, Delta. Set a watch and I'll prepare a secondary team to assist."

Locke finally looked up. The blood vessels in his left eye had ruptured. His face was a reddened mask of anger and hate as he came to his feet. "Rally Bravo Team and have them gear up." He plucked the knit cap from his head and tossed it aside. "Tell them I'll be leading them in for the recovery."

To their credit, Davidson and the SWAT members who observed the carnage on the monitors said nothing as Locke exited the MCC and slammed the RV's door.

They watched as he marched purposefully toward the tent that Bravo was using and disappeared inside.

"Should we offer assistance, Director?"

Davidson raised a brow at Ford. "I don't think now is the time." He cleared his throat and came to his feet. "But it wouldn't hurt to remind Simon that he's got other assets standing by."

"Wait…did he just volunteer us to die?" Murphy asked, not realizing his voice carried.

Ford shot him a stern stare. "You really don't know when to keep your thoughts in your head, do you?"

Davidson squared his shoulders and approached the Bravo tent. He pulled the flap open just as Locke was stepping out. "The fuck do you want?" His tone of voice carried more venom than even Davidson expected.

"I just wanted to express our condolences." He cleared his throat and stepped back. "And to remind you that you have other resources at your disposal, should you need them."

Locke glanced over Davidson's shoulder at Ford and Murphy watching from the bullpen. "I think we got this covered, Director. But should the need arise, I'll be sure to let you know before I commandeer your men."

Davidson placed a gentle hand on his shoulder. "Simon, we have more than just SWAT teams out here." He glanced toward the chopper. "We have air support and a damned good pilot to boot."

Locke gave him a "duh" look. "Fat lot of fuckin' good a chopper does me underground." He pushed past him, spun and marched toward the hard cases of supplies they had brought and throwing the cover aside as he rummaged through the contents, searching for body bags.

Director Davidson sighed heavily and turned to his men, offering them a mere shrug.

"Looks like you get to live another day, Murph." Ford pushed past, leaving him to contemplate his actions.

"What?" Murphy asked as he fell into step behind him. "We're all thinking it."

Ford paused outside the mess tent and gave Murphy a tight-lipped smile. "You know, you can't have it both ways."

"What do you mean?"

"You can't bitch about being sidelined then whine about being 'sent to die' should your services be needed." Ford stopped before he said something he couldn't take back. "You can't be satisfied."

"You saw what happened to Locke's guys in there." Murphy kept his voice low. "I'm all for taking the fight to them, but not in their own damned living room."

Ford spun on him and spread his arms wide. "This whole mountain is their living room. They know every hill, every rock, every tree…hell, probably every blade of grass that's out here. There is no place out here that isn't 'their home.' You got to get that fact through your head." Ford dropped his arms and scoffed. "The only way you get to face them and they don't have the home field advantage is if they invade downtown Albany."

Murphy stared at him open mouthed as Ford spun and picked up a tray. He glanced around the mess tent then set the tray back down. "I think I've lost my appetite."

Murphy watched him leave and stared after him. "How could he even have an appetite after what we just watched?"

14

FOB Dog Town

Director Davidson sat in the MCC and watched as Bravo and Delta Teams carried out the remains of their fallen. The drone displayed high definition images, and he paused to catch a solemn moment where Locke knelt beside one of the body bags and bowed his head. A moment later he made the sign of the cross and came to his feet.

Davidson knew the man's pain all too well. Having lost men to the same enemy, he also knew the metallic taste in the back of the throat that came from pure hatred. He turned the volume down on the team's coms and sighed as they loaded the body bags into the back of three Kawasaki mules.

The ATVs had been converted to carry their members over rough terrain for long distances. The rear dump beds had been converted into crude bench seats, but they were hastily removed for this task. He couldn't help but noticed the reverence the men used when loading the bags in the bed.

"I'll never get used to this part." He pulled the headphones off and set them aside before coming to his feet and stretching his back. "I never thought I'd be okay with using a nuke on American soil, but right now…" he trailed off, unwilling to say aloud his true thoughts.

"Trust me, Director," the tech beside him raised a brow at him. "Commander Locke is about to go scorched earth."

Davidson met the man's gaze and realized he meant every word he'd said. "They have it coming."

"What gets me, though?" The tech pushed away from his console and lowered his voice. "They had Delta dead to rights in those mines. Why'd they stop with just Charlie Team?"

Davidson took a deep breath and let it out slowly. "And why were we allowed to make our recovery? Where did the assailants go?" He stepped back to his post and sat down carefully. "Delta inspected the area that Charlie Team was…" he cleared his throat nervously, "where they engaged the enemy. There were no exits. Hell, the entrance to that alcove was little more than a crack in the wall."

The tech nodded slowly. "I've done comparisons on their heat signatures. These things they're facing are *huge*." He glanced to the rear of the MCC to ensure none of the other techs were listening in. "I mean, some of them are nearly twelve feet tall and the weights that I've extrapolated? Between eight hundred and twelve hundred pounds."

Davidson sat back and nodded. "That goes hand in hand with the lore."

The tech stood quickly and lifted the fold-down cover on a cubby above his work station. He pulled out a three inch binder and handed it to the director. "These are the compiled government files on the monsters." He glanced back again to ensure nobody was watching. "They aren't even being honest with the people that know about them."

Davidson's face twisted. "What do you mean?"

The man nodded toward the binder. "Read it. Just… you didn't get it from me."

"Won't it be missed?"

The tech scoffed. "Negative. I compiled that as I hacked their servers." He grinned widely. "Nobody but you knows it exists. I tried to get Locke to read it and he told me I was 'surfing down conspiracy theory rabbit holes' and threw it in the trash. He didn't want to know."

"Why would you—"

"Just read it, Director." He cut him off. Nodding to the screen he whispered, "They're returning. You don't want to have that in here when Locke returns."

Davidson nodded quickly and tucked the binder into his jacket. He slipped from the MCC, went straight to the logistics building, and pulled the door shut behind him. He sat down at his desk and turned on the desk lamp before deep diving into what the government really knew about sasquatch.

DAVIDSON DROPPED the binder in front of Ford and Murphy. "Did you know that there are seven distinct subspecies of Gigantopithicus Americansus?" His face formed a sneer. "That's just here in North America. They believe that there are as many as *eight* more subspecies scattered over the globe."

Ford gently set his rifle to the side and closed the cover of his cleaning kit. "Come again?"

Davidson paced the small tent and breathed heavily. "They've known about these things for so long," he scoffed as he turned back and pointed at the binder, "they have sequenced the goddam things' DNA."

Ford slowly came to his feet. "Okay, Director. I believe you."

"They knew, Ford." He stopped pacing and leaned his head back, his eyes closed as he tried to gather his thoughts. "They knew that the 'tribe' of these rock giants here in the Catskills were some of the most aggressive out there."

"I believe it, after seeing what they've done." Murphy was confused by the director's sudden anger. "But, sir…what's your point?"

Director Davidson paused and held his hands out while he gathered his thoughts. "They didn't tell anybody. *ANY*body. Hikers have gone missing in these mountains for decades, and not a peep. They not only knew about all of this, but they deliberately sent Gamboa's team out here without so much as a goddamned warning."

Ford came to his feet and met the man's gaze. "We know. We realized all of this when Locke and his men claimed they knew everything there was to know about these things."

Davidson scoffed. "Ha! Locke doesn't know half of what he thinks he knows." He leaned closer and lowered his voice. "They didn't brief him on any of this. And I bet this isn't even everything."

Murphy's brows knit. "Come again?"

Davidson handed him the binder. "One of Locke's techs hacked their servers and downloaded all of the classified files on these things."

Murphy chuckled as he sat down. "And you think he didn't show this to Locke already?"

"He threw it in the trash. He's too ready to swallow the government line as gospel."

Ford picked up the binder. "Is there anything in this that can give us the edge on these things?"

Davidson sighed heavily and sat on the foot locker at the base of Ford's cot. He thought for a long time then shrugged. "I dunno. Maybe."

Murphy picked up the binder and flipped through it. "I don't get all of the secrecy. It's not like they're UFOs or aliens." He paused and looked up at Davidson. "Are they?"

Davidson shook his head. "The DNA says that they're our closest primate relative. Even closer than chimps."

"Maybe that's why?" Murphy flipped through more pages. "They don't want to tick off the religious folks. Bible thumpers can get real pissy when you start talking evolution and—"

"They wouldn't care." Ford sat back on his bunk and scratched at his goatee. "If the missing link were out there, they'd be more than happy to supply the data… even if that missing link were still alive and stomping around in the woods." He glanced at Davidson. "Does it say in there why it's classified?"

Davidson shook his head. "If it does, I missed it."

Ford pushed to the edge of his cot and lowered his voice. "Let me take my team out tonight."

"Locke won't allow anybody but his teams—"

"Screw Locke," Murphy said a bit too loudly. "I'll take the new Echo Team as well and—"

"Wait a second." Ford came to his feet. "Just a few hours ago you were complaining about getting dead."

"That's if Locke is the one barking orders." Murphy raised a brow at him. "Give me my own team and I'll deliver. Just not with Garden Gnome Scarface yelling in my ear."

"They're not 'the new Echo.' We don't recycle team names in the field." Davidson didn't look up right away. When he did, he looked exhausted. "Murph, your team is Victor."

"Not Foxtrot?"

Davidson shook his head as he came to his feet. "Negative." He sighed as he eyed the two men. "Call it superstition, but I'm calling an audible on this one. You're officially Victor Actual." He turned to Ford and raised a brow. "If I authorize an op, I need to know you can get by Locke's men."

"It's not his men I'm worried about. It's the sensors he's placed around the perimeter." He leaned closer and whispered, "Any chance you can make a couple of them not work if we narrow a time window?"

Davidson sucked at his teeth as he considered what it would take. "I can't say for sure. I'd need the help of someone inside the MCC."

Murphy came to his feet again. "What about the guy that gave you the intel?"

"Maybe." Davidson glanced through the open tent flap. "Locke and his men are back. Give me a few hours to try to make it happen." He turned back and met Ford's gaze. "What do you have in mind?"

Ford smiled and it didn't reach his eyes. "Stirring the pot and pissing off the mountain monkeys. See if I can get them so mad they make an attempt on Dog Town."

Davidson stared at him wide-eyed. "And you think this is a good game plan?"

"Have you seen how many men are inside the perimeter armed to the teeth? They wouldn't stand a chance in a full frontal assault."

Davidson considered his plan and offered a slight shrug. "I'll consider it. Meanwhile, I'll see if my new friend in MCC can cause a malfunction tonight."

"That's all we ask."

THE LARGE RED-BEARDED man stood closest to Locke as he made his speech. "At dusk, I'm sending in everything we got." He eyed each of the men as he spoke. "I want their fuckin' heads for Charlie Team."

A round of "ooh-rahs" chorused around him.

"I want every goddam one of them dead or dying by sunrise." His voice turned deep and low as he growled, "Even the goddam babies. Don't leave any for a fuckin' zoo exhibit. Don't put 'em on the fuckin' endangered species list…put 'em all on the fuckin' *extinct* list!"

"How do you plan to draw them out?"

Locke turned and shot Davidson a dirty look. "Let's just say we left a few surprises for them."

A muffled round of laughter murmured through the group as Locke worked his way around the assembled men. "Just make sure you're in MCC watching the drone feeds."

"And you're certain they'll—"

"Just do as you're fuckin' told!" Spittle flew from Locke's mouth as he yelled.

Davidson took it all in stride. "Any chance you'll want to utilize the two SWAT teams I have here?" He raised a brow at the smaller man. "They're standing by and ready to get dirty with the rest of your men."

Locke's face twisted slightly just before he broke into a toothy grin. "Why not. Tell your boys to gear up and be ready to insert at dusk."

Davidson was genuinely surprised, but nodded. "I will."

Locke turned back to his men and paced in front of them. "Tonight we bring hell down on these beasts. If they won't come out and play, we'll go in after them."

"If they're half as vicious as they're supposed to be, they'll want blood after what we left for them," one of the men stated. "They won't be able to help themselves."

Ford edged in next to Davidson and whispered, "What did they do?"

"I've no idea."

Ford noted the large red-bearded man near the front and smiled. "I think I know one person I can ask."

Once the crowd dispersed, Ford trotted up next to his soon to be best friend. "I'm Ford." He held his hand out. "We were never formally introduced."

The large man took his hand and smiled. "Bodie. Gil Bodie."

Ford sidestepped and leaned in, lowering his voice.

"What were they talking about? What did they do that they think'll make the woodboogers strike?"

Gil grinned and looked away, stroking his beard. "I heard they left a few gifts for them." He gave Ford a knowing look. "From what some of the guys on Delta said, they wired up the entire mineshaft." His face turned stoic when he met Ford's gaze. "They also booby trapped the bodies that were taken back."

Ford's brows rose and he felt a chill run down his spine. "The same bodies that they appeared to pray over?"

Bodie nodded. "All of them."

"Holy smokes." Ford felt his chest tighten. "If—and this is a big 'if,' but—if they hold their dead in some kind of esteem…"

"Exactly." Bodie shrugged. "Locke's idea of poking the bear actually involves poking bears."

"I guess we'll find out if his tactics are effective."

Bodie glanced to either side then lowered his voice to a near whisper. "It's not the first time I've seen Locke stoop to a new low. He's pulled all kinds of shit in the past that was overlooked because it worked."

"What do you mean?"

Bodie crossed his thick arms over his chest and gave Ford a knowing look. "We've been called in to operate in all kinds of places, all over the world. We've dealt first-hand with all kinds of people. I can tell you, with all certainty, that Locke's methods often cross the line."

"I don't think I'm following you."

He took a deep breath and blew it out forcefully. "Desecrating graves is minor compared to some of the shit he's pulled." He saw the confusion on Ford's face and decided to elaborate. "Locke has a way of knowing just how to truly piss off his opponent. Whether it's hypothetically kidnapping a child, depredating a religious site, killing a close friend or family member, or even…" he sighed as he trailed off. "Let's just say that has a way of getting his enemy to lose their shit and go off halfcocked."

Ford didn't realize his mouth was hanging open until he tried to speak. "Wait…you're serious?"

Bodie gave him a slow shrug. "In his line of work, nobody seems to care *how* a job gets done, so long as the desired result is achieved."

Ford felt his mouth go dry. "And he thinks that blowing up—"

"No." Bodie cut him off. "Not thinks. He 'feels' it. Somehow he just knows what buttons to push and this time, the button to push was booby trapping their passageways—and their dead." He gave him a knowing look. "You know as well I do, it's not just their warriors that traverse those tunnels."

In Ford's mind, he could see families travelling the tunnels, possibly going to pay their familial respects, and the damage that properly placed explosives could do. He turned to Bodie and raised a brow. "What do you think?"

"I think he's just crazy enough that I'm not going to be the one to call him on any of it." He stepped back and shrugged. "I have a family too."

15

FOB Dog Town

Ford finished loading out his tactical vest then closed his eyes. As he placed a hand on each pouch, he recited the contents, ensuring that he would instinctively know where to reach as the need arose.

Murphy stepped into the tent and dropped his gear on the foldout table. "I've got the creeps about this."

"How so?"

He leaned back and peered through the tent flap before lowering his voice. "Just some of the comments that Locke's people have made. I have a feeling that they won't be watching our backs."

Ford chuckled as he reached for his carbine. "I think your paranoia is catching up with ya."

"I'm serious, Dave. These guys? They just ain't wired right."

Ford paused and took a deep breath. "They're highly skilled operators, granted. But they're still human and there's no way they'd just stand by and watch as one of those things—"

"I'm talking about *them* doing something." Murphy's eyes portrayed honest fear.

Ford cocked his head and opened his mouth to reply when a muffled explosion sounded in the distance. "What the hell? Did they insert without us?" He grabbed his rifle and slipped through the tent flap with Murphy hot on his heels.

"What the actual fuck was that?" Locke yelled as he marched across the bullpen.

One of the original techs turned the drone camera in a 360 degree arc, homing in on the explosion. "Ah… looks like one of them found the booby traps we left for them."

"Booby traps?" Locke stepped closer and glared at the man. "The only goddam booby traps that are supposed to be out there are the ones my fuckin' men left in the mines, and they wouldn't be detectable above ground."

Davidson stepped between Locke and the technician. "He's talking about the munitions that my men placed before you—"

"You had the goddam forest charged and didn't fuckin' think to inform me!?" Locke's hand slipped up to Davidson's throat in a blur, a survival knife in his grip. "Tell me you didn't just fuckin' say that!"

"Woah!" Ford brought his carbine up and stepped towards the pair. Immediately Locke's men reacted. In a split second thirty rifle barrels were pointed at Ford, but the man refused to lower his weapon. "Let's put the knife away and talk about this before anything escalates."

Locke's eyes darted to the side then bulged when he saw Ford pointing a weapon in his direction. "You better lower that goddam weapon, boy, or my guys will ventilate your fuckin' skull." The pure hatred that seethed within his words was more than evident.

"I'll lower mine when you put that knife away."

"One…" Locke counted and his men stiffened, bringing their rifles to aim.

"Just lower the knife," Ford repeated calmly.

"For God's sake Simon, what are you doing?" Davidson asked, the blade scraping at his throat.

"Two…" Locke continued, his eyes locked with Ford's.

"Keep counting, asshole." Ford brought his red dot to center on Locke's forehead. "At this short a distance, I can't miss, and I can guarantee you that even if I'm shot, I can still pull this damned trigger."

Locke's eyes made a quick scan of the area then slowly stepped back from Davidson, his knife lowering. Ford's barrel slowly lowered and he continued to watch as Locke slipped the knife back into its scabbard.

"You almost lost a goddam team leader, Mike."

Davidson rubbed at his throat and stepped away from him. "That would be a shame considering I've already lost a friend today." He raised a brow at Locke. "I don't even know who you are."

Locke spun and jabbed a finger in his face. "Why the fuck didn't you tell us that your people had planted charges in those woods?"

Davidson stiffened and squared his shoulders. "It was in the summary report I provided you when you first got here."

Locke continued to glare at him. "You wrote it down." He scoffed. "On fuckin' paper."

"It. Was. In. The. Report." Davidson glared at the shorter man. "Everything we've done since we've been here…every man lost, every tactic attempted. I even included the GPS position for each and every one of those munitions. It was all in the report. The very report *you* signed off on as 'read and received' shortly after your arrival."

Locke huffed and stepped away. "Somebody get me that goddam report." He shot a hateful glare at Davidson as he stepped away. "Apparently it's too much fuckin' trouble to just open your goddam mouth and tell people that you mined the playing field."

Murphy stepped a little closer to Ford and cleared his throat. "Still think I was 'off' on my assessment of these guys?"

Ford felt his hands begin to shake as the adrenaline burned off. "They only did what I did." He shot Murphy a frightened look. "Trying to protect their boss."

"Which, by the way, was totally fucking cool what you did." He turned and stared at Locke storming toward the MCC. "What Napoleon there pulled, not so much."

"And they were friends."

Murphy scoffed. "With friends like that, who needs enemas?"

"You mean enemies."

Murphy grinned. "Not when they're as full of shit as that guy."

"Double check that your PDA shows all of the hotspots." The tech stood in the middle of the operators as they went over their gear. "Per Locke's order, you are to give each of these munitions a wide berth. Let the monsters find them instead."

Les Palmer approached Ford as the tech continued the quick primer. "Director Davidson assigned me to your team but…" He shrugged. "Why am I not gearing up with the rest of them?"

Ford barely looked up at him. "You're the only chopper pilot in Dog Town. I want you standing by to bring that bird in the air, should the need arise."

Palmer scoffed. "Locke would never authorize me—"

"Screw that crazy old man." Ford pulled him aside and locked eyes with him. "You stick with Davidson. He and I already talked, and if shit hits the fan, you bring that bird in with the Vulcan blazing. Got me?"

Palmer swallowed hard and glanced at Locke, who still seemed to be steaming over the earlier incident. "Men like that can ruin your career by killing you and burying you in a remote, unmarked grave."

"Exactly why I want air support standing by." Ford clapped the man's shoulder. "Odds are we won't call on you, but I consider you my personal condom. Better to have you and not need you…" he trailed off.

Palmer chuckled. "Only you could make this situation even more awkward."

"Just be ready." Ford stepped around him and motioned for his team to converge. "We're in Quadrant

Three. We placed those charges and we have a digital map, thanks to Locke's guys. I don't need to tell you to stay sharp out there."

Murphy appeared at his side. "Quad Four. You?"

"Three." Ford double checked his loadout once more. "You ready for this?"

"Born ready." Murphy grabbed his arm and pulled him closer. "Stay close to the three-four border and I'll do the same. I don't want any of…" he nodded his head toward Locke. "You know. I don't want to have to stress about catching one in the back."

Ford shot him a sardonic grin. "I don't think you're the one they'd be aiming at." He stepped away and gave him a knowing nod. "See ya on the border."

A new voice broke over their coms. "Attention all teams. We have major activity brewing on the outer perimeter of our surveillance area. Tangos making a slow but steady approach and should reach the hot zone in minutes."

One of Locke's men guffawed, "Told ya they'd react!"

Ford glanced at Murphy and nodded. "Stay tight."

"Tighter than a tick's ass, brother."

Davidson came over the coms sounding all business, "All tactical teams stage in your respective quadrant. Prepare for insertion."

Locke glared at the MCC and clenched his jaw tightly before slamming a magazine into his weapon and charging it. "Let's move, ladies."

As THE TEAMS slowly approached the edge of the clearing, wood knocks could be heard in the forest. From one side of the FOB to the other, the knocks notified all teams that the beasts were surrounding the camp. The slight Fall breeze carried the musky stench of the creatures into the camp and more than one of the operators groaned as the smell washed over them.

Murphy glanced at Ford and shook his head. "I got a bad feeling."

"Just keep your head on a swivel. I'll see you once this is over."

An explosion reverberated through the trees near Quadrant One, and Murphy could just make out the rising dust and smoke. "Scratch one wood ape."

"Coms are hot, Victor Actual. Cut the chatter," Locke barked.

Murphy growled low in his throat and shouldered his rifle just as another munition blew in Quadrant Three.

Ford brought his rifle to bear on the location of the blast but couldn't see anything through the darkness of the trees. "Tangos are closing ranks," the tech advised. "They appear to be taking known trails now."

Any minute now… Ford continued to scan the tree line, straining eyes and ears to detect any movement.

"Tangos have stopped advancing. Holding at perimeter minus ten yards." The tapping of the tech on the keyboard came across the coms as they brought up the standby drones. "Second wave of air surveillance deployed."

Ford craned his neck and barely caught the tiny flashing red light as a drone whisked by overhead. "Eye in the sky. The more the merrier." He brought his rifle up and peered through the optics. The drones were masked by the dark, but every once in a while, a small flashing LED would mark their location.

"What are they waiting for?" a disembodied voice asked rhetorically.

The forest erupted in a cacophony of hoots, whelps, howls and pounding as the Genoskwa shouted their war cries. Both Ford and Murphy felt the hair on their neck stand on end and a sudden wave of nausea hit them as their heads began to pound. Murphy lowered his weapon and gripped the sides of his temples. "What the actual fuck is going on?"

"Infrasound," Ford nearly yelled as he fell to one knee. "Oh my god…I'm gonna hurl."

The infrasound struck each man differently. Some were barely affected while others were nearly incapacitated. More than a handful bent over and vomited as the infrasound messed with their inner ear.

"Open fire on them sumbitches!" Locke yelled over the coms. Almost immediately a barrage of small arms fire sent thousands of rounds across the short clearing and into the woods surrounding Dog Town.

Ford had trouble keeping his balance as he tried to shoulder his weapon. He fired blindly into the trees and nearly gasped when the infrasound ended. He felt weak as he struggled to get his feet back under him.

"All teams be advised, we've picked up and analyzed the source of the infrasound attack." The technician's voice sounded tinny in their ears. "Working on a white noise solution to counter the effects. Stand by."

Ford fell to his knees, leaning his head back and trying to pull the cold air deeper into his lungs. "Christ, that hurt."

As if on cue, the war cries died, leaving the forest eerily silent. The total lack of sound gave the men a creepy feeling of impending doom. Murphy glanced across the open field and watched as Ford slowly came to his feet. "Something isn't right, Dave."

"Stay the course, John." Ford huffed as he got his feet back under him and brought his rifle up again. "They're fucking with us."

"Negative." Both men turned to see Bodie standing at the head of his team. "They're simply using every weapon in their arsenal." He spat to the side and dropped to the kneeling ready position, his barrel steady on the trees. "Be ready for anything."

A loud curse from Murphy's left had him searching for the source and he noted one of Locke's men staggering, his hand to his head. "What the hell?" Murphy squinted in the low light, trying to make out what was happening. He nearly jumped when a large stone landed directly in front of him and it took him a moment to realize the Genoskwa were throwing rocks now.

"Incoming!"

Ford slowly backed away, unable to see the approaching rocks in the dark until they were nearly on him. He barely dodged a barrage of smaller stones and was about to order his team further from the tree line when one of them caught a large stone in the side of the face.

"Medic!" Ford called out as he rushed to the man's side. As he knelt beside him, he could see that the side of the man's face was bloodied and both his helmet and skull were crushed on one side. "I need a medic over here!"

"Withdraw!" Murphy called out. "Back! Back away!"

"You move your people when I tell you to move your goddam people!" Locke screamed into the coms. "Stand your fuckin' ground! Open fire on these goddam things!"

"Screw this," Murphy grumbled as he grabbed his closest teammate. "Back away. Get out of their range!"

Ford slowly came to his feet once he realized his team member was dead and turned to see Murphy and his squad moving up the slight incline away from the trees. He'd turned to order his own team back when a tree fell between him and his men.

Spinning quickly, he saw another tree violently strike the earth where Murphy had been standing just moments before. "Retreat!" Ford called out. "Back! Back!"

He didn't see what struck him, turning out the lights. He barely had time to register the ground under him before everything went black.

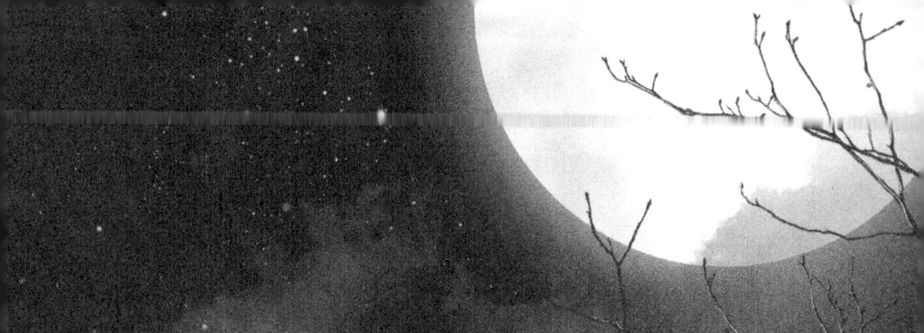

16

FOB Dog Town

Men scattered as large stones and even larger trees rained down on their positions. In the near total darkness, their NV goggles were proving less than adequate. Their ability to focus natural light on incoming projectiles was so limited that most of the men stripped the goggles and were trying to adjust their vision during the attack.

Screams of pain echoed through Dog Town as men were assaulted with anything the Genoskwa could grip and throw. More than once, Les Palmer heard the gurgling death rattle of men after a sickening impact, and his adrenaline levels rose to dangerous new highs. He finally turned and ran for the logistics building and threw open the door.

Davidson's techs were working furiously at their stations, doing everything they could to keep drones in the air and reporting the monster's positions to the men along the perimeter.

Les glanced at the small hardened building and knew that the director must be in the MCC. He slammed the door and ran the short distance to the RV hosting Locke's techs and stepped inside. Director Davidson was doing his level best to report movements without shouting into the coms.

"Sir, let me gear up and support the teams."

Davidson barely glanced over his shoulder before calmly stating, "Denied." He keyed the coms again and reported another group skulking along the edges of the tree lines.

Les Palmer stepped closer and gripped the director's arm. "Then let me take the bird up. I can wipe out most of them before they ever leave the trees."

"Negative, Palmer!" Davidson cupped his hand over the mic mounted to his headgear and shot the man a dirty look. "Like it or not, Locke is still in charge of this operation and that bird doesn't fly until he orders it. He knows it's available."

"But sir—" Palmer heard his voice crack as he spoke. "I can't just sit here and do nothing."

"Ford ordered you to stand by. I suggest you do just that." He turned back to the screens and cursed before announcing, "They've located our drones and are using projectiles to drop them. We've lost three eyes in the sky already."

"Sir…" a tech pointed a shaky finger at a monitor. One of the creature's faces grew large in the frame as it snarled at the drone. The huge wide mouth opened and a moment later, the drone feed went to static.

"Jesus Christ!" Davidson plucked his earpiece out

and sighed. "Ugly motherfuc—how many cameras are still functional?"

Before the tech could answer, a small explosion went off and one of the helmet cams turned to the closest noise maker Locke had set up along the perimeter. "It's running back to the woods, sir."

"That's one. Only a couple hundred more to go."

"Director!" Palmer yelled. "Let me off the chain!"

Davidson ground his teeth as he stared at the man. "Do your preflight checklists, and *stand by*."

"They're already done, sir."

Davidson nodded. "Then warm up the batteries."

Palmer broke through the door and ran back to the makeshift landing pad. In a flash he was inside the chopper and had turned the power on, watching as the lights and gages came to life on his dash. He quickly tugged on his flight helmet and switched the frequency of his radio to match the coms of the troops on the ground. A moment later, he wished he hadn't as the screams and cries of broken warriors bled into his ears.

Palmer's finger rested on the switch to start turning over the engine and he waited, praying that Locke, Davidson or Ford's voice would call out for him to bring the rain.

"Come on, dammit. I'm *right here!*"

Ford groaned as he tried to roll over and cursed when something stabbed into his side. "Christ, I'm pinned." Images of Barlow and McCoy impaled on tree trunks flashed in his mind and he fought the urge to panic. "Murph!"

He had to force himself to breathe normally and rubbed his face in the soft moist earth, trying to determine if his coms were still attached. "Dammit Murph... I'm pinned down."

"I gotcha, Dave!"

Ford almost cried when he heard Murphy's voice hovering over him. "Something hit me, Murph. I'm pinned down."

"Yeah, buddy. Hairy assed primate done Paul Bunyan'd your ass."

Ford's mind raced as he tried to imagine what Murphy meant. "Say again?"

"They threw a fuckin'—" Murphy grunted as he tried to roll the large pine over and off of his old boss. "They threw a tree at you, bud." He stood shakily and held a hand out. "Here."

Ford winced as he rolled over and reached for Murphy's hand. "I think one of the limbs..." He raised his BDU blouse and his undershirt was darkly stained. "I think one of the limbs used me like a pin cushion."

"Yeah you're bleeding like a stuck hog, brother." Murphy jumped as another stone struck near his feet and he quickly grabbed Ford's arm, pulling him farther up the incline. "We need to give the bastards space. Apparently the White Sox haven't thought to recruit out here."

Ford couldn't hear most of what Murphy was saying as the dozen or so men surrounding them continued firing into the woods. Ford pulled back from his grip and stared at the ground. "I lost my weapon."

"We'll get you another one, just as soon as a field medic checks you out."

"I'm good." Ford pulled away from him and staggered slightly as he tried to get his bearings. "I need a weapon."

"You need your head examined is what." Murphy grabbed him roughly and pulled him up the hill. "Get checked by the docs and I'll give you my rifle." He grinned at him broadly. "It's like new, barely used, only shot by a little old lady on Sundays after church. Damned thing still has that new gun smell."

"You're goofy," Ford groaned as he stumbled up the hill.

"I guess that makes you Mickey." He tugged harder. "Come on, dammit."

As they entered the bullpen Murphy yelled for a medic and plopped Ford down near the logistics building. "I'll be right back."

Ford watched him run off as two medics surrounded him. "Where are you going?"

"I got a special delivery for our hairy assed friends out there." Murphy ran down the incline and plucked a fragmentation grenade from his vest. As soon as he reached the first few boulders that the wood apes had thrown at them, he pulled the pin and launched it toward the tree line.

He stepped back and waited for the body parts to fly then nearly fell to his knees when the grenade exploded yards from the trees. "Dammit to hell," he groaned. "Somebody tell me they have an M79 and a pouch full of grenades."

Simon Locke cursed as he slammed a fresh magazine into his rifle and sent three round bursts into the trees. "Dammit Mike, tell me we're having an effect here!"

Davidson's voice came over the earpiece calm and collected. "We're seeing numerous heat signatures staying still and their heat fading, but not to the extent you'd expect for the number of rounds you're expending."

Locke called for a ceasefire and stepped back from the line of stones and trees that had been launched at them. "Back off. Make 'em fuckin' work for it."

"Sir?"

"Draw them out. If they want to throw sticks and stones, they'll have to break out of the shadows and make themselves seen." He turned and pointed to the crest of the incline. "I want snipers at the high points, constant fuckin' scan on the trees. Give 'em ten yards before you initiate." He spat to the side and sucked at his teeth. "I want as many of the bastards with balls to make themselves seen."

Palmer's voice came over the coms. "You've still got a bird with a fully armed Vulcan at your disposal, sir."

Locke turned around and glared at Dog Town. "Fine. You want to put that goddam thing in the air so fuckin' bad, go ahead. But when these fuckin' things turn tail and run for their tunnels, you better follow 'em inside and kill 'em all or I'll shoot your ass out of the air my fuckin' self!"

A moment later the whine of the engine starting could be heard coming from Dog Town and Locke growled under his breath as he squatted down and rested his rifle across a tall boulder. "Mike, put the drones that are still in service as fuckin' high as they'll go. I wanna know if these goddam things turn tail and where they go!"

"Copy that."

Locke sat back and stared at the tree line, mentally daring the bastards to step out. "Come on, ya smelly motherfuckers. Show yourselves!" He stood and fired another three round burst into the trees. "What are they doing, Mike?"

"They're holding fast in three quadrants."

"What about the other quad?" Locke was afraid he wouldn't like the answer.

"No eyes on it. They took down the two drones covering Quad Two."

"Of course they fuckin' did," Locke groaned to himself as he squatted again. "Can you allocate another to cover that quad?"

"Negative. All drones down but three. They're orbiting as high as we can get them to cover the most area."

Locke sighed and rubbed at the grit in his eyes. "Understood." He turned to the man on his right and raised a brow. "How many of them fuckin' things did we bring, anyway?"

The man scoffed. "Apparently not enough sir."

"Apparently not." Locke stood and stared at Dog Town. The chopper was spinning up and the running lights flashed across the face of the tents. "I'm not risking it all on a fuckin' Huey."

"Sir?"

"I'm taking the fight to them." He spat again and

stepped away from the broken trees and boulders. "Here I am ya fucktwits!" He fired another three round burst into the trees as he marched toward the darkness of the woods.

"Locke, *what are you doing?*" Davidson's voice rose in pitch as he watched the heat signature march across the open expanse. "You're too close! Tangos are fifteen meters!"

Locke plucked the earpiece out and let it dangle as he continued marching toward the trees. "Come out, come out wherever you are!" He fired another three round-burst ahead of himself then stopped just ten yards from the edge. "You fuckin' cowards!" He switched his rifle to full auto and emptied the magazine into the woods, screaming as the rifle belched fire into the darkness.

As the last round fired, he ejected the magazine and slammed a fresh one into the well. "I ain't afraid of you! You hear me!"

"Somebody drag his wrinkled ass back from those trees!" Davidson screamed into the coms. "Pull him back!"

Locke spat in the direction of the trees then turned and began marching back as two of his men ran towards him. "Fucking cowards don't have the balls to—"

His men stomped to a stop in front of him just as Simon Locke's face went slack and he fell forward. The two men reached for his arms and barely acknowledged the wooden spear protruding through his vest, just above the trauma plate in his carrier.

One of the men screamed for a medic as they dragged his body from the tree line. A rain of spears flew from the shadows and pinned both men in place as Locke slipped from their grip.

"Dammit to hell!" Davidson threw his microphone across the MCC and turned to punch one of the cabinets.

"Sir!"

Davidson turned to see the man pointing. "Look."

LES PALMER PUSHED the chopper for all she was worth. As soon as she was airborne, he pointed her to the closest edge of camp and started his run.

Swooping down in a lazy arc, he fired the Vulcan in short bursts, hoping to preserve as much ammunition as he could. With a cycle rate of 6,000 rounds per minute, the six-barreled rotary cannon could level the forest in seconds.

Les ground his teeth as he pulled the chopper up and swept to the side, lining up for another strafing run. "They're breaking back to the woods." Les didn't recognize the tech's voice, but he was determined to keep the monsters in his sights.

"Copy that," he grumbled as he swooped low for another run.

His thermal imager wasn't high definition. Basically, he saw a wall of warmth just inside the tree line. That was his target. He adjusted his grip on the fire control stick, making slight side to side sweeps as he let the cannon rip holes through anything with a heartbeat.

THE REVENGE

FORD RECOGNIZED the sound of the Vulcan as it came to life. He craned his neck and smiled when he saw the orange line of death descend from the sky and the loud *bzrzrzrzrzt* the Vulcan screamed as it rained hot 20MM rounds into the forest.

He sat back and chuckled as the medics attempted to stitch up the hole in his abdomen. "He finally got to fly the damned thing." He clapped one of the medics on the shoulder. "This will be over real soon, now."

"I don't know why Director Davidson and Commander Locke didn't open with the chopper," the medic commented.

Ford cringed as the hooked needle pierced his skin. "I think they were afraid they'd all run and hide."

The medic scoffed. "Isn't that the whole idea? Hurt them so bad that they don't ever mess with humans again?"

Ford winced again and shook his head. "Yeah, I don't think they think that way."

"Who's to know?" The medic finished the stitches and sat back to clip the line. "You're stitched up, but I'd be careful. That puncture wasn't deep but it was big around. You could tear those really easy."

"Thanks." Ford sat forward and pulled his BDU over the wound. He slowly came to his feet and walked to the edge of Dog Town, watching as Palmer swooped low and rained hell onto the monsters. "Get 'em, buddy," he whispered.

He leaned on the corner of one of the Tahoes to watch the show and nearly dropped when something shot from the trees and pierced the acrylic polycarbonate of the chopper's windshield. "No…no, no, no!"

He stumbled to the edge of the bullpen and watched in horror as the chopper pulled a hard right and plummeted, deep in the woods.

Ford held his breath and waited for an explosion or fireball and actually breathed a sigh of relief when neither occurred. "We gotta send a rescue party!"

Men staggered back into the bullpen, nursing broken bones and some carrying the dead. Ford tried to get their attention. "Hey! We gotta send somebody to—" His words were cut off as Bodie gripped his shoulder.

"Ain't nobody going into those woods tonight, friend." He gave him a solemn look and slowly shook his head. "Your buddy didn't survive that."

"You can't know that," Ford felt his mouth go dry as he spoke. "You…you can't."

Gil sighed and pointed to the smoke rising above the trees. "Whatever they launched at the chopper, the pilot lost control. The only way he's going to do that is if he's dead."

"No…you can't know that. They might have broken something and—"

"They threw it through the cockpit." Gil gave him a knowing look. "Your friend was dead before he hit the ground."

Ford pushed away from him. "I'll go myself."

"Then you'll be joining him." Gil gripped his arm and held him in place. "Let's say he survived the crash. Those things are thick as fleas on a dog's ass out there. You know they were on him faster than…" he trailed off. "Your friend is gone."

Ford felt his knees go weak and his slid to the

ground. “We...but we have to try.” He heard his voice crack as he spoke.

Gil squatted next to him and patted his shoulder. “The minute the sun is up, I’ll go out there with you. If he’s still with the chopper, we’ll recover his remains and give his family something to bury.”

Ford looked up at Gil and nodded weakly. “Thank you.” Bodie patted his arm before he stood and trudged back to his tent.

17

FOB Dog Town

Director Davidson stood solemnly on the steps outside the logistics building. He could barely look at Locke's men. The survivors of the night's skirmish were in worse shape than he had feared. Too many men from both camps had been injured by the blunt force attack of the wood apes, and far too many had been killed.

When he finally looked up, he cleared his throat. "I knew Simon Locke long before he became the tip of the spear for Haze Gray." He glanced down the hill where Simon had been killed and shook his head. "I have no idea why he'd act so *recklessly*."

"He hoped to draw them out, sir."

Davidson nodded gently and pursed his lips. "Still, tactically, it wasn't his smartest move." He suddenly squared his shoulders and stared out at the men. "I know that he was your leader. With him gone, I fear that there's little to hold you here. I wouldn't blame any of you for cutting your losses and—"

"I ain't going nowhere until they pay for his death." The men turned to watch West saunter toward the front of the assembly. "As his 2IC, I'm prepared to take over where Simon left off." He looked out across the assembled men. "Those who are wounded or unable to fight will be transported out with the dead. I'll call HQ and get us replacement operators."

"I'll be taking back control of the operation," Director Davidson announced. When West didn't react, the men assumed the two had already hammered out this tiny detail. "Those of you who have a problem with that can take it up your chain of command and Commander West can deal with it." He raised a brow as he stared out at the men. "In the meantime, I'll be coordinating with all of the team leaders and section leaders. We need to go over every bit of data we've assembled so far and use that information to devise a workable plan of attack."

Murphy raised his hand high to get the director's attention. When Davidson nodded at him, he stepped closer. "Remind me again the desired goal of this operation, sir?"

"We are to neutralize the threat posed by these creatures."

"And now that they've called in reinforcements of their own?" Murphy narrowed his gaze at the man. "I mean, I have absolutely zero love for these things but where do we stop? Do we eradicate every living bigfoot that haunts these woods, or do we take it to the next forest and kill those as well?" He shrugged animatedly. "I'm just trying to get an idea the end goal here, sir."

"We'll know it when we get to it." The look on Davidson's face challenged Murphy to push the subject. "In the meantime, get some rest. Have your injuries tended to. Get a hot meal inside you and expect retaliation at any given moment. This isn't over."

"You heard the man." West nodded to his teams and watched as they dispersed. Once they were gone he turned to the director. "My men have cleared the battlefield, but what about your chopper pilot?"

Davidson stared out towards the still smoking crash site. "I believe one of yours escorted one of mine to recover the body." He looked away. "If there still is one."

West turned and stared toward the rising smoke. "Is it true those things eat people?"

Davidson nodded. "That's the lore, anyway."

West slowly nodded. "Then the ones they put on display for us to find were definitely them sending a message."

"Oh, yeah." He stepped down from the stairs and stood next to him. "They kill ours, we retaliate. They kill more, we kill more." He sighed heavily. "Maybe Murphy is right to question where it ends."

West turned and locked eyes with him. "It ends when the last of their kind is splayed out as a hair skin rug in my fucking den."

DEEP in the Catskills

. . .

Bodie hacked at some sticker vines and pushed through brush. "I can smell it. We're close."

Ford felt the sweat break out on his forehead and winced with each step. His hand pressed firmly to the bandaged wound in his gut. "How close is close?"

Bodie tugged back some vines and paused. "Oh yeah. We're there."

Ford stepped up and peered around him. The main cockpit of the chopper lay on its side, broken bits and pieces scattered throughout the woods. "Is this it?"

"The part that matters." Bodie stepped over a fallen tree limb then reached back for Ford's arm, helping him over. "Easy, buddy."

Ford paused at the side of the cockpit and took a long pull from his canteen. "I don't know if I want to look inside."

"I gotcha." Gil gripped the broken landing skid and hefted himself up and onto the side of the cockpit. He eased to the door and peered through the side window. "Uhh…empty."

Ford's head shot up. "Empty?"

"Yeah, but…" Gil slid off the side of the chopper and walked to the front. He gripped a three inch thick wooden spear and tugged it from the broken polycarbonate. The tip was splintered and soaked with blood. "The inside of that bird looks a lot like this." He held the spear out for Ford to inspect.

"How much blood?"

Bodie dropped the spear and shook his head. "Too much."

"Then where's his…" Ford trailed off, already knowing the answer.

"My guess is they either took him to…I dunno. Make an example of? Or to snack on."

Ford lowered his head and squeezed his eyes shut. "Thank you for coming with me."

Bodie gripped his shoulder and squeezed gently. "I got your six." He glanced back at the bird and tsk'd. "Your boy did some serious damage with that thing before they got him, ya know."

Ford allowed himself a smile. "Yeah, he spent some shell casings, that's for sure."

"It was a hell of a sight to behold up close." Bodie stepped back over the log and extended his hand once more. "Reminds me of that sound the Warthog makes when they rip a hole in the sky."

"Sounds like a giant zipper to me." Ford fell into step behind him as the pair made their way back along the same trail.

Bodie chuckled to himself. "My old C.O. used to say it sounded like freedom to him." He shot Ford a crooked smile. "Hi, we're from America, and we're here to free the shit out of you."

Ford chuckled then gripped his gut again. "Oww, don't make me laugh."

Bodie kept his head on a swivel on the way back out. Occasionally he'd stop and inspect the damage to the trees and tried to determine if it was from their gunfire, the Vulcan on the chopper, or the monsters themselves.

Just before breaking back out into the clearing, Bodie paused and bent low. "This was where one of the trees were." He used a stick to flick at the dark, moist soil. "Those things literally gripped a trunk, pulled it from the ground and then *chucked* it at us."

"Pretty incredible, eh?"

He stood again and squinted in the shadows, feeling eyes on him from deeper in the woods. "Yeah. Pretty damned incredible." Without taking his eyes off the shadows, he cleared a limb and held it for Ford to step out into the clearing.

As the two slowly made their way back to Dog Town, Bodie quietly stated, "We're being watched."

"I feel it, too." Ford quickened his pace and made a wide arc around some of the trees scattered in the clearing. "I'd hate to meet one of those things face to face with nothing but my wits to protect me."

Bodie chuckled. "I'd definitely be in trouble. I don't have enough wits to damage air with." He glanced back at the woods and sighed when they entered the bullpen.

As the pair paused outside the logistics building, Ford extended his hand. "Thanks again. I don't think I could have made it that far on my own."

"Any time." Bodie glanced toward the two-ton truck being loaded with body bags. "You going to medical to get that properly looked at?"

Ford shook his head and offered a tight-lipped smile. "My place is here. I don't know why, exactly, but I can't leave until the job is done."

"Respect."

"How ya holding up?" Murphy fell onto the cot next to Ford.

"Still breathing." He shot him a crooked smile. "Thanks to you. I guess now I owe you one."

"Shoot…you owe me more than one." Murphy

kicked his boots up and crossed his feet as he lay back on the rickety bed. "So what are you burning brain cells over?"

Ford winced as he twisted to face him. "I'm remembering stories from my childhood."

"Oh, those are fun. Are we talking the Little Red Riding Hood type or Daddy's a Mean Drunk type?"

"Neither, actually." He slowly sat upright and stretched his back as carefully as he could, paying attention to the stitches in his gut. "I was remembering stories about how pioneers had to deal with huge populations of ground hogs."

Murphy's face fell. "Oh, well, as long as it's an important story, then…" He rolled his eyes.

"I think it applies." Ford sighed and rubbed at his eyes. "I mean, I think it could."

Murphy sat up and eyed him. "Speak."

Ford took a slow, deep breath and began. "So, I don't remember where I heard it, or if I read it, but—"

Murphy rolled his hands at him, urging him to get to the point. "Sometime today would be good."

Ford chuckled. "Right. So, they poisoned them."

Murphy's brows rose and he stared at him blankly. "Right. So…yeah. Good story, bud."

"No, I'm saying…I don't remember actually *how* they did it, but why couldn't we do the same?"

"Good luck getting Poppa Squatch to convince the others to go Jim Jones."

Ford shot him a "duh" look. "We know they go underground. We know where some of the tunnels and mine entrances are. So we gas them out."

"Locke tried that with explosives and you see how well that worked."

"Bombs go boom and that area is cleared. Poisons can linger. They can kill much later."

Murphy shrugged. "Why not just poison the water supply?"

"No, water flows. You don't want to go killing everything in the woods, just the monsters."

Murphy scoffed. "I'm not so sure that descriptor can be limited to just the 'squatches nowadays."

"Pay attention, Murph. I'm serious. I think it could work."

Murphy sighed heavily as he came to his feet. "Okay, so we gas their underground. What about the others?"

Ford shrugged. "Surely there's some kind of nerve agent we could fog the woods with."

"Nerve agent?" Murphy studied him for a moment. "You're serious, aren't you?"

Ford nodded gently. "I am." He followed Murphy as he paced the tent. "I'm ready for this to be done with. No more losing good people trying to hunt something that can hunt you back."

Murphy rubbed at the stubble on his jaw and slowly shook his head. "I'm really thinking that this is a terrible idea. I mean, one shift of the wind and we gas ourselves."

"We can wear gas masks."

"Nerve agents can be absorbed through the skin, pal."

"So we use something else. Something deadly but that has to be inhaled." Ford slowly came to his feet. "Come on, man. There has to be a CIA guy somewhere that knows the right stuff to use."

Murphy's head bounced as he connected the dots.

"Oh, I'm almost certain the CIA has people who do nothing else but stay awake at night dreaming up new and creative ways of killing people using poisons, but…" he trailed off. "It's not like we can just call the agency and say, 'can we speak to your resident assassin that deals with poison gas?' They'd put you on every watch list they have."

"So make Davidson call." Ford grinned. "He needs to be on a few watch lists."

"Yeah, not funny." Murphy sighed as he stopped pacing. "Okay, I think I can see where you're going. We need something other than this spray and pray that we hit them with a lucky shot." He turned and gave him a confused look. "But poison?"

Ford shrugged again. "It worked on the ground hogs."

"These aren't ground hogs, Dave. These are intelligent hominids that are mean as hell and have the strength to throw boulders like we throw beach balls."

"All the more reason to napalm their asses."

"Napalm? Come on, man."

Ford grimaced as he reached for his BDU blouse and tugged it on. "I want to present it to Davidson. If he likes the idea, he can figure out the details."

"And if he doesn't like it?"

Ford paused at the tent flap and shrugged. "I'm just trying to think outside the box here, John."

Murphy laughed as he turned to follow him. "Maybe we can convince him to use a tactical nuke."

"You're still not funny."

Murphy scoffed as he pushed him through the tent flap. "Up yours, dude. I'm hilarious."

18

FOB Dog Town

Director Davidson rubbed at his jaw, thinking. Commander West stood across from him, arms crossed while assessing the wounded agent before them.

Ford winced as he tried to stand up straight. "I think it might be a good play."

Davidson glanced at West who remained stoic. "I'm not sure the Bureau is ready to face any kind of environmental negativity. Still…" he trailed off, eyes searching West.

Commander West remained stoic but finally cleared his throat. "It's not a bad idea, per se, but I think the director is right. There's a high probability of backfire there that the Bureau would never live down."

Ford nodded slightly. "You honestly don't think there's a chemical agent out there that is effective but would break down quickly in nature?"

Davidson shrugged. "If there is, it's beyond my

knowledge base." He sat down heavily and rubbed at his temples. "The problems we're facing are simple. We shoot one and two more come to the funeral." He raised a brow at him. "Literally, it would seem."

West placed his hands on his hips and nodded. "We need to find out where they're coming from and how they are getting there. I sent one of the drones on a recon trip, looking for these things traveling here to reinforce their numbers. I thought maybe if we could find out which direction they were coming from we could possibly intercept with charges rather than have our men face them in the woods."

Ford nodded. "Makes sense. I take it you didn't find anything?"

West slowly shook his head. "The surrounding woods were empty. If they are traveling here from outside the immediate area, they're doing it underground or they're being so damned stealthy about it that they're not even leaving a trail."

"So, we have an ever increasing number of combatants, no way to identify their source, and no idea where they actually call home. Or *if* they have a central location they call home."

Davidson came to his feet. "I'll definitely take your suggestion under advisement." He held his hand out. "It's not a terrible idea, just...I'm not sure we have anybody with that knowledge base."

"CIA might." West pushed away from the table and gave the pair a knowing look. "I might have a source I could contact." He turned to Davidson and shrugged. "That is, if you want to go down this road."

"It can't hurt to reach out and pick their brain. It seems we've started a battle with no real plan to win."

"I'll make a call." West turned and stepped out of the logistics building.

Davidson turned and faced Ford. "You shouldn't be out here. You can barely stand."

"It's just a puncture wound. The docs said it wasn't that deep, just tore up the skin real good."

"I saw you were in pain just standing up." He stepped closer and lowered his voice. "I understand the desire to stay in the field with your guys, but—"

"Director," Ford interrupted. "My body might be in a bit of pain, but my mind is a more effective tool for you right now. I'm taking the antibiotics and the Ibuprofen like the docs said." He gave him a lopsided grin. "Worst case scenario, if we fall under attack, I'll climb my happy hiney on top of the MCC and set up a sniper's nest."

Davidson chuckled as he turned for the door. "Just be careful, and spread the word to the team leaders and the section heads. I want to have a sit down with them at fourteen hundred."

"Subject of the meet?"

Davidson scoffed. "I want to pick their brains for tactics, strategy, our next move. Facing a bunch of bigfoots wasn't exactly covered at Quantico."

MURPHY HELD a chair for Ford who walked very carefully between the rows before sitting down. "You look like shit, bud."

Ford scoffed as he sat down. "Thanks. You're no ten, yourself."

"You know what I mean. You okay?" He held a hand out to touch Ford's forehead and was quickly brushed aside.

"You're not my mom."

"Somebody needs a nap." Murphy crossed his arms and sat back while the other team leaders filed in. "What's the pow-wow about?"

"Davidson wants a confab, toss some ideas around for what to do next." Ford grimaced and held a hand to the bandaged wound.

"I take it you told him about poisoning ground hogs?"

"They weren't thrilled with it."

"Okay people, settle down." West stood in front of those assembled, arms crossed and with a stern look in his eye. "This is Q&A 101. For us, as much as you."

Davidson stepped toward the front while sifting through papers. He handed them off to West and took a deep breath. "It would seem we're at an impasse. The more of these creatures we kill, the more show up to take their place. It's like fighting a damned hydra." He looked out over those assembled and sighed heavily. "For what was supposed to be a quick eradication operation, it's gone to shit in a hot second. We've lost entirely too many people out here, and I'm beginning to wonder if it's worth it."

"They speared Locke and two more of our guys like they were hunting frogs." One of the mercs came to his feet, his face a mask of anger. "That's not counting what they did to two of your guys, impaling them like that. These aren't just animals, they're monsters, and I, for one, think that erasing these things is definitely worth it."

A round of "ooh-rahs" and grumbled agreement came from the mercs assembled.

West held a hand up, bringing the noise back down. "Nobody said anything about quitting or pulling up stakes, so settle down." He stepped closer and raised his voice. "We're here to discuss possible tactics."

"Send us out in four-man teams." A merc in the back came to his feet. "Small teams can maneuver more silently and watch each other's backs easier. We pick 'em off in hit and run exercises."

"Too many of them out there. The last thermal reads we got from the drones indicated over a hundred." He turned to Davidson and nodded. "And that was after your boy lit them up with the Vulcan. Techs estimated he took out over two thirds of the creatures."

"There was three hunnerd of 'em in the woods?"

West searched the faces to see who asked but couldn't identify. "At best count, yes."

"I thought there was only supposed to be a couple dozen of these things."

Davidson stepped forward and raised his voice. "Best we can tell, they've called in reinforcements from neighboring clans, apparently." He shrugged. "Simon claimed that their clans are usually kept to smaller, more manageable numbers, but they do interact with others and will come when there's a common threat. We are that common threat."

"So what do we do about them?"

"Kill them."

West held his hand up again. "If you want to say something, raise a hand or stand up. I want to know who I'm addressing." He kicked a foot up onto a crate and rested an elbow on his knee. "We had a suggestion made this morning that might have traction."

Murphy nudged Ford. "I bet it's yours."

"I made a call to some people I know in the spook business. There might be a chemical agent we can utilize to our benefit."

"Chemicals?" one of the men in the front asked.

"Basically GB, but more manageable." West grinned. "I know, it sounds odd, but—"

"You wanna use sarin gas?" A merc in the front row stood and stared open mouthed. "That's asking for trouble."

"Not sarin exactly…" West trailed off. "The agent they're talking about reacts like sarin but breaks down in a few days when exposed to nature. The risk of environmental contamination is negligible."

The man slowly sat down, but he appeared cautious. "So, no poisoning waterways or…?"

"No. If the area is sampled just three days later, they'll find a few trace compounds, but nothing that ties together to GB." He gave him a reassuring nod. "I've been assured that the stuff is a hit and run. Effective, but quick to break down."

"We're still not sure that we're going to go this route," Davidson added. "There are a lot of things to take into consideration and a lot of contingencies that have to be in place before we'd pull the trigger on something like this."

Gil Brodie raised his hand and slowly stood. After clearing his throat he glanced around the room. "Anybody here ever hear of the 'wasps nest'?" He looked to West and could almost see a light bulb pop on over the man's head. A slow smile formed as Bodie looked to

Director Davidson. "Imagine a swarm of tiny HK drones. HK, as in hunter-killer. They use some kind of computer algorithm that can track a subject and when they get close, they explode."

West chuckled and nodded as he turned to Davidson. "Think tiny flying Claymores. They have steel balls inside that destroy body armor. I think they'll work well on these mud encrusted monkeys."

Davidson seemed to perk up. "And we can get our hands on these…HK's?"

West shrugged. "I'll make a call." He paused then added, "They aren't cheap. Keep in mind, they're designed to be used once, destroyed completely if used as intended, and there are hundreds of these things in a swarm."

"Right now, cost is the last thing on my mind. If we can save just one more human life…" he trailed off.

"Okay then. I'll see if I can get them." He turned and shot Bodie a wink. "Good thinking."

THE CLATTER of multiple men eating in the mess tent created a low din as Ford and Murphy sat with Bodie. "Where'd you learn about this 'wasps nest' stuff?" Ford quietly asked.

Bodie sipped at the hot coffee and shrugged. "There was this op in a certain third world shit hole. The locals called in an American contractor to remove the head of a resistance group."

"Were you and your boys the contractor?" Murphy asked.

"One of several. The contractor I'm talking about used a lot of state-of-the-art and experimental stuff." He shrugged. "I can't believe now that I laughed when they brought out these drones."

"Why's that?" Ford shifted uncomfortably.

"They were about the size of a softball. Made this ungodly whine when they first fired up, but once they were in the air, they were damned near silent. Used these funny looking little propellers. I think he called it toroidal, but it was like a figure eight. Quiet as a humming bird, once it was airborne."

"And they carry Claymores?" Murphy asked.

"No, actually they *are* the Claymore. The plastic explosive is packed inside around the battery. The shell is this ceramic coated, segmented steel that acts like shrapnel and…" he shook his head as he remembered the scene. "I was observing through these long range field glasses to verify the right guy was targeted and," he scoffed. "Nothing left but his boots. The dude exploded like a balloon filled with red confetti."

Murphy raised his brows and glanced at Ford. "Sounds like we could use a couple hundred of them."

"If they are in close proximity to each other, one wasp could conceivably take out numerous targets. Especially if it's head shots."

Ford gave him a questioning look. "If West can procure these, how long would it take to actually get them here?"

Bodie sat back and thought about it. "The contractor is based out of DC, but they have a field office in New York." He raised a brow. "If they have them available, they could be here in a matter of hours."

Ford sighed as he sat back. "This could be over sooner rather than later."

Murphy came to his feet and refilled his coffee. "It sounds too easy." He sat down and eyed them both cautiously. "Paint me a pessimist, but these things are crafty. They'll find a way to counter the wasps, I just know it."

"You're right. You're a pessimist," Ford grumbled.

"I'm just saying. These things are supposed to be dumb animals. Like, we should be able to sneak up on them, pop 'em in the head and be done with it. Instead, they encase themselves in some kind of cement body armor. They hunt our people with spears the size of fence posts and throw boulders like we lob grenades. Hell, they crush people under trees." He turned to Ford and scoffed. "Fucking trees, man. I mean, who does that?"

"Apparently the Genoskwa do."

"I'm just saying, man. If there's a way to counter these flying bombs, they'll find it. Probably have home-made baseball bats just waiting to bunt the damned things back at us."

"Is he always like this?" Bodie asked as he sipped his coffee.

"He needs to eat a Snickers," Ford laughed. "He's not himself when he's hungry."

"Screw you both." Murphy sat back and eyed the guys going through the chow line. "It's not that I don't want this to work, I'm just not gonna hang all of my hopes on it."

Bodie shrugged. "Maybe they'll use the wasps in conjunction with this sarin gas stuff."

Ford sighed as he sat forward and planted his elbows

on the table. "I know it was my idea to poison these things, but *sarin*?" He glanced at Bodie. "That stuff scares me."

"Do you buy his story that it's 'like' sarin but not *actually* sarin?" Murphy asked.

Bodie shrugged. "Who am I to question? West is a decent enough guy. God knows he's more mentally stable than Locke ever was…but is it beyond his capabilities to lie to get the job done?" He shrugged. "He stood by and watched as Locke pulled all kinds of sketchy shit over the years to get the job done." He gave Ford a knowing look. "Lying about a chemical agent in order to win? I don't think that's beyond him."

"Not to mention the manufacturer's guarantee the stuff breaks down, I mean, they don't have anything to lose by exaggerating their claims," Ford said.

"Great," Murphy groaned. "Just what I wanted to hear."

Ford leaned in and lowered his voice. "Regardless of what the label says, if it comes to it, we take every necessary precaution around that stuff." He stared them both in the eyes. "Agreed?"

Bodie and Murphy both nodded. "Agreed."

19

FOB Dog Town

Director Davidson stood back as the contractor, Larry Davis, gave his spiel, explaining the nuances of the wasps nest and the drone's capabilities. Commander West practically stood over the man's shoulder, grinning from ear to ear with excitement.

"Do you have an approximate number on the targets?" Larry asked, looking at Davidson.

The director shrugged. "Best guess, a hundred or more."

West plucked one of the drones from its foam enclosure and held it up to eye level. "But if we're lucky, we can dispatch more than a handful with each one of these babies."

Larry plucked the drone from his hand and replaced it carefully. "They're not toys."

West chuckled. "Yeah, they actually are. You just shoved a bomb inside them."

He closed the lid on the carry case and planted a hand on top to keep West from playing with them. "I'll have to have more airdropped in, if your target package is over fifty."

West gave him a curious look. "You said you brought a hundred drones. Why would you need more?"

Larry raised a brow at him. "Did you not listen to the pitch? For crowd eradication, the effective rate of kills drops to less than sixty percent."

"And why is that?" Davidson asked as he took a tentative step closer. "It would seem that it should be higher rather than lower with more targets."

"You would think." He latched the case and pushed it to the side before sitting on the table. "For a single kill, the effective rate is over ninety percent. Reason being, the target has no knowledge of the planned assassination, and if the drone is even noticed, it's considered more of an oddity, rather than a delivery vehicle, before it's recognized as a possible threat. However, with mass killings, once the first few drones are triggered, the other targets become aware of their existence. Their lethality is registered and active attempts are made to avoid them. Hence the terminal efficacy rate drops significantly."

Davidson sat back and wiped a calloused hand over his face. "I was really hoping this would be a one and done scenario."

Larry scoffed. "Hardly. The best case scenario is a full frontal by the enemy. The drones are dispatched en masse and triggered almost simultaneously. Even then, we're looking at less than eighty percent lethality."

Murphy stood and raised a hand. "Question." He stepped towards the front and gave Davidson a knowing look. "What if the drones are used in combination with another attack?"

Larry shot him a questioning look. "I suppose that would depend on the other attack."

Murphy shrugged. "The sarin-like gas that Commander West mentioned."

"Ah, yeah." West stepped out from behind the table and addressed the squad leaders in the room. "My guy says the gas is available and in quantity. But I'm not sure how you intend to use both."

Murphy shrugged again. "I have no idea how the gas is normally used, but if we could get it in some kind of launchable package, like a smoke grenade, we hit the tunnels and mines during daylight hours while the creatures are supposed to be resting. As they exit the tunnels, the drones strike."

"We don't know all of the tunnel entrances though," Davidson replied. "There's no way we could coordinate that."

Larry Davis held a finger up as his mind raced. "Actually…depending on how wide a field of play we're talking about, we could set the parameters into the drones' AI software, launch them into the known tunnels first, then station people strategically to gas grenade the ones that exit."

Davidson slowly shook his head. "I'm not big on having people release the gas out in the open. I'd rather the gas be used below ground. Limit the risk to personnel."

"We may not have that luxury, Director." The contractor shrugged. "I'm open to try this however you deem appropriate, but I think using the gas for stragglers would be the best combination."

Ford sighed heavily. "Snipers set up a hundred yards apart in the thick. Their effective range will be shit with all the timber, but with carefully placed shots, they should still be somewhat effective." All eyes turned to him as he spoke. "Use the gas in the known mines and tunnels. Snipers will pick off those that escape above ground. Send the drones to pick off the ones that get by the sharpshooters."

West nodded. "I have the snipers."

"And the gas," Davidson added. He looked at Larry. "Thoughts?"

Larry Davis thought heavily then shrugged. "The snipers will have to remain stationary until all of the units are either utilized or recalled, but it should work." He glanced at West. "Part of the parameters entered into the Wasp AI is movement. If your snipers try to run for whatever reason…" he trailed off, leaving the rest unsaid.

"They're professionals. They'll follow orders."

Larry nodded. "Great. Then no worries."

"How soon can we be set up to implement?" Davidson asked.

West checked his watch. "Gas should be arriving within the hour."

Murphy raised a brow. "And in what form? Ready for deployment?"

West shrugged. "We'll find out when it gets here." He turned back at Larry. "If you really think you'll need more of these, you should arrange for a drop as soon as possible. It may come down to these flying bombs being our primary line of defense."

"I'll make a call." He turned away and pulled out his satellite phone, punching numbers as he walked away.

"So this is the plan?" Ford asked.

"It's your plan," Davidson reminded him. "Second thoughts?"

He groaned as he came to his feet, his hand pressed to the wound in his gut. "Reminds me of the old adage about using a cannon to swat a mosquito."

"If that mosquito is ten feet tall and over a thousand pounds, you should use two cannons."

"Drones are programmed and standing by." West pulled the door shut behind him as he stepped into the MCC.

Director Davidson checked his watch again then double checked by glancing at the clock mounted above the monitoring station. "Shouldn't your chemicals have been here by now?"

West paused and checked his own watch. He instinctively reached for the satellite phone and punched in a number. As he waited for the line to pick up he braced against the counter. "They should have been here over an hour ago." He held the phone out and shook his head. "Goes to voicemail."

"Maybe the road in is too rough for them?"

West's eyes hardened. "I'm thinking they ran into trouble." He pushed off the counter and reached for the door. "Mind if I call in your SWAT teams to respond?"

Davidson shrugged. "I don't care but—"

"My men are being prepped on the insertion points." He held the door open. "You're sure you're good with it?"

"Go. Check the roads. Maybe they had a flat or something."

"Or something." West disappeared and Davidson spun to watch him on the monitor. He walked across to the SWAT team tents and entered. A few moments later Murphy exited with him and Ford followed more slowly.

Davidson winced then exited the MCC. "Ford!" He waved the man over. "You need to stay on light duty. Why don't you monitor the MCC, and I'll escort your team with West."

Ford's face fell. "It's probably nothing."

"Let's hope. But in the meantime, I'd feel better knowing you weren't taking any unnecessary risks." He gripped the man's shoulder. "Let's call it an order."

Ford groaned as he turned for the MCC. "Great. Sidelined on a simple babysitting job."

"*Potential* babysitting job." Davidson trotted to catch up with Murphy as he entered the armory. "I'm filling in for Ford."

Murphy raised a brow. "How long since you've been SWAT rated and qualified?"

Davidson rolled his eyes. "Stow it Murphy. I still do the annual quals at the range so my certification is valid." He tugged a plate carrier on and tightened the straps. "Besides, I'm still technically your boss."

Murphy chuckled as he tightened the straps on his thigh holster. "Okay boss. Just remember, you lead Delta. Victor is still mine." He checked the chamber of his weapon before holstering it. "Catch you at the truck."

Davidson watched as Murphy and his team exited the armory then glanced at Delta Team. "Relax fellas. Odds are this is a nothing trip." He grabbed extra mags for his carbine and slipped them into the pouches on his vest. "We'll be back before you know it."

WEST GRIPPED the dashboard as the scene came into view and the driver slowed the two ton truck. "Give us a wide berth." West felt his chest tighten as he realized he hadn't brought MOPP gear. He keyed his coms and tried to keep his voice even as he addressed the truck following. "We've got a problem. If anybody thought to bring MOPP gear, now's the time to put it on."

"Sitrep?" Davidson's voice sounded tinny over the hand held radio.

"Truck's overturned and there are bodies." West blew his breath out hard and opened his door. "A lot of bodies—and not just human."

Murphy appeared at his side with a filtered mask. "I'll take a look."

"Hold up." West gripped his arm. "Sarin can be absorbed through the skin. Don't touch anything."

"I thought it was 'sarin-like.'" The accusation wasn't missed in his voice.

"Treat it the same." West released him and Murphy turned to slowly advance.

Davidson appeared at West's side. "There were only two masks in the truck." He watched as Murphy made a slow advance, his carbine at the ready. "I'm not seeing anything in the air."

"You probably wouldn't." West stooped and picked up a pinch of dirt releasing it in the air. "Breeze is from the south. It should be blowing anything aerosolized away from us."

"Thank god for small favors." Davidson stepped out and fell into step behind Murphy.

"Hey, shouldn't you wait until he gives us the all clear?"

Davidson turned and shot him a "duh" look. "At this point, how would he know?"

West groaned and grabbed his own rifle from the cab of the truck. "Stay here until we call for you. Radio the other truck and tell them all to stand by." He slammed the door behind him and followed Davidson toward the overturned truck.

Murphy was bent low, inspecting the corpse of the closest sasquatch. "Whatever this stuff is that West ordered, it looks like it worked fast."

"That's not sarin." Davidson stepped closer to the truck and peered through the windshield. The truck was lying on the passenger side and the driver was splayed across the passenger side window. "Driver has foam coming out of his mouth and nose."

"So does the bigfoot." Murphy did a double take. "Shouldn't you be masked at least?"

Davidson shrugged. "I figure if it's still here and active, we were exposed the moment we crested that hill." He stood back and counted. "Four bodies. I guess the creatures meant business."

"Big males." Murphy tugged the mask off and hooked it to his belt. "I can't breathe in that thing."

Davidson made his way to the rear of the truck and used the barrel of his rifle to push open the rear double doors. A short glance inside and he quickly backed away. "There are canisters everywhere." He put as much distance as he could between the truck and himself. "I can't even hazard a guess how secure they may be."

Murphy whistled and Davidson stepped around to the side. "Whatcha got?"

"One of your canisters I think." He pointed with his barrel to a small plastic container.

West stepped closer and hunkered low, studying the container. "I'm guessing when the monsters attacked, they panicked and tossed one of these out of the truck."

"So how'd it get back into the truck and kill these two guys?"

West shrugged. "No idea. I suppose the wind." He stood and sighed. "I can't even guess if the stuff inside is contaminated." He shrugged at Davidson. "I mean, if they opened it inside and then threw it, the other canisters might be covered. I just have no way of knowing."

Davidson stepped away and keyed his radio. "Send one of the trucks back and bring up anything we can use for decon. Have all personnel in MOPP gear. I want this scene decontaminated and the chemicals inside readied for deployment."

"Copy that." The rear truck started and began to back away. It was only after it left that Davidson realized it had taken most of their armed personnel with it. "Surely they wouldn't try to attack the same place twice." He glanced at West. "I mean, since they already lost four of their own."

West shrugged. "I guess we'll find out." He turned and peered into the tree line. "Let's just hope they don't drag their feet getting back here."

Murphy cleared his throat. "We could have the truck drop some of the guys and have 'em march back if you really think there's a chance of…" he paused, sniffing the air. "Yeah, unless these guys can stink against the wind, I think we're being watched."

"I'll take the high ground." West called the other truck closer and climbed up onto the running board. Hiking his foot onto the hood, he scrambled onto the rear box of the truck and began surveilling both sides from on high. "I'd give your left nut for a couple of drones with thermal right about now."

"As long as they just watch, we're good," Davidson commented, his eyes scanning the trees.

Murphy was about to reply when the first wood knocks echoed from the shadows.

20

Deep in the Catskills

The brisk fall breeze played no part in the cold chill that ran down each man's spine as wood knocks echoed from either side of the makeshift road. The trees seemed to come to life as knocks reverberated around them, slowly encompassing their position.

The driver of the two-ton quickly exited the vehicle and took up a defensive position near the front of the tipped over chemical transport, using the edge of the hood as a rest for his carbine. "I thought these things were supposed to be nocturnal."

"They are," Murphy slipped in beside him and covered the other side of the trees. "I reckon somebody forgot to remind them."

Davidson felt his mouth go dry as he took up position near the rear double doors. "I'm beginning to think they use those wood knocks as a call to arms."

"Fuck!" West cursed as he scanned both side of the

tree line from the top of the box truck. "I got nothing up here."

Davidson keyed his radio, praying the two-way could reach the FOB. "Delta Actual to Command. We need reinforcements up here NOW!" He listened carefully, praying for a response and felt his stomach drop as only static played over his earpiece. "I think we're on our own."

"These two ways are only good up close, director." West brought the scope to his eye and adjusted the reticle. "We're just going to have to cross our fingers and hope the boys don't drag their feet getting back here."

"It's my fault," Davidson practically whispered into the coms. "I sent the men back to get MOPP gear. If I'd been thinking, I'd have left some of them here for support."

"No time for second guessing, director. Stay alert," West replied calmly. "Live and learn, sir."

"Yeah," Davidson scoffed. "It's that first part I'm starting to worry about."

"Movement!" the driver yelled from the front of the truck just moments before a large rock bounced off the undercarriage.

"Here it comes," Murphy grumbled as more rocks began launching in their direction. "Take cover!"

West dodged to the side as another rock flew towards him. "They're smart! They're staying in the shadows."

Davidson cursed under his breath and stepped out from the rear of the truck. He leveled his rifle on the tree line and opened fire, randomly peppering the area. "Keep 'em guessing!"

Murphy shrugged and opened fire on his side, sending a barrage of three round bursts into the darkest regions of shadows. He smiled when he heard a pain filled howl echo back and increased his rate of fire, praying his rounds found even more of the monsters.

West held his fire until he saw movement in the trees. Once that movement was verified, he painted the area with full auto fire and expanded his field of fire in case the creature moved and he'd missed it. He slammed a fresh magazine into the carbine and continued scanning the area, praying the gunfire carried far enough for his men to hear and spur them to respond.

The driver followed suit and began firing into the trees, using as much of the truck as he could to shield himself from further attack. "Any chance we could use the shit in the back of this thing against them?"

"I wouldn't risk it," West replied over the coms. "Until we can guarantee that none of it was contaminated, I wouldn't touch it."

The driver cursed as he slammed another magazine home. "For fuck's sake, did nobody bother to bring gloves?"

West laughed as he painted the other side of the road with hot lead. "It's not just gloves. If the back of the truck was contaminated, you'd need full hazmat gear just to go inside."

"Great," Davidson grumbled. "And here I was sticking my head inside to assess the damage."

"You're still breathing, director," West replied. "I think you're good to go."

"Cease fire!" Murphy called out, holding a fist in the air. "Hold fire." He slowly came to a full standing position and strained to peer into the shadows. "Have they fallen back?"

"I'm not seeing anything," Davidson replied.

"I never saw anything to begin with," the driver added.

"I've got no movement," West answered as he stepped toward the edge of the box truck. "I can't hear shit, though."

The driver stepped out from behind the nose of the overturned truck and wiped the sweat from his brow. "Nothing like bringing rocks to a gun fight, eh, Commander?"

He turned and threw a mock salute to the man atop the box truck then flew back ten feet and slammed to the ground as a thick wooden spear tore through his chest. He lay prone in the dirt and blinked rapidly as his mind tried to override the instant shock and make sense of why he was suddenly splayed out on the rocky ground.

"Dammit!" Murphy cursed as he knelt beside the driver, his hand going to the man's neck. "Take cover!"

West stared at the scene below; it took a moment for his brain to connect the dots. He instantly flopped to the ceiling of the box truck and slid to the edge, pushing the barrel of his rifle out enough to expand his field of view. "Contact!"

West opened fire on any movement in the trees and rolled to his side to eject the empty magazine and slam another into the well before raining hell on the shadows once more.

Davidson tucked in tight to the rear of the truck and prayed that it wasn't contaminated as he sprayed the area with hot lead. He found himself trying to hold his breath and finally dropped to one knee, using the rear bumper for whatever shielding it could provide. "We're sitting ducks out here!"

Murphy gripped the driver's carbine in one hand and his own in another and stepped out, firing both rifles at the same time, cutting down small saplings as he spun side to side. "Get some!" he yelled. When the driver's carbine emptied, he tossed it aside and slammed a fresh magazine into his rifle. "Come on you mangy pieces of shit!" He continued spraying the woods with hot lead and slowly backed to his original position, using the truck as shielding.

"Slow your roll, Murphy!" West called into the coms. "Conserve your ammo."

"If I'm going down, I'm going down fighting!" Murphy slammed another fresh magazine into his rifle and charged it.

"Hold fire and take cover!" West barked into the coms. "Find cover and sit tight. Our people will be back shortly."

"Tell that to your man, West." Murphy loosed another barrage of hot lead into the shadows. "They kabobbed his ass when we thought they'd left!"

"Fuck you, Murphy," West growled to himself. He rolled to the other side of the box and peered out across Murphy's field of fire. He caught movement high in the trees and swung his barrel up toward the target. Without taking the time to scope the movement, he fired in the general area and a moment later a large, hairy blur fell to the ground with a crashing thud. "You're welcome, Murphy!"

"Christ!" Murphy yelled then scanned the tree tops. "They're up high!"

"No shit," West called back. "Head on a swivel!"

As the firing slowed and eventually came to a stop, Davidson slowly allowed himself to stand, his knees shaky as he came to his full height. "Have they withdrawn?"

"Last time we thought that we lost a man," Murphy quietly replied.

"Stay alert," West whispered as he scanned the trees.

With their ears still ringing from the barrage of gunshots, the three men found themselves holding their breath, straining to listen for the monsters in the woods.

"I can't hear anything," Davidson quietly stated.

"Just ringing," Murphy added.

West slowly rose to his knees and peered into the shadows. "Sun's starting to go down. My guess is they're calling in reinforcements."

Murphy pressed a hand to his temple. "Oh, shit…I don't feel so good."

Davidson felt his mouth water as bile rose in his throat. "Dammit. They're still out there."

West cursed and pressed his hand to his forehead. "What the hell? They can do that at will?"

Murphy dropped to one knee and lowered his rifle, the barrel still smoking. "Ford said it's infrasound. Too low to hear but…I'm gonna be sick."

West cursed and wished he had a grenade launcher. "Jeezus…how do they…" he leaned to the side and retched over the edge of the box truck.

A moment later and the infrasound attack ended, but the woods came alive with hoots, hollers, whoops and screeches. The three men suddenly felt isolated and alone as the woods became a bohemian boom box.

Davidson lifted the rear door of the truck he was tucked behind and scanned the interior. A white metal box stood out and he grabbed it, pulling it closer. Jerking the lid open he rifled through the contents and pulled out a flare gun. The orange plastic pistol reminded him of a water gun and he set it aside as he rifled through the contents, searching for a flare. He sighed as he removed the flare and quickly loaded it. He stepped aside and pointed the flare straight up, firing it into the evening sky.

"What the hell?" West called over the coms. "Where did that come from?"

Davidson slid to his ass and leaned against the rear bumper. "Last ditch effort to call for reinforcements." His voice sounded small and tired over the coms. "I'm almost out of ammo."

Murphy continued to spit to the side, his mouth refusing to stop watering. "I know why they do the infra-sound…to make you sick enough that you volunteer to be eaten just to get it over with."

"They don't just eat you," West replied. "They like to keep you alive and torture you first."

Murphy spat again then took a deep breath, doing his best to settle his insides. "I got a 9mm strapped to my thigh that will remove that possibility." He took another deep breath and let it out slowly. "But I'll take as many of them as I can out with me first."

As if on cue, the woods suddenly fell silent and the three men stiffened. Even the birds and insects refused to break the silence. West peered over the edge of the box and noted just how quickly the area was darkening. "I say we use this lull in the action to get the hell out of here. We can come back when we have more men and more firepower."

"I thought we were defending your stupid sarin," Davidson replied.

"Let 'em have it! It was meant for them anyway."

West slid to the front of the box and down onto the cab of the truck. He slid down the windshield and off the hood of the truck, landing beside the driver's door. "Move it!"

He pulled open the door of the truck and breathed a slight sigh of relief when the keys dangled in the ignition. He slammed the door and twisted the key in one motion, checking his side mirrors for the other two men. "Move it!" he yelled into the coms again.

A moment later he saw the silhouettes of both men rushing for the passenger door and he pulled the truck into gear, holding the brake until they had one foot in and were scrambling up into the cab. The side mirror exploded just as Davidson pulled the door shut and West stepped on the gas pedal.

He flipped on the lights and had to resist the urge to stomp the brake when a dark, imposing figure stood in the middle of the path, large enough to block the light. West gunned the engine, lurching the truck forward even faster. The figure made a twisting motion before stepping out of the way.

A half-second later, the windshield exploded, raining shards of glass inside the cab. West felt something warm and wet spray across his arms and when he glanced to the side, Murphy gripped the spear that impaled his throat, his eyes wide as he tried to force air into his body.

"Murphy!" Davidson twisted in his seat and tried to grasp the sharpened tree limb that pierced John's neck, but the point of the spear was imbedded in the rear metal of the cab, unmoving. "We gotta do something!"

West reached forward and pushed out the shattered glass that impeded his view. "Nothing we can do, Director!" He glanced at Murphy again and watched as his hands fell to his sides, his eyes lifeless. "He's already gone."

Davidson tugged once more at the spear then noticed the spark missing from Murphy's eyes. He sat back and sighed, his body shaking as the adrenaline burned off. "He deserved better than this."

West glanced in his remaining side mirror then slowed the truck, satisfied the creatures weren't giving chase. He allowed himself a moment to breathe then nodded in agreement. "How about we bring back every swinging dick that can carry a gun, grab the sarin and make these monkey motherfuckers pay?"

Director Davidson sat back in his seat and nodded solemnly. "We'll rain Hell down on them."

21

FOB Dog Town

Ford watched solemnly as the men removed Murphy's body from the cab of the truck. He felt his jaw quiver as his anger grew until he found himself in the armory, gearing up for war.

"What are you doing?"

He turned to see Director Davidson standing in the entrance, Murphy's blood still drying on his clothes.

"You know what I'm doing." Ford began loading magazines into his carrier pouches. "I can still pull a trigger."

"This is no time to start taking unnecessary risks."

Ford scoffed. "Define 'unnecessary.'"

"You know damned good and well what I'm saying." Davidson stood beside him and gripped his shoulder. "He was my friend, too."

"No," Ford corrected. "You were his boss." He spun and locked eyes with Davidson. "He was *my* friend."

Davidson stepped back and lowered his eyes. "He wouldn't want you to risk your own life—"

"It doesn't matter what he'd want. He's gone." Ford took a deep cleansing breath and let it out slowly. "I'm going out there. If I have to, I'll stand rear guard while the men transfer the chemicals. But nothing is stopping me from being there."

Davidson squared his shoulders. "I could order you to stay behind."

Ford slid the pistol into his holster then turned and faced him. "But you won't. Because you don't want to bring your last remaining team leader up on insubordination charges." He stepped around the man and exited the armory tent.

Davidson sighed heavily as Ford marched across the bullpen and stepped into the back of the truck with the remaining SWAT members. For a brief moment he considered charging Ford, just to keep the man from hurting himself. Then, he placed himself in his shoes and knew he had to let him do this.

He stepped back into the armory and reloaded his empty ammunition pouches. He double checked his weapons once more, then, for good measure, he flipped open the lid on the fragmentation grenades. He stood in silence for a moment, contemplating the numerous ways this could go wrong before he plucked four of the devices from the crate and clipped them to his vest.

"Go big or go home."

As THE LAST licks of sunlight streaked across the purple sky, men took up positions every five feet along the makeshift road, their eyes scanning the darkness of the woods. The fallen bodies of the sasquatch had been removed by their kin, leaving the truck and the two dead humans behind.

Ford stood near the rear, closest to the transport truck, as men in hazmat gear methodically washed each of the plastic containers then stacked them neatly into crates to be transported to the FOB. He couldn't help but wonder if any of this, even absolute victory, was truly worth the cost.

Dale Archer's voice echoed in his mind, reminding him that they had been warned. That they should stay away, no matter the cost.

Now, Ford could see the man's point.

None of this was worth the price they'd paid in blood. Was vengeance on a feral animal worth any man's life? Were these creatures worth the effort?

He had to push the questions from his mind before he lost heart and ended up like Archer, refusing to take action. Instead, he let his anger build. He let his hatred grow. He found himself clenching his jaw so tightly that he feared cracking a tooth.

By the time the op was over and the hazmat team was loading up to leave, he found himself wishing the monsters had made an appearance and given him a chance to vent his frustration—no—his RAGE against them.

Once the trucks had pulled to a stop at the FOB. Ford found himself stationed at the large screen outside the logistics building, his eyes constantly searching for heat signatures that might approach the perimeter.

He wanted a fight.

Even as the night air chilled and others donned jackets, Ford warmed himself in his righteous anger, his eyes glued to the monitor, praying that a monster would be stupid enough to make an approach.

Director Davidson watched as Ford stood vigil over the monitor and sighed. "I've never seen him like this."

West glanced at the man then lowered his voice. "I noticed that he and Murphy had gotten close to one of my guys. I could send him over and have him do a little recon. See if your boy can be unwound before he snaps."

Davidson nodded slightly. "That would be good. Maybe your guy can defuse him before he does something to hurt himself."

"Give me a minute." West walked over to his team's tent and entered.

A moment later, Gil Bodie stepped out and made his way towards Ford. "Sorry about what happened with Murphy." Gil kept his voice soft and solemn. "That's a shit hand to be dealt."

Ford nodded slightly, his eyes glued to the monitor. "Thanks."

Gil took a deep breath. "Want to talk about it?"

Ford shook his head. "Right now, I just want a little vengeance."

"So say we all." Gil sat next to Ford and looked up at the man. "Might as well take a seat. It might be a while before any of them decide to approach the perimeter."

Ford crossed his arms and planted his feet. "I'm good."

"No, brother, you're not," Gil stated softly. "You're letting this eat you up inside." Ford shot him a hateful stare and Gil shrugged slightly. "Hey, man, I've been there before." He sighed. "Odds are, I'll be there again before I'm dead."

Ford narrowed his gaze and set his jaw. "I've lost men before."

"I'm sure." Gil leaned back in the chair and stared at the monitor. "We do dangerous jobs. Every day is a chance to lose a friend. A coworker. Hell, even our own lives." He raised a brow and looked up at him. "But we've gotta be careful not to let the hate suck us in."

"Why the hell not?"

Gil ignored the tone and addressed the question. "Because once we allow ourselves to become emotional, we lose our edge." He sat forward and planted the front legs of the chair. "When we allow ourselves to get worked up, we lose rationality. I mean, look at Locke. The guy had decades of cool-headed action under his belt, but the moment he let his anger take over, he did something rash. And it got him killed." He glanced at Ford and saw the first crack in the anger armor. "If Locke had kept his wits about him, operated by the playbook, he'd still be here. We'd still have his decades of wisdom to fall back on and, at the least, we'd have one more trigger finger to put into play." He sighed heavily as he rocked the chair back again. "But instead, he set aside those decades of experience, let his emotions get the better of him and he got stupid. Stupid gets you killed." He glanced at Ford again and raised a brow. "And you only got to get stupid once to lose the game."

Ford rolled the words around in his mind a moment and slowly his armor fractured. He felt the anger drain and his limbs felt weak and heavy. Gil slid a chair under him just as he lowered himself and sat down, holding his head in his hands. "How do I tell his wife?"

Gil patted the man's shoulder. "You tell her whatever the bureau tells you to tell her." He sighed heavily and leaned closer. "Glad to have you back, brother. For a moment there, I was afraid you were lost."

Ford sat up and tears were forming in his eyes. "John had been my 2IC for years."

"I know."

"This was his first command." He glanced at the Victor tent. "His team was made up of survivors from the other teams and…" he trailed off, the words refusing to form.

"I get it, man." Gil glanced toward West and gave him a curt nod. "Believe it or not, I've been there. I was just lucky enough to survive."

Ford leaned back in the chair and stared up into the sky. "We've lost so many on this fuckin' op."

"Oh yeah we have. And believe me, I'm right there with you when you start asking 'Why?' Is it worth it? I get it."

Ford leaned forward again and glanced at him. "So? Is it?"

"What? Worth it?" Gil shrugged. "Whether it's terrorists, monsters or just bad people that the world would be better off without, it's my job to respond."

"That doesn't tell me if it's worth it."

Gil chuckled. "No, it doesn't, does it." He shrugged.

"I guess I'll figure that part out when I'm old and writing my memoires."

Ford held his hand out and it was shaking. "I'm just so damned mad."

"Good." Gil gripped his hand and held it steady. "Let the adrenaline burn off then screw your damned head on straight and do your job the way you were trained to do." He let his hand go and locked eyes with him. "Remember, it's okay to be angry. Just use that anger as fuel to keep going when you don't think you can anymore. Don't use it as an emotional crutch to get into the game, use it to get yourself out when there's nothing left in the tank."

Ford nodded slowly, trying to put his words into perspective. "How'd you get so smart?"

Gil actually laughed. "I've never been called that before. Usually, it's the opposite." He took a deep breath and let it out. "I guess…just being where you are too many times in my life. Others who were much smarter than me talked me down before I did went off half-cocked." He shrugged. "I'm just paying it back."

Ford nodded solemnly. "Thanks."

Gil clapped his back. "Any time, brother."

WHEN DAWN BROKE the techs were still assembling the gas bombs. The components that were shipped with them had no instructions, and the people who knew how to build them were zipped up in body bags, waiting transport out of the Catskills. Thankfully, satellite internet and experts were prepared to come to the rescue in the middle of the night.

"We've got two remote units that we can use to set the gas. They're not much good over the rougher terrain, but the old mines should be simple work for them," West announced to his teams.

"I'm guessing we'll be humping the bombs into the other tunnels?" Bodie asked.

"Unless you can teach 'em to walk in on their own." West smirked at him. "No need to sweat the hump. These things have triple redundancy. You could shoot one, and unless you ruptured the stainless steel container, you're safe."

Bodie scoffed. "I'm more worried about running into one of the woodbooggers."

"That's why you'll be traveling in teams."

Bodie hiked a brow. "Yeah, that didn't much help Charlie Team."

West sighed and crossed his arms. "Do you have a better idea for setting the charges?"

Bodie shook his head, accepting the question as an invite to shut his pie hole.

West turned back to face the men assembled. "The wasps nest drones are currently set to manual, and they'll be escorting you through the labyrinth of tunnels. You'll have to plant signal repeaters along your path, but Mr. Davis, our contractor, will let you know when those are necessary." He turned to face Larry. "Anything you'd like to add?"

"Sure." Larry stepped up and faced the men. "Usually the wasps are preprogrammed to key in on movement then utilize AI to verify the target with facial recognition.

Since you'll all be moving, we have to do this manually with remotes. I'm bringing your techs up to speed on the project as we speak." He cleared his throat and stood taller. "If you encounter resistance, the plan is to *not* detonate the drone unless it is absolutely necessary to save a member's life." He raised a brow as a low murmur went through the crowd. "We don't want the creatures to connect the dots on the drones until it's too late. If a drone is incapacitated for any reason, leave it. As long as the signal repeaters are within rage, we can detonate remotely at a later time."

"You're wanting all the drones to go boom at the same time?" Bodie asked.

"If it's possible, yes." He stepped forward and held his hands up. "Look, guys, if it comes down to saving any of you, we'll use the drone as it was intended and suffer any consequences from that later. We're not about to sacrifice a soldier's life just to get a tactical advantage on these things."

"He's right. What the drones can't do, the gas will." West crossed his arms and studied the men before him. "Primary goal here is to plant the charges and get every man back safely."

Larry nodded as he stepped back. "You've still got time while I finish the training with your techs." He glanced at West. "Muster at…?"

"Eleven hundred. If all goes according to plan, you'll be in and out in time for lunch."

"And if it doesn't go as planned?" Bodie asked, a sly smile forming.

"Then I guess you'll have to improvise or skip your midday meal." West waved them off. "Be geared up and ready to rock at eleven."

22

FOB Dog Town

Ford winced as the med tech peeled the bandage from his wound. "Yuck. This is starting to get infected." He held the gauze pad up and Dave saw the yellowish green goo mixed with the brown-colored dry blood.

"Just slap some triple antibiotic ointment on it and wrap it back up."

"You need a broad spectrum antibiotic." The med tech turned and rifled through his case. "I've got pain pills but no antibiotics." He looked up and stared across the bullpen. "There may be some in the triage tent."

"Do you have a triple antibiotic ointment in there?" Ford nodded to the case.

"Well, yeah, but—"

"Then let's start with that." He leaned back and raised his arm, stretching the skin around his wound. Once the gauze was taped back into place, he'd be less likely to pull it loose with movement. "I'll go to the triage tent and see if they have a z-pack or something."

"Amoxicillin, if they have it." The tech smeared the clear ointment over the weeping wound then pressed a fresh bandage over it. "Or even Keflex. Azithromycin is over prescribed these days. Odds are it wouldn't help."

"Understood." Ford stood and pulled his undershirt down before buttoning his BDU blouse. He stretched slightly then smiled to himself when the tape didn't pull. Turning for the triage tent he noticed Bodie exiting the Haze Gray tent.

He trotted up to him and nudged him. "What's the word?"

"We insert at eleven." Bodie paused and stared across the perimeter, the early morning sun casting moving shadows that made him overly cautious. "West has some kind of remote control unit that can set some of the charges, but for the most part, it will be us." He gave Ford a knowing look. "We're supposed to have the drones provide support."

Ford bristled. "We…my team could provide support." He'd almost volunteered Murphy and his team until he caught himself.

Gil shook his head. "West has it all planned out." He noted Ford's face fall then quickly added, "But the techs will be remotely flying the drones. I can't say for the others, but I'd appreciate a set of eyes like yours keeping a close watch on our six."

Ford nodded slightly. "Consider it done."

"Sweet. What say we fill up on caffeine and over cooked powdered eggs before we start this day."

Ford chuckled. "Why not? If the Genoskwa don't see you coming, they should sure smell you."

FORD HOVERED over the tech's shoulder as Bodie and his group inserted into the tunnels. Streaks of steel gray flashed across the monitors as the AI powered drones jockeyed for position around the team.

He pulled one side of his headset away, "Christ, those things sure cut in close."

The tech chuckled. "It's a trick of the helmet cams. The drones are probably a good meter, meter and a half away. They're just highly reflective and show up like that under NV."

"Considering the damage they can do, they might as well be in their shirt pocket." Ford pulled a roller chair closer and sat beside the tech. "Feel free to tell me to piss off if I get in your way."

"If Gil wants your eyes on the team, then you're good." The tech slipped over a bit, making more room. "This is a shit ton of data to be covering alone."

Ford glanced at all of the monitors. "Okay, which are the screens for the mines?"

"The tracked delivery vehicles are those two." He pointed to the top right. "They've got two fire teams per." He pointed back down to the lower monitors. "These are the squad monitors. Mostly helmet cams."

Ford's eyes bounced between the two sets of monitors. "How far apart are they?"

The tech shrugged. "About a click and a half." He finished tapping at the keyboard then leaned back in his chair and reached around Ford. He pulled a topographic map and handed it to him. "Check that. The tunnel entrances and the old mines are marked. We're pretty confident that the two tie in at numerous intersections, but we aren't sure just how far the tunnels go under the mountain."

Ford surveyed the map, occasionally looking up at the monitors. "How deep are they going?"

The tech shrugged. "Yeah, that I don't know."

"Raptor Two, set a repeater." Davis stared at the signal strength meter and spoke into one of the many microphones. He continued to study the signal strength of the numerous readouts then keyed a different mic. "Raptor One, set a repeater."

Ford raised a brow. "I don't suppose any of the signal repeaters that were set before are still operational?"

The tech shrugged. "I'm guessing from his orders that they were either damaged or the batteries died."

The headset gave a short static burst then a voice came over the speaker, "Holy cow that stinks." Ford sat up and stared at the screens again. "Where are they?"

The tech pointed to the center monitor. "About twenty yards from where Charlie Team bought the farm."

Ford keyed the mic, "Stay alert Raptor Three. You're closing in on Charlie Team's last activity area."

"Nice choice of words, Ford," Bodie whispered into the coms. "Thanks for the heads up."

Ford didn't realize he was holding his breath until they'd given the area a wide berth. One of Raptor Three's members scanned the area with a mounted torch then, using hand signals, gave the all clear. "Good." He sat forward and continued to stare at the monitors.

"Raptor Three, set a repeater," Davis marked the

area on his readout then went back to studying the strength meters.

"Approaching delta," Bodie whispered. "Tagging Raptor Two."

Ford zoomed in on Bodie's helmet cam and could just make out the members of Raptor Two stepping into the tunnel from the mine. "Charges set to delta."

Bodie handed them the air monitor and flipped on his red-lensed torch. As the member from Raptor Two held it at head height, the tiny impeller began to turn and a digital readout gave them wind direction and strength. "I think we're good. What little circulation we have in here should carry the aerosol much deeper into the caverns."

"Drop the last of the charges," Bodie quietly ordered. "Prepare for exfil." The Raptor Two member handed him back the air monitor and Bodie stepped into the mine to watch them prep the tracked machine for the return trip. "West was right. Back in time for lunch."

"Don't jinx us, Bodie."

"Contact!"

Both Bodie and the Raptor Two member spun, looking for who called out. The men in the mine suddenly came alert and suppressed weapons fire echoed through the hollow chambers.

Bodie had a limited field of view of the mine but saw something very large and dark flash across the opening. Their orders had been clear. At the first sign of occupancy, respective team leaders were to exfil their unit immediately. The men who made contact had no expectation of backup.

Bodie ground his teeth as he considered ignoring

those orders. He gripped the man closest to him, "Everybody out! Double time it!" He released the man and stepped towards the opening of the mine.

"Gil! What are you doing?"

Bodie turned back and pointed to the exit. "Go, now! I'm going to flank this thing and give Raptor Two a fighting chance!"

A moment later and he disappeared into the tunnel.

Ford was on his feet and trying to study the different helmet cams as men ran through the passages, making for daylight as fast as their feet would carry them. "Bring up Bodie's helmet."

The tech tapped a few inputs to the keyboard and Bodie's helmet cam came up, the NV view artificially altered with color. The image bounced as Bodie ran through the mine until he slid to a stop behind a very wide, hairy creature holding the control arm of the tracked delivery vehicle and swinging it like a club.

Bodie immediately brought the barrel of his carbine up and aimed center mass before delivering numerous rounds into the mud encrusted monster. The creature appeared to stiffen then spun, swinging the metal arm behind it in an attempt to squash whatever had stung it.

Bodie had just enough clearance to avoid being hit but dodged regardless. As his shoulder impacted the stone covered mine, he opened fire again, this time aiming for the tree trunk-sized legs. The creature immediately howled and launched the metal arm at him.

Bodie rolled to the side and cursed as the arm impacted the rocks beside him, sending shards of aluminum and stone into his face. He rolled again and leveled his barrel on the monster, firing low once more.

The muffled report of numerous suppressed weapons echoed through the mine as the creature fell into a full-on rage attack. It launched itself at the retreating Raptor Two team and scooped up the closest the man, swinging him unmercifully like a bat, knocking more of the soldiers into the solid rock walls of the mine.

As the creature cleared a path to the front, it turned and launched the corpse of the solder back towards Bodie before limping for the mine exit. Bodie barely avoided the wet splat of the man's impact and scrambled to get his feet under him to give chase.

"Tango is headed for the east mine entrance!" he yelled into the coms.

"Raptor Three, why the hell are you in the mines?" West practically screamed over the coms. "You are assigned to the southeast tunnel, over!"

Bodie ignored the call and did his best to avoid the bodies littering the ground as he ran after the beast. He rounded a bend in the mine, knowing that he was closing on the giant. He barely had fifty yards before the mine entrance would open to the forest.

As he rounded the bend and the light from the entrance came into view, Bodie slowed to a stop and stared. The mine was empty.

"There's no way that thing outran me here." He did his best to control his breathing and strained to listen. "He's gotta be here somewhere."

Ford's voice came quietly over the coms, "Check for a blood trail. You know you peppered its legs."

Bodie flipped his NV up and turned on his torch, pulling the red lens from the flashlight before sweeping the ground. A slight reflection indicated Ford was right. He bent low and ran his finger across the dark stain. "Yeah, it's blood." He rubbed his fingers together then smelled the familiar coppery scent.

Moving slowly and scanning the light ahead of him, Bodie made his way towards the mine entrance. "Head on a swivel, Gil," he mumbled to himself. "This thing could be anywhere."

He avoided the edges of the mine and paid careful attention to any jutting edges that might hide a side tunnel. He refused to be fooled like Charlie Team had been.

Following the blood, he suddenly came to a stop. The trail ended, a small puddle across one of the rail ties being the last of it. He carefully scanned both sides of the mine, but there was no escape. "Where the hell did he go?"

A familiar buzz flew by his head and Bodie spun, his flashlight reflecting the ceramic coating of a dozen wasp drones coming to the rescue. "Thought you could use backup," Ford's voice whispered in his ear.

"Thanks, but…the blood trail just stops," Bodie replied. He made sure his helmet cam displayed what he was seeing as he panned both sides of the mine. "No side tunnels, no gaps, nothing. He just vanished."

"Look up," Ford suggested.

Bodie leaned back, panning his light across the ceiling. "Son of a bitch." He stepped to the side and could see smears of blood on the rocks above. A hole in the ceiling connected another tunnel to the mine. "I guess I'm not used to thinking three dimensionally."

The drones circled quickly then zipped into the opening one by one. "Davis wants to explore a bit." Ford said. "You need to vacate the mine. At the first sign of activity, they intend to release the gas."

"Understood." Bodie turned and made for the exit. As he stepped out into the full light of the noon day sun, he stopped and stared.

"You had orders." West stood with the full squad of Raptor One around him. "You went against those orders."

"I was trying to provide support for Raptor Two." Bodie slung his carbine and set his jaw. "I was able to wound it and—"

"Raptor Two was dead the moment that thing locked onto them." West's face was stoic. "All you did was piss it off a bit before it beat those men to death."

Bodie opened his mouth to argue but closed it when West shoved a finger in his face. "If I can't count on you to follow orders, you will be relieved of duty."

Bodie locked eyes with him then slowly nodded. "Understood."

The muscle in West's jaw ticked as he glared at the man. "You're lucky your team made it out without resistance. Otherwise, we'd be having a completely different conversation."

Bodie lowered his eyes and swallowed the epithet that threatened to shoot from his lips. 'Yes, sir."

"Get your ass back to the FOB and prepare for debrief." West spun on his heel and stormed away, Raptor One in tow.

Bodie sighed heavily and began the long trudge back

to base. "Don't sweat it," Ford said quietly. "You did the right thing."

Bodie quietly scoffed. "Got any openings at the Bureau?" he joked.

Ford's voice suddenly became solemn. "Actually, as of right now, I'd say we have a lot of them."

23

FOB Dog Town

Bodie stood back while West and Davidson monitored the screens. Ford slipped in next to him and gave him a gentle nudge. "I see you still have most of your ass. I'm a little surprised West didn't chew it all off."

"Funny." Bodie crossed his arms as he continued to stare at the monitors. "We've got movement inside but not much. They're wanting to wait until there are larger numbers."

Ford nodded absently. "Makes sense." He nudged him again. "You do know there's like an eighty inch big screen outside with the same readouts."

Bodie nodded. "I like hearing them talk out their thoughts." He gave Ford a sideways glance. "It helps me to come up with better ideas."

Ford leaned to the side and lifted the light blocking curtain, checking the number of men assembled around the monitor outside the logistics building. "Most of your guys are absent."

"They've set up sniper nests around the known exits." He sighed to himself and lowered his voice. "We have no way of knowing how many exits there are. This last part, to me, is the weakest link in the whole plan."

"I'd bet good money the gas and drones will take out most of them." Ford checked his watch then sighed. "We've still got a couple hours before sundown. Want to go for a walk?"

Bodie hiked a brow. "You do know there are snipers set up all through those woods."

"I was thinking the perimeter of Dog Town." He crossed his arms as he continued studying the screens. "Fewer ears out there."

With Bodie's interest piqued he reached for the door of the MCC. "After you."

Ford held his hand tightly to the bandaged wound as he stepped down. Once the door was shut, he turned and made his way through the bullpen with Bodie following. As the pair passed the last of the tents, Ford glanced around to ensure they were alone. "Tell me something." He cleared his throat. "If you were a semi intelligent being and somebody did to you what we're about to do…if you survived, what then?"

Bodie sighed heavily as he sat on one of the rock outcrops. "I'd load for bear and go on a shooting rampage."

"And if you were one of them and had no guns?"

"I'd use whatever God and Mother Nature provided." He glanced at Ford. "You think this is a bad move?"

Ford slowly sat beside him. "Part of me wants blood. ALL of their blood." He glanced at Bodie and shrugged. "Another part of me knows that if we escalate then they will as well."

"Blood for blood." He shrugged. "A tale as old as time." He scratched at his chin. "What are you really thinking?"

Ford hung his head and sighed. "A very good friend of mine survived an encounter with these things." He paused a he gathered his thoughts. "He's convinced that they 'allowed' him to live so that he could tell us to leave them the hell alone."

Bodie nodded gently. "I suppose that's possible. If they're really that smart, you'd think they'd try to find a way to…" He shrugged. "I dunno. Communicate with us."

Ford scoffed. "I think that's exactly what they did when they let my friend live." He took a deep breath and blew it out slowly. "I just worry that we've jumped head first into a battle that there might not be an end to." He thrust his hand out towards the woods. "And how rare are these things? Most folks consider them legend or myth. We find out they're real and what do we do? Exterminate them all?"

Bodie chuckled to himself. "Yeah, that don't make a lot of sense, does it?" He glanced at Ford again. "So, if you were in charge, what would you have done?"

Ford hung his head again. "Like I said, part of me wants blood. The other part wants to wash my hands of this mess."

"And therein lies the conundrum. You lost your best friend to these things so you want to mount their heads on a wall."

Ford nodded solemnly. "While another part wants to

pack up and leave. And there's no regret with that thought. That's what really drives me nuts."

Bodie leaned back on the rock and let the setting sun warm him. "That regret would hit you later."

Ford shrugged. "Maybe." He squinted as he stared towards the horizon. "I don't know if I'm really having second thoughts or—" His words were cut off by an explosion in the woods.

The two men turned to each other. "That wasn't the mines," Bodie stated.

Ford felt his mouth go dry. "Those are the munitions we planted outside the perimeter." He pushed up from the rock and scanned the tree line, searching for a rising dust cloud. "There." He pointed.

"How did they escape the tunnels without getting gassed?" Bodie asked.

"How did they get past the sniper nests?" Ford felt his stomach fall. "Maybe they don't actually stay underground. Maybe they just use the tunnels to travel unseen during daytime?" His face paled as realization struck. "Did we just dump the majority of our assets outside the wire for nothing?"

"I WANT thermals in the air NOW!" Davidson barked as he used the joystick to adjust the cameras on the sentinels.

Ford stood in the open doorway of the MCC. "Sir, that explosion was on the opposite side of the camp from the mines."

"We know," Davidson replied absently, his eyes scanning the tree line. "We're trying to determine if it was a lone lookout or the scout for a planned attack."

Bodie nodded to West. "I can recall my men and have them inserted in—"

"Negative!" West pulled his chair out and fell into it, his hands reaching for the keyboard in front of him. "Once we have verification from IR, I'll consider options, but until then…" he trailed off as he leaned closer. "We've got numbers to the south."

Davidson's voice sounded calm as he replied, "And huge forces to the north and west."

"I think it's safe to assume they're surrounding us," Ford stated. "Director, I recommend we arm up every remaining man in Dog Town and have them standing by, should the natives attack."

"Do it." Davidson continued to track the movements on the screen. "Tell them to stay close to the bullpen. If they want to throw trees and boulders at people, they'll have to step out of the shadows."

"Yes, sir."

Ford spun and pushed open the door with Bodie hot on his tail. "Natives?"

Ford shrugged. "I'm pretty sure they were here first."

Bodie keyed his radio. "Sniper teams, stand by. All remaining personnel report to your respective armory and gear up. Hostiles at the perimeter!"

Ford stopped in front of the Bureau's armory tent and glanced at Bodie. "Load heavy."

"You know it!" Gil disappeared into the Haze Gray armory and Ford stepped aside as personnel darted back and forth.

When an opening made itself available, he slipped inside and donned his tactical vest, stuffing the pouches with magazines before plucking an M4 from the rack. "Load heavy!" he shouted before stepping out in the quickly darkening evening.

"Agent Ford?"

Ford spun to see a man wearing a cook's smock. "What?"

"I'm not weapons qualified, sir. Am I supposed to—"

"Unless you can beat an eight hundred pound gorilla to death with a spatula, grab yourself a fucking weapon and turn to!" Ford pushed past the man and paused just outside the door of the armory, his wound throbbing.

"You alright?"

He turned to see Bodie staring at him questioningly. Ford nodded. "Yeah, just pulled some stitches getting my tac vest on." Bodie almost looked as if he believed him as he pushed into the chaos.

Ford stepped out and followed him, nearly certain the largest bundle of heat signatures were to the northwest. "How long you gonna keep your snipers out there?" Ford yelled as he trotted to catch up.

"Not my call." Bodie glanced back towards the MCC. "If West has more than two brain cells in his head, he's already ordered them to make a slow advance and catch these things in a pincer."

"And if he hasn't?"

Bodie shrugged. "Then I guess we're going to find out just how bulletproof these beasts are."

"I CAN FEEL their eyes on us," Bodie quietly stated.

Ford gave him a barely perceptible nod. "I guess they're waiting for the sun to fully set."

"Or reinforcements." Bodie sighed and leaned away from the optics of his rifle. "I'm getting a headache staring through this thing."

Ford smirked. "Wanna trade?"

"Red dot?" he scoffed. "I'll deal with the headaches."

Ford stretched his neck and continued scanning the shadows of the trees. He shivered slightly as the cool fall evening drew colder. "I could sure go for a coffee right about now."

"Make mine a double," Bodie murmured. "Hey, hold up. What's this?"

"Where?"

"Just beyond the large rock outcrop." He shifted slightly and turned the reticle of his scope while Ford pulled his field glasses up.

"Is that…?"

"One of our snipers. What the hell is wrong with him?"

Ford felt his stomach fall. "He's dead, Gil."

"He's standing upright…" he trailed off as realization struck. He looked away and winced. "Dammit."

Ford watched as the man bounced up and down like a rag doll just at the edge of the scrub, limbs flailing and head lolling to the side. "They impaled him."

Bodie stiffened and shifted his grip on the rifle. He sighted in the area and attempted to guess where the creature holding the other end of the pole might be before squeezing off the first round.

Ford watched as the sniper's body fell to the ground

and an unearthly howl echoed through the woods. "I think you got him."

"Didn't kill it, though." Bodie cursed as he continued to scan the shadows. "Come on you big hairy bastard…step out and let me ventilate your skull for ya."

Another shot cracked to their right and Ford instinctively turned to see. He turned up the gain on his coms and listened as his men reported seeing the snipers' bodies marionetted along the edge of the trees. He groaned to himself and turned down the gain. "Either they found your snipers first or they caught them sneaking up on them."

Bodie shuffled away from his prone position along the flat rock and shot him a sideways glance. "What are you saying?"

"I'm saying that Bureau coms are alive with sightings of your snipers—" he gave him a knowing look, "—just like the one we saw."

"Son of a bitch," Bodie swore. He ran a gloved hand over his face and clenched his jaw. "How could they get the drop on so many sniper nests?"

Ford offered a slight shrug. "How does something that big move through the woods silently?"

Both men's coms came alive as West barked in their ear. "We have reliable reports that our snipers were ambushed." His voice softened slightly. "Do your best not to react when the monsters attempt to use their remains to get a rise from you."

"Too late," Bodie grumbled to himself.

"The tangos have our encampment surrounded with significant numbers and we are about to release the gas in the tunnels. There is sufficient activity to warrant the release, although the specimens are smaller. Possibly females or youths." He actually sounded disappointed by the casualties he was about to cause. "We'll be reserving a portion of the gas canisters for when the main forces return to the tunnels."

Davidson's voice came over the coms. "Do your best to preserve ammunition, but give 'em hell boys. The moment those things emerge from the trees, mow 'em down."

Ford sighed and glanced at Bodie. "Gassing the families? Why does that not sit right?"

"Because it's not the prize we're after, is it?" He nodded towards the trees. "We want those murderous motherf—" he stopped himself before he could begin a rant. He took a deep breath and let it out slowly. "If we don't thin their numbers significantly, I'm certain we'll find out just how human-like they are when they find their loved ones dead underground."

"Always rainbows and sunshine with you, isn't it?" Ford smirked as he turned his attention back to the trees. He pulled the field glasses away and watched the last rays of sunlight lick across the purple night sky. "Shit's about to get real, bud."

"I'm ready to put an end to this."

Ford opened his mouth to reply when the first war calls came from the woods. Hoots, hollers, howls, barks and whoops combined into a cacophony of noise backed by deep, echoing wood-thumps. "How do they get so damned loud?" Ford practically yelled.

"Lungs the size of sofa cushions would be my guess." Bodie squinted in the low light and pressed a hand to his temple. "Not this shit again."

Ford pressed a hand to his wound as he doubled over, his mouth watering. "I hate this…" He spat as his mouth filled with more saliva. "I don't need to be barfing with this stomach wound."

"Fuck this." Bodie crawled back to his position and levelled the rifle on the trees across from him. "Eat lead, you knuckle draggin' pieces of shit!" He screamed as he opened fire on the shadows, emptying his magazine and slamming a fresh one into the well. Almost immediately, the men to either side of them opened fire, splintering the scrub at the edge of the tree line into kindling.

Round after round sliced through the woods, cutting down anything in its path until the firing slowed, the shooters either holding back to conserve munitions or to reload.

Ford spat again and leaned back, sucking in the cold night air. "Finally. Relief."

"Heads up!" Bodie nodded toward the trees again as a sniper's body was flung from the shadows. It landed on the ground crumpled in a distorted heap, the man's bones obviously shattered. A moment later something else flew from the darkness and rolled across the grass.

Bodie knew what it was before he flicked on his torch, but felt the need to verify. As the light fell on the lump, he felt his chest tighten. The sniper's head lay wide eyed, staring into the night sky.

24

FOB Dog Town

"Where the fuck are my exploding drones?" West yelled across the MCC.

Larry Davis tapped furiously at the keyboard in front of him, his jaw clenched. "They're stuck underground and I'm having trouble getting a radio signal to them." He pushed away from the keyboard and huffed. "They're running on AI right now, searching for moving targets inside the tunnels."

"I need them in the forest! NOW!"

"I realize that, Commander, but at the moment, they're autonomous. Until I can get a signal recalling them, they're stuck on search-and-destroy."

"Fuck!" West threw a clipboard across the RV. He spun slowly as the gears in his head turned. "If we redeploy one of our IR drones, can you piggy back or relay a recall signal off of it?"

Larry Davis slowly began to nod. "Yeah. Yeah, I

think so."

West clapped one of his techs on the shoulder. "Do it! Deploy the closest IR drone we have and get those damned wasps into the fight!"

The tech reached for a joystick controller and began relocating the drone to the mine entrance. "Uh, sir?" The man slowed the drone near the edge of the woods. "How will the drones differentiate our people from the creatures?"

"We'll deal with that as soon as they're back in radio range." He glared at the tech. "Move it!"

Davis prepared a target package to upload to the wasps and paused. "I can limit their range to the camp perimeter and into the tree line, but if any of your snipers are still alive…" he trailed off, unable to finish the sentence.

West stared at the heat signatures surrounding the camp and slowly shook his head. "None of our snipers are still breathing." His voice was calm and even. "Are we in position?"

"This is as deep as I dare send the drone, sir. The radio signal should reach the wasps."

West nodded to Davis. "Send it."

Davis finished tapping in his commands and hit enter, watching as the wasps began to uplink their video footage through the IR drone. "I've got a shit ton of bodies here, Commander." He froze one of the images and sent it to the large overhead monitor.

West squinted in the near zero light of the scene and crossed his arms. "Can we enhance that video any?"

Davis tapped at the keyboard again and the image switched to NV, glowing green as it outlined the bodies scattered throughout the chambers.

"Oh shit. They're juveniles," the tech staring at the screen mumbled.

"Little ones grow up to become big ones." West marched past him and pulled a chair up to another station. He tapped at the keyboard and brought up the video feeds from the nearly released wasps. "Now the fun really begins."

Davis cleared his throat nervously. "Commander, I think I can tie in the thermal readouts to the wasps and narrow their target packages."

"Do it."

Ford had barely turned to look when another charge blew to his left. He gripped his rifle tighter and peered over the edge of the rock outcrop he used for cover. "They must be thick in those trees if they're hitting all of our munitions."

Bodie grimaced as he focused on the moving shadows. "Not enough of your munitions, I'm afraid."

A large stone arced across the twilight sky and landed with a heavy thud in the clearing between the camp and the trees. "That woulda left a mark." Ford took a deep breath and shimmied up the rock a bit more, levelling his weapon across the top. "I don't think they're going to come out of the woods. They know that's their advantage."

"Can't say I blame them." Bodie scanned further right before pulling his face away. "They're not stupid, that's for sure."

Both men spun when a man to their left cried out,

falling over and gripping his shoulder. "What happened?" Ford called to his partner.

"Something hit him." The agent scanned the area around them and lifted a softball sized stone. "This."

Ford cursed under his breath. "They know they'll have to throw smaller rocks if they want to reach us."

Another man to their right howled and crumpled, his hands instinctively dropping to his leg. Bodie squinted in the low light and realized the man's femur had been broken. "Oh, that's not good." He slid down the boulder and locked eyes with Ford. "They can hurl rocks hard enough to break a man's leg?"

Ford cursed under his breath and keyed his coms. "All units, drop back. Retreat to the edge of Dog Town." As soon as he rolled to the side one of the Haze Gray personnel fell face forward, a large wooden spear thrust through his middle. "Fuck me!"

"Double time it!" Bodie yelled into the coms. "Fall back!" He came to his feet and held his hand out for Ford. "Move it, Bureau!"

Ford didn't register the pain in his wound as the adrenaline rushed through him, pulling himself to a standing position and quickly trotting back towards the camp. As he reached the outer edge of the first tents, he spun and dropped to a knee, laying down cover fire for his men as they retreated. "Move it!" he yelled as he ejected his empty magazine and slammed a fresh one into the belly of the rifle.

Bodie appeared on the opposite side of the main thoroughfare and provided cover fire for the men scrambling up the hill. "Let's go, let's go, let's go! Double time it!"

Both men held fire when a fireball erupted across the

clearing and a huge Genoskwa body flew from the tree line into the grass outside the woods. Ford stared dumbfounded for a moment then glanced at Bodie. "We didn't set any charges that close to the perimeter."

Another explosion went off high in the canopy and a large figure fell from the taller branches as yet another charge exploded deeper inside the woods. Bodie slowly came to his feet and shouldered his weapon, peering through the scope. "Drones." A slow grin formed as more explosions echoed through the woods. "The wasps."

Ford breathed a sigh of relief and used the butt of his rifle to help him come to his feet, his wound suddenly aching. He limped into the main thoroughfare and watched as the last of the men raced to the safety of the tents. "About damned time something worked in our favor."

Bodie closed the distance and gave him a disapproving look. "Brother, you need to get to the med tent and have them take a look at you."

"I'm fine."

"Like hell." Bodie nodded toward Ford's middle. "You're leaking again."

Ford slid his hand to the bottom of his tactical vest and pulled away a bloody glove. "Well, shit." He wiped absently on his trousers and opened his mouth to say something witty when he began to collapse, crumpling into Bodie's arms.

"I gotcha, buddy." Bodie lifted the man and began walking him to the med tent. "Medic!"

"Morning, sleeping beauty."

Ford cracked his eyes open and groaned. "Aww, you think I'm a beauty."

"Dream on, Alice." Bodie came to his feet and raised a brow at the man. "You're lucky I brought you in when I did."

"Yeah," Ford coughed and winced, gripping the fresh bandages around his middle. "I guess I owe you one."

Bodie handed him a cup with a straw. "Docs say you need rest."

"Naw. I'm good. All I need is coffee." Ford sat up slowly and took a long drink. "This isn't coffee."

Bodie set the cup down and slowly sat. "They had to give you two units of plasma to get your blood pressure back into the 'realm of the living.'"

"Okay, now you're exaggerating." Ford grinned at him. "I don't have that much blood in my caffeine system."

"Joke all you want, but Davidson has grounded you. In fact, he said if he had any trucks going out today, you'd be on one."

Ford's face twisted and he glared at Bodie. "What of the dead? Isn't he going to bus them out?"

Bodie's eyes lowered to the floor and his face twisted. "The last truck that tried to go out found the remains of the truck before it." He looked up again and shook his head. "The driver was torn to pieces and the bodies of the fallen were scattered all over the place." He cleared his throat nervously and sat back. "The driver returned and reported what he found. Davidson and West both agreed that, for now, we'll keep our fallen in the chiller and bus them out when we all leave."

Ford sighed heavily and lay back on his cot. "That's assuming there will be an end and we'll get to leave."

"Yeah." Bodie stood and glanced toward the door. "I'm gonna get chow. I'm sure they have you on Jell-o or some such. Want me to sneak you back something?"

"Coffee."

"I meant something solid."

Ford grinned at him. "If it's made right, coffee can be a solid."

"Alright smart ass." Bodie pushed off the support and crossed his arms. "I'll see what I can do."

Ford pulled himself up and slid his feet off the edge of the cot. "Actually, I think I'll just come with you."

"Docs said you need to rest."

Ford gripped the IV in his arm and pulled it out, dropping it to the ground. "Yeah, I'm a bad patient and I'll rest when I'm dead."

Bodie hiked a brow at him. "That might be sooner than you think if you don't listen to the professionals."

"I am a professional." Ford glanced around for his clothes. "A professional with my ass hanging out of a gown, but still…where the hell are my clothes?"

"Covered in blood. Probably in the burn bags by now."

"Great." He clapped Bodie's shoulder. "You go ahead. Grab some chow. I'll join you as soon as I find some pants."

"Definitely pants first. We do have a dress code around here." He turned for the door and shot the attending nurse a knowing look. "He's ready for discharge."

"No, he's not."

"Tough." Ford stepped around Bodie and made for

the exit. "I feel great. Thanks for topping off the tank, doc. I got things to do."

The nurse tried to argue but Ford made a hasty exit, leaving Bodie behind to catch the brunt of the nurse's argument.

Moving directly to his tent and being careful not to rip stitches getting his fresh clothes out, Ford used a flashlight and peeled back the dressing, peering at his wound. "Staples this time. Nice." He felt sweat pop out on his forehead as he fought with the hospital gown. He actually had to sit down and catch his breath between articles of clothing.

"Boss, you don't look so hot."

Ford looked up to see one of his men standing at the foot of his cot. "I'll be okay. I just need some caffeine."

"Yeah, no." The man stepped closer and appeared genuinely concerned. "You're paler than a brand new tube sock." He reached for a shaving mirror and handed it to him. "You should be back in the infirmary."

Ford stared at the image reflected at him and barely recognized the face. Unshaven, dark circles around his eyes and pale skin, he looked like Uncle Fester. "Still handsome." He tossed the mirror to the next cot and reached for his socks, trying not to pass out as he bent over and pulled them on.

"Seriously, boss. You should get checked out and—"

"I've already been," he replied through gritted teeth. "They stapled me up and pumped me full of blood." He turned and glared at the man. "I'm good."

The man held his hands up and slowly backed away. "Whatever you say, boss."

Ford had to stop in the middle of tying his boots and catch his breath. His fingers shook and felt like swollen sausages as he attempted to do anything that required dexterity.

The moment he was finished dressing, he planted his hands on the edge of his cot and tried to come to his feet. His legs shook and his knees felt like gelatin as he stood. Ford gripped the metal locker next to his bunk and struggled to catch his breath.

"Took ya long enough."

Ford nodded slowly as Bodie stepped closer. "Maybe you should get that rest they suggested?" He held a paper cup under his nose. "I brought you coffee." He raised a brow at him. "Is that a good enough bribe to get you to lay down for a bit and catch your breath?"

Ford slowly lowered himself to his bunk and reached for the cup. "I'll need more than this."

"Then you wouldn't be able to sleep."

Ford scoffed. "Watch me." He sipped the coffee then tossed the cup back, swallowing it like a large shot of whiskey. "Yeah. More." He handed Bodie the cup again and smiled. "Lots more."

Bodie sighed as he took the cup and set it aside. "You rest. I'll fetch more." He helped Ford to stretch out on his cot then turned for the exit. "I'll just bring a carafe next time."

"Big one." Ford sighed as he lay his head back on the pillow and closed his eyes. "Great big one."

Bodie set the antibiotics the nurse had given him down next to Ford and chuckled as he turned to leave. "I'll have them put it in an IV bag for ya."

Ford smiled, his eyes closed and held a hand up, giving him a thumbs up. "I'll just wait here for—"

25

FOB Dog Town

Ford groaned as he attempted to roll over and his eyes shot open. Lifting his head he glanced around. "How long was I out?"

Bodie looked at his watch and sighed. "Counting today, three weeks. All the 'squatches are dead. You're the last living Bureau guy, so I guess that makes you the boss." He came to his feet and reached for the coffee cup. "Oh, and we've all been awarded hero medals for saving mankind from the big, bad, stinky monsters."

Ford blinked at him in confusion. "Really?"

"No, dipshit." Bodie handed him the cup. "You've been out about seven hours."

Ford took the cup of lukewarm coffee and swallowed it greedily. "I'm so thirsty."

"Probably because you ripped out your saline IV when you left the med tent." Bodie crossed his arms and glared at him. "Davidson convinced West you needed a babysitter so I was voluntold to watch you. I've been right here by your side, the whole time."

Ford stared at him blankly. "Really?"

"Fuck you, dude. I offered." Bodie took the cup and poured the last of the warm coffee into it. "You really need to ingest something more than bean juice. Maybe some solid food and a liquid that isn't a diuretic?"

Ford groaned as he sat upright and slid his boots off the end of the cot. "I'm okay." He held a hand up holding Bodie at bay. "Really." He planted his feet and hung his head, breathing deeply. "Any kind of action from the bigfeets?"

"A couple of scouts hovered near the edge of the tree line, watching us. West had Davis deploy some of the drones. Got one, but the other slipped away." Bodie sat back down and braced his elbows on his knees, watching the man. "We figure there must be tunnel accesses all through the hills. That's the only way we can explain them just disappearing from thermals."

Ford took a deep breath and let it out slowly. "Do we know if any of them have returned to the mine?" He looked up, his eyes asking what his mouth couldn't.

Bodie nodded slightly. "About an hour after you passed out, they raised a hell of a ruckus. Howling and screaming at the top of their lungs." He seemed to go pale as he retold the events. "Loud enough it echoed through the woods. It carried all the way from the mines to here."

Ford's brows rose. "Oh, shit."

"Yeah, 'oh, shit.' I think attacking the non-combatants raised this altercation to a whole other level."

Ford looked up at him questioningly. "How did Davidson respond?"

Bodie shrugged. "I wasn't in the MCC, but word is that he got pretty unnerved by it all. One of the techs said they had a downed drone in the entrance of the mine that was still providing video feed." He cleared his throat nervously. "The males went into a full blown tirade. Beating the walls and nearly caused a cave-in."

"And West?"

Bodie shrugged. "West isn't wired like the rest of us. He's a lot more like Locke. The 'whatever it takes' mindset runs deep in him, so he wasn't fazed."

Ford took a deep breath and winced. "I almost wish you weren't joking earlier."

"About?"

"That I was the ranking Bureau member." He looked up at him and sighed. "I'd call a strategic withdrawal."

"Probably be a smart idea." Bodie shook the thermos and came to his feet. "Word is that the trees took out more drones than they did 'squatches."

"How many are left?"

Bodie shrugged. "I'm only hearing rumors from inside the MCC, but…" he locked eyes with Ford. "Less than a third of what Davis brought here."

"Any idea how many Genoskwa were killed?"

Bodie clenched his jaw for a moment. "Less than a dozen." He sighed heavily as he leaned against the steel locker separating the cots. "And worse, thermal scans keep showing an ever increasing number of the things. It's like they're streaming in from parts unknown." He gave him a knowing look. "Last read I got was hundreds of heat signatures surrounding the camp, and that was before the bodies were discovered underground."

Ford groaned as he looked away. "Like ants. The more you kill, the more they swarm from underground."

"Yeah." Bodie sucked at his teeth. "I'm gonna refill the thermos. Try to rest and we can continue catching up when I get back."

Ford watched him exit the tent and slowly fell to the side, closing his eyes as his head hit the pillow.

"RADIOS ARE DOWN AGAIN, SIR." The tech pulled off his headphones and tossed them aside. "The whole setup's beginning to fail like clockwork."

"Can you boost the outbound signal?" Davidson leaned closer to the monitor and stared at the readouts.

"Negative, sir. Whatever is going on, it almost acts like the transmitter is being grounded. No matter how much we boost the signal, nothing is getting through."

Davidson stood and continued to stare at the readouts. "You said it's almost like clockwork?"

The tech nodded then tapped at his keyboard. "Okay, here, there was no interference for about fifteen minutes, then here," he tapped again and the image changed, "we had almost forty-five minutes of dead time. If you go back over the last two days, it's nearly identical."

Davidson's face twisted in confusion. "That sounds almost mechanical. Are we being jammed?"

The tech shook his head and removed his head phones again. "No, sir. It's not that precise. Sometimes we'll have signal for up to thirty minutes, other times, less than ten. Same for the dead air. Sometimes it's as long as an hour, sometimes it's as short as thirty minutes."

Davidson sighed. "Can you think of any natural phenomena that would cause sporadic interference like this?"

The tech shrugged slowly. "Honestly, sir, this one has me stumped."

Davidson nodded then began to pace. "Okay, let's start compressing our logs and reports into data packages. Every time there's an opening, we send a data burst to HQ. Anything new, we add to the end of the data burst."

"Sir? Resend the same data over and over?"

Davidson nodded. "In case any of it doesn't make it through in previous bursts. For posterity."

The tech raised a brow at him. "Are you afraid we'll not make it out of these mountains, sir?"

Davidson stiffened slightly but offered the man a gentle smile. "I just want to make sure that all of the i's are dotted and the t's are crossed." He gave the man a knowing look. "As many casualties as we've had out here, the powers that be need to know how hard to bring the hammer down on me."

Commander West smiled as he entered the MCC. "Support is on the way." He fell into the chair opposite of Director Davidson and intertwined his fingers behind his head as he rocked back.

"What kind of support?"

West's smile widened. "I finally got through on the

satellite phone and called in a few favors. Once they heard that Locke was KIA, the other unit commanders were more than happy to send their support." He sniffed hard as he leaned forward. "Seems they felt a certain debt to Locke after he saved their asses over the years."

"What kind of support?" Davidson asked again, slower.

West came to his feet and stretched his back. "We have a couple of gunships headed in. Both have dual Vulcan cannons and a metric shit ton of ammo." His face fell slightly and he shrugged. "I tried to get ASMs, but they just weren't available."

Davidson's mouth fell open. "You…tried to order…*missiles*?"

"They were deployed." West shrugged. "But hey, you've seen how effective the Vulcans are, so, we should be golden."

Davidson wiped a heavy hand over his face and leaned on the counter. "You do realize that once they hear us start up those choppers, they'll scatter like cockroaches. We'll never see them as long as those birds are in the air."

West shot him a tight-lipped smile. "This ain't my first rodeo, Mikey." He clapped the man on the back as he reached around him for the coffee pot.

"What do you intend to do?"

As West poured a cup of coffee, he fought back the smile forming. "They're going to stage about five miles from us. Them wood apes won't hear a thing, or if they do, they won't consider it a threat since it's so far off." He sipped the hot liquid and locked eyes with Davidson. "Once they've formed up along our perimeter again, I'll call for a strategic withdrawal of our forces and signal the birds to come in and grind them into hamburger." His smile widened. "From behind."

Davidson's eyes widened. "So…the area *beyond* the birds' target will be…" he trailed off.

West nodded. "Us." He shrugged again. "Danger-close is acceptable if it gets the job done." He set the coffee down and clapped Davidson on the shoulder again. "No worries, Director. We'll inform our people well ahead of altercation. They'll know what to do."

"And if they can't, for whatever reason?"

West offered a slow shrug. "Survival of the fittest?"

Ford was sitting up on the edge of his cot slowly chewing a sandwich when Director Davidson stepped into the Delta Team tent. "I'm glad you're here. We need to—" He came up short when he saw Bodie sitting in the corner. "I…uh, didn't realize you had company."

Bodie raised a brow at him. "I was told to babysit, so I'm babysitting."

"Right." His eyes shot between the two men as he tried to think of any other reason to be in Ford's tent.

"What do you need, Director?" Ford asked before biting off another chunk.

"I, um…" he cleared his throat nervously. "Uh, it wasn't really important."

Bodie leaned forward, his eyes locked to Davidson's. "It sounded important when you came in." He glanced at Ford. "Is it because I'm here? I can hit the head and—"

"No, no." Ford held a hand out to stop him. "Anything you can say to me, you can say in front of him."

Davidson lowered his eyes and took a deep breath. "Even if it deals with his commanding officer?"

Bodie's ears perked. "Especially if it deals with him." He swept his hand to the side, offering a chair. "Please."

Davidson glanced around the tent to ensure none of the men were present before taking his seat. "So it seems that Commander West has ordered a couple of strike helicopters."

Bodie broke into a toothy grin. "Finally. An end to this nonsense."

Davidson held a hand out to stop him. "Except, he also shared his proposed tactics." He glanced at Ford and gave him a knowing look. "He's starting to sound more and more like Locke."

"How's that?" Ford asked.

Davidson glanced around again then leaned in closer, lowering his voice. "He wants to stage them off a bit, and the next time the creatures make a stand in the trees, he wants to come in from behind to strike."

Ford glanced at Bodie and both men shrugged. "Okay. And?"

Davidson gave him a "duh" look. "If they're striking from *behind* the creatures, what is directly *beyond* them?"

Both men thought for a moment; you could almost see the shock of realization when it struck. "Okay, so…" Ford swallowed the bite in his mouth. "Where are we supposed to stage that is bulletproof?"

Davidson shook his head and lowered his voice. "He said 'survival of the fittest.' Doesn't sound like he cares what happens to any of our staff."

Bodie groaned as he sat back. "He learned that from

Locke." He met Ford's gaze and grimaced. "Long story, but…let's just say the job got done."

Ford set the sandwich down and rubbed at his eyes. "Do the men know?"

"Not yet, but West claims he's going to inform them so that they can take whatever measures they deem necessary." He scoffed. "In other words, he's going to leave them to their own devices."

"There's just too much open ground." Bodie came to his feet and peered through the mesh window. "The tents won't offer any defense. The closest thing to protection is the logistics building and the MCC, but…" he turned back to them. "If they're attack helicopters then they'll likely have Vulcans. Nothing short of heavy armor plate will stop those rounds."

"There aren't enough rock outcroppings out there." Ford could feel his hands shake as his anger grew.

"By all rights, you should have been out of here yesterday." Davidson shot Ford a dirty look. "If the trucks could still leave without…" he trailed off.

"I wouldn't go anyway." Ford crossed his arms defiantly. "I'm the last team leader you have, and even though there's barely enough men left to make a full team, you need me."

Davidson sighed and wiped nervously at his brow. "You're not wrong."

"Foxholes," Bodie quietly stated. He turned to meet their gazes. "We need to have the men start digging foxholes along the edge of Dog Town, facing the perimeter and stack as many rocks and sandbags along the outer edge as they can." He clenched his jaw as he ground his teeth. "We repair as many sentinels as we can and get them operational again. We dig foxholes for the men to take cover in and we do it ricky-fuckin'-tic." He reached for his coat and slung it over his shoulder. "Because I know West, and the moment he can use those choppers, he will. The men be damned."

Davidson came to his feet and held Ford's shoulder, preventing him from rising. "We'll take care of this. You stay here and try to heal. We don't need you manning a shovel."

Ford sighed and melted back into his cot. "I'm not arguing."

Davidson glanced at his watch. "I doubt they'll be here by tonight, but we'd best get started. We've only got a few hours of daylight left."

Bodie stepped around the director then paused. He turned back to Ford with a smirk. "No worries, sunshine. I'll make sure my foxhole is big enough for you, too."

"Don't forget to add the mini bar."

"And the disco ball." Bodie shot him a wink. "You bring the nachos."

"You bring the ladies, I'll bring the booze."

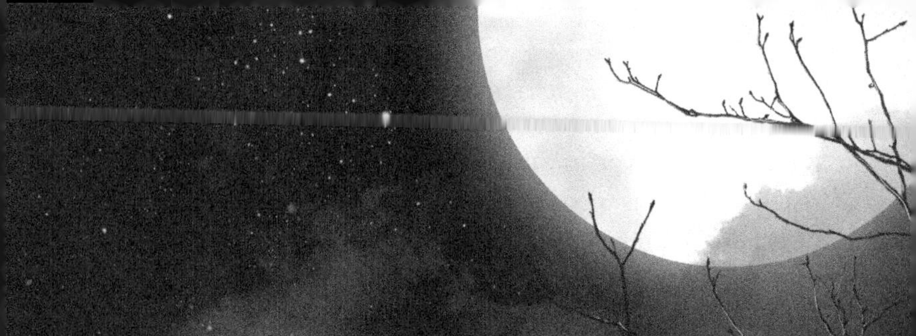

26

FOB Dog Town

"We're down more than fifty percent of our manpower." Bodie sighed as he ripped open an energy bar and settled in against the side of the foxhole. "I saw the list before coming out here."

Ford hung his head and tried not to think of the casualties they'd suffered. "I'm certain our numbers are even lower."

Bodie chewed slowly and glanced towards the setting sun. "Maybe those gunships are a good thing."

Ford shrugged. "If they arrive in time. I don't guess West gave you an ETA?"

Bodie shook his head. "Just that they're on the way. I don't know if that means they're in the air as we speak or if they were approved for use but haven't even been fueled yet." He sighed and leaned his head back. "I guess we'll find out when the 'squatches find out."

"Joy." Ford craned his neck and peered past the sandbags. "Where's the booze?"

Bodie popped the last of the energy bar into his mouth and stuffed the wrapper into his blouse pocket. "Supply chain issues." He sat up and peered into the tree line, hoping to catch movement. "I put in for a mini bar and they sent energy bars instead. You'd think this was still the military or something."

Ford brought the scope to his eye and peered into the shadows. "Probably for the best. I forgot the nachos anyway."

"Movement." Bodie shifted slightly and reached for his IR binoculars. "Just beyond those large pines." The whine of a high speed drone buzzed overhead and he watched as it appeared closer to the tree line. "Here we go."

He waited for the drone to make its kamikaze run but the thing hovered in place along the edge of the trees. Slowly bobbing in the air, it spun right, then left, searching for the heat signature that was its target.

"What happened?" Ford asked.

Bodie shook his head. "Either a false reading or the damned thing went underground before the drone could do its thing."

He continued to study the drone through his binoculars and barely caught the flash of a heat signature deeper in the trees. "I think there's another one."

Ford pushed up and peered over the sandbags. "They learned from our previous attacks." He reached for his ear bud and switched to the MCC channel. Constant chatter about disappearing heat signatures deeper in the woods was the subject of the moment and he could hear the drone operator's frustration. "Yeah, they're toying with the boys in the MCC. Heat signatures are popping up and disappearing all over the place."

Bodie sighed as he slid back into the foxhole. "Strange, innit? I've gone up against all kinds of bad guys in my career. The one sure-fire thing about them is, they're all stupid. They make obvious mistakes that single them out, we strike and make them go away." He glanced at Ford. "But these things?"

"They're fucking smart."

"Yeah, they are." Bodie pulled his canteen and took a long swallow, wiping his mouth on the back of his sleeve. "A little too smart if you ask me."

"Hold on…" Ford held a finger up and pushed his ear bud in a bit more. "There's chatter about a window opening…radio data burst…." He glanced at Bodie. "Any idea what that is?"

Bodie shook his head. "I know they've been having all kinds of issues with the long range radios. Maybe that's it?"

"Data bursts?" Ford plucked the ear piece and let it dangle. "Who are they sending data bursts to?"

"Probably HQ in the city." He gave him a knowing look. "Most likely telling them to stay the fuck out of the forest 'cuz the wood monkeys are handing us our collective asses."

Ford stretched his neck then reached into his pocket for a pain pill. He tossed it back and swallowed it, wincing as his staples pulled with each movement.

"You okay?"

Ford leaned into the wall of the foxhole and nodded. "Yeah, I'm good." He glanced around the foxhole and nodded approvingly. "Nice grave. I like how it's made for two."

"I just figured I'd save the survivors from having to dig them." He shot him a crooked grin. "Forever together. I hope you don't snore."

"Hard to snore once they fill it back in with dirt." He slid to the side and brought his barrel up around the edge of the sandbags. "Why are they holding back? They know how to avoid the drones. They should have made a move by now."

"Like I said. They're smart." Bodie glanced overhead at the clouds moving in. "Please tell me it isn't supposed to rain."

"Not tonight." Ford rubbed at his knee. "At least, that's what my internal barometer says."

"Good." He slid back into the foxhole and cradled his rifle over his knees. "It's a bit chilly to be swimming."

Ford opened his mouth to warn him about skinny dipping when the forest erupted with hoots, hollers and screams. The wood knocks seemed rhythmic, almost like a drum beat as they increased in tempo. Ford chuckled to himself. "Ask and you shall receive."

Bodie sighed as he readied his rifle again. "Time to make the doughnuts."

"It's like blinking Christmas lights out there," Davidson grumbled as he studied the monitors.

Larry Davis scoffed. "The heat signatures fade in then fade out too fast for the drones to react, even running with AI." He pushed his chair back and shot Davidson a frustrated look. "If it were just my drones, I'd think it was a software glitch, but yours are doing the same thing."

"Uh, Director?" One of the techs leaned back and motioned to him. "The fallen drone by the mine?"

"What of it?"

"You might want to see this." The tech stood and vacated his seat, motioning for Davidson to sit.

Davidson fell into the chair and stared at the screen. "What am I looking at?"

The tech mumbled an apology then leaned across and tapped at the keyboard, causing the image to rotate ninety degrees and display an upright image. "There ya go, sir."

Davidson watched the night vision images and felt his blood run cold. Medium-sized creatures carried the dead bodies of smaller ones past the camera and formed a line toward the rear of the cavern. One by one they bent and placed their dead into holes in the ground. "What the hell am I watching?"

The tech cleared his throat nervously. "They're burying their dead, sir."

Davidson leaned back in the chair and stared open mouthed. "I never would have…" he trailed off.

"It doesn't matter," West growled as he entered the MCC from the rear of the RV. "Terrorists bury their dead, and they're barely a step up from animals." He pushed his chair between two of the working techs and fell into it. "Hell, some of the bastards we've faced would need a couple steps up the evolutionary ladder to be considered an animal. How about you turn your fuckin attention back to the task at hand, huh? How many of the woodboogers are staging out there?"

"A lot, Commander." One tech leaned away from his station, revealing heat signatures winking in and out on the screen. "I don't know how they're masking themselves from our sensors, but it's flashing like lightning bugs out there."

West shot him an evil grin as he checked his watch. "We just have to keep 'em busy a couple more hours. Then Haze Gray will take care of them for us."

"Your choppers are inbound?" Davidson asked.

"As we speak. Fully fueled, fully loaded and armed for bear."

Davidson felt his mouth go dry as he glanced at the monitor of the perimeter again. "And you warned the men to be ready for this little display?"

West's face fell as he leaned forward. "Seems like somebody beat me to it." His eyes narrowed at Director Davidson. "No matter, though. They got the word and apparently dug themselves foxholes to stay out of the line of fire."

Davidson scoffed. "Imagine that. Men who actually want to stay alive. What a novel concept."

West felt his temper start to flare and turned his chair to face the man. "As I recall, it was your request for assistance that got me and my men out here in the first damned place. Do you have any idea how many of my assets have been lost due to your—"

"Don't you mean Locke's men? It was Simon Locke who answered my call, and he was the commander of this team of specialists, was he not?"

West felt the muscle in his jaw twitch as he glared at him. "Regardless, they're under my command now." His features suddenly relaxed and he smiled, the act of which unnerved Davidson more than the man's angry displays. "But if you'd rather deal with this problem on your own, I will gladly call for a withdrawal of our resources." He came to his feet and planted his hands on his hips. "What do you say, Director? Are you and," he scoffed, "what's left of your teams, ready to deal with this on your own?"

Davidson refused to take the bait. "If you want to cut and run, West, be my guest." He slowly turned back to the screens and focused on the assembling forces in the forest. "I've got more important things to do than get into a pissing match with you."

West smiled broadly. "Yeah, that's what I thought." He sat back down and checked his watch again before reaching for the radio. "We have helicopter gunships incoming. ETA one hour, forty five mikes. All personnel are ordered to do nothing, repeat, do nothing to engage the tangos. We just have to keep them along the perimeter long enough for our brothers to fly in and grind them into dogfood for us." He took a long breath and smiled again. "With a little luck, this standoff ends tonight. That is all." He tossed the radio to the counter and leaned back in his chair, crossing his hands behind his head as he rocked back and forth. "I feel like pancakes." The techs all turned and gave him a confused stare. "I think when this is over, I'm gonna find a pancake house and eat till I'm ready to pop."

"DID YOU CATCH THAT?" Ford rolled his eyes. "'Keep them at the perimeter,' he said."

Bodie scoffed. "Yeah, I'm sure they'll listen to us if

we ask them to just wait." He continued tracking the moving shadows along the edge of the tree line. "Y'all just hold tight while we bring in a couple of gunships to kill you. That should work, right?"

"Works for me." Ford shifted slightly and winced, absently reaching for his bandaged side. "I'll be glad to sleep in my own bed when this is over."

Bodie glanced at him. "Do you think it will ever really be over?"

Ford cocked his head to the side and studied him. "What do you mean?"

Bodie sighed and pulled his eye from the scope. "The next poor fucker that hikes through these woods…" he shrugged, leaving the statement hanging.

Ford nodded knowingly. "I read Archer's report. He went through everything that Gamboa left behind and even did some research of his own on these things. The way it read to me, they've been at war with mankind since before Europeans ever set foot on this continent." He glanced at Bodie and shook his head. "We might have reignited this conflict, but we didn't start it."

"Blood feud." He chuckled under his breath. "Maybe they're cooking moonshine in those hills and the Indians moved in on their territory?"

"Wrong movie, bud." Ford slid back into the foxhole and leaned against the wall. "I don't feel so good."

"No shit. You had a tree branch shoved into your guts and…" Bodie turned and spit, his mouth watering heavily. "Fuckers are doing that thing again."

Ford groaned as he rolled to the side and pressed a free hand to his temple. "Fucking infrasound." He spat into the dirt. "I'm gonna have to start shooting into the trees to get 'em to stop." He spat again and tried to quell the desire to throw up. "If they make me toss cookies and I rip these damned staples—"

Bodie spat again and tried breathing through his mouth. "What you gonna do? Kill 'em?" He spat again. "This is getting ridiculous."

"Fuck this mess." Ford pushed up from the ground, tossed his rifle across the top of the berm, and was preparing to fire randomly into the trees when gunfire erupted on either side of their foxhole. "Well," he slid back behind the berm, "somebody beat me to it."

Bodie spat again and pressed both hands to his head. "Only they ain't stopping."

Ford crawled away from the berm and heaved, holding his wound as tightly as he could. "Dear lord, no…"

Bodie plucked a grenade from his vest and pulled the pin. "I can't take their shit anymore." He released the lever and threw it as hard as he could toward the trees, yelling, "Frag out!" He slid below the berm and pressed his hands to his temples again.

When the grenade went off, all hell broke loose as the men in their foxholes opened fire, slinging hot lead blindly into the trees. The order to cease fire echoed through the coms as the firing slowly died down.

Bodie looked up at Ford still gagging and trying to spew. "I think it's over."

"Tell that to my gut." He sat back and spat again, his hand clenched tightly to his wound. "I actually felt sorry for the hairy bastards for a minute, what with gunships coming to kill them and all, but now?" He chuckled as he fell back onto his butt. "Those choppers can't get here fast enough."

"Yeah, because trying to kill us isn't worth slaughtering them wholesale, but making us seasick? That's a straight up death sentence."

Ford took a deep breath and rolled up on his knees, his hand still pressing his wound tightly. "This time, yeah." He took another deep breath and blew it out forcefully as he walked on his knees back to the forward berm. "I knew I should have brought the booze."

Bodie slung his rifle back up over the berm and assessed the damage. "I still see movement in the trees." He squinted and leaned forward slightly, staring at the treetops. "Those suicide drones are acting like they don't know what the fuck to do."

"Huh?" Ford glanced at him questioningly.

"They're buzzing back and forth across the treetops…I guess they're searching?"

"Or they're lost." Ford came up on his knees and peered over the edge with his binoculars. "Huh. I wonder if the techs piloting them are high?"

"Something ain't right." Bodie shifted his weight and tried to focus on the small metallic balls with the blinking red LEDs. "Yeah, they're acting all sorts of weird."

"Maybe whatever is messing with the long range coms is messing with their signal, too." Ford scanned along the tops of the trees all across the perimeter. He focused further down the line and watched as a drone suddenly bobbed up them shot across the clearing toward the foxholes. "Uh-oh."

"What?"

The explosion that echoed through Dog Town was entirely too loud and the screams that followed sent a chill down Ford's back. "We need to run."

Bodie watched as Ford completely ignored his

bandaged wound and scrambled to the rear of the foxhole. He didn't wait to find out why they were making a hasty retreat and quickly followed suit. "Where the hell are we going?"

Ford glanced over his shoulder just as another drone exploded closer to the bullpen. "The drones are locking in on our heat signatures!"

"*The fuck?!*" Bodie turned and watched as another foxhole exploded and men began to scramble away from the perimeter. "How the fuck did they do that?"

Ford slid to a stop by the showers and jerked open the rickety wooden door. "Beats the fuck out of me, but I'm not taking any chances." He reached out and grabbed Bodie, pulling him into the outdoor shower stall. He hugged him tightly then pulled the chain, dumping the Fall air-chilled water down onto their heads in a continuous pour.

Bodie watched nervously as a drone buzzed past and impacted the side of the mess tent, exploding near the double front doors. "Son of a bitch."

Ford swallowed hard as the sound of drones buzzing through the air increased, like a hive of angry hornets. He activated his coms and barked into the mic, "Kill the drones! Kill the drones!"

27

FOB Dog Town

"What the hell are they doing?" West barked as he came up out of his chair.

"They're…they're…they lost our signal!" Larry Davis typed furiously at the keyboard, his face pale as his worst fear came to life. "They've all switched to AI and falling back on their original program."

"What original program?" Davidson asked nervously.

"They're searching out ANY heat signatures and attacking."

"Shut them off!" West marched the short distance and stood behind Davis. "Shut them off NOW!"

"I'm trying!" Larry typed furiously, sweat breaking out across his forehead as he struggled to regain control of the flying bombs.

West angrily pulled his sidearm and pressed it to

Larry's temple. "Shut them down, now," he stated quietly.

Larry knew the implied "or else" was silent but deadly. "*Don't you think I'm trying?* Something is interfering with the signal. It's like they're being jammed!"

A tech pushed his chair back and turned to West. "Commander, we've lost long range coms again. Whatever it is, it's probably what's affecting the drones."

"I don't care what's causing it." He pulled the hammer back on the pistol and pressed harder to Larry's temple. "Make it stop."

"I'm trying!" Larry typed furiously then leaned back, staring at the screen. "Wait. I think...maybe..." He typed again, his fingers a blur across the keyboard. When he finished, he slammed and held down the enter button and swallowed hard, his eyes scanning the monitors. "That's it!" He breathed a sigh of relief and turned to face West, the pistol now pressed to his forehead. "They're down."

West locked eyes with the man then glanced at the monitor. All of the drone feeds read "inactive." "How many people did we lose?" he asked quietly.

"No idea yet, sir." The techs operating the overhead surveillance drones were fighting to regain control of the units. "I think I have control of the cameras again. Wait one." West continued to hold the pistol on Larry's forehead as the tech worked behind him. "Oh, no..."

West felt the weight of the pistol as his arm dropped and he turned to face his technician. "How bad is it?"

"Bad, sir." The tech pushed his chair back and allowed West to study the screens. Rapidly cooling heat signatures were scattered across the empty space between the perimeter and Dog Town. The second drone zoomed in on the bullpen and the damage done to the mess tent and two of the secondary living quarters.

"Fuck me," West groaned. "We've bombed our own goddam camp." Davidson pushed up from the monitors and reached for the door. "Where the hell do you think you're going?"

Davidson's jaw ticked as he ground his teeth. "To render aid, if I can." He glared at West and hated the man for his callousness. "Those are our people out there." He gripped the door tighter. "Or is this just another example of 'survival of the fittest?'"

West rolled his eyes and turned his attention back to the monitors. "What are the creatures doing?"

The tech beside him nervously glanced between the two men before turning his attention back to the screens. "They're holding at the tree line, sir."

"Well then, maybe it's safe for you to..." he trailed off as he realized that Davidson had already left.

Director Davidson walked carefully through the bullpen, his eyes taking in the total carnage of the drones. Wailing could be heard in the distance and wounded personnel were straggling in from the perimeter.

He spun a slow circle, taking in the damage done; it took him a long moment to realize the lack of people moving through the camp. "Where is everybody?" he asked himself as he made his way to the edge of the bullpen.

He glanced out along the gentle slope of the hill the camp was built on and noted the steaming piles scattered across the area. It took his brain a moment to realize those were human body parts scattered across the ground, their heat escaping as steam in the cold night air.

"Director?"

Davidson turned and blinked at Ford as he worked his way slowly toward him. "Why are you wet?"

Bodie came up from behind. "Brainiac here thought it was safer to soak us in a cold shower."

"It worked, didn't it?" Ford shot him a crooked grin.

Bodie pulled his boonie hat off and squeezed the water from it. "It did something."

"Cold shower?" Davidson studied the two men as his mind tried to connect the dots.

"Remember in *Predator* when Arnold coated himself in mud?" Ford shrugged. "It was the closest cold thing I could think of."

Davidson patted his shoulder. "Good thinking." He looked past the man at the wounded slowly making their way towards camp. "How many were hit?"

Ford lowered his eyes. "Too many. I heard a lot of explosions out there."

Bodie glanced across the bullpen then clapped Ford's shoulder. "I got wounded. I'll catch up later."

Ford nodded as he darted off then turned back to Davidson. "What happened?"

The director slowly shook his head. "I'm not sure. We lost the long range radios and the drones just did their own thing. Davis said they fell back on original programming or some such. Just started targeting the closest heat signatures."

"And the bigfoots weren't the closest?" Ford's exasperation wasn't missed.

Davidson shrugged. "I watched the monitors, Dave. Their heat signatures were fading in and out like Christmas lights. They probably couldn't get a lock on them." He glanced over Ford's shoulder to the tree line. "You don't think...surely they can't have a way to mask themselves from our sensors."

"They're hillbilly apes. I'm sure their spears are considered their greatest achievement."

Davidson nodded slowly. "Yeah. I'm sure you're right."

Both men froze when horrific screams echoed through the camp followed by gunfire. They spun towards the noise and saw men running into camp at full speed. "What's going on?" Davidson yelled over the din.

"They're attacking!" a soldier yelled as he ran towards the gunfire.

Ford's face fell and he gripped his weapon. "They're taking advantage of a bad situation."

Davidson pulled his sidearm and fell into step with him. "Just as we would, if the situation were reversed."

The two men rounded the edge of the logistics building and saw a wave of hairy giants closing the gap between the trees and the camp. "Holy shit!" Ford shouldered his rifle and began emptying rounds into the swarm of giants.

Davidson took aim and fired into the crowd as spears began flying through the air. He gripped Ford's vest and pulled him back around the corner of the building just as the first spears struck, wedging deeply into the wall of the logistics center. "We gotta fall back and regroup!"

"So fall back!" Ford shrugged out of his grip and spun his barrel back around the corner, firing into the monsters.

"Both of us!" Davidson pulled at him again and Ford began walking backward, firing into the rapidly closing wave of beasts, changing mags as they emptied.

An explosion erupted in the middle of the monsters and Ford barely caught a glimpse of Bodie lobbing grenades into the oncoming wave of hair and muscle. "Bodie!" he screamed over the roar of charging beasts, but his voice was drowned out.

"We need to regroup!"

Ford spun and glared at Davidson. "Regroup what?" He extended his arms and scoffed. "There's not enough of us left to regroup!"

Davidson's jaw clenched and he glared at the man. "This isn't Custer's last stand. I said REGROUP!"

Ford growled low in his throat then spun and emptied his mag into the wave of monsters tearing men limb from limb as they made their way towards the camp. "Move!" Ford yelled, clapping him on the shoulder. "I got your six!"

Davidson moved to the side of the alleyway as those who were initially wounded in the drone attack rearmed and turned to go back out and face this new threat. "I can't tell what the hell is going on," he growled. "I need intel."

Ford slapped at his vest and cursed as he came up empty. "I need ammo."

"Go. Grab me a carbine," he turned towards MCC, "I'll be right back."

Davidson slammed the door open and stepped inside. The entire MCC was a madhouse as techs called out surges in the line of attack and which of the sentinels were still active and attempting to push back.

West stood over the entire crew barking orders. "Where the hell is my backup? Who's defending our western flank?" He turned to Larry Davis and pointed a finger. "Get those goddam drones back into action!"

"I-I can't. They're dead until we can reset them." Davis inched away from him, afraid he'd pull his pistol again.

"I need a sitrep!" Davidson yelled over the cacophony of noise. "Where are our primary forces?"

"They were blown to hell by those goddam drones!" West yelled back.

"They've breached the perimeter, sir!"

"Order our forces to push them back!" West gripped the man's shoulder so tightly that the tech cringed. "Now!"

Davidson took a deep breath and stepped forward. "Where are they?" He pointed to the monitors. "The bulk of our people?"

The tech gave him a grave look and shook his head. "Scattered, Director. It's a literal free for all out there."

A loud and heavy thud struck the side of the MCC and West's eyes bugged. "The fuck do they think they're doing?" He pulled his pistol and kicked open the door, firing as soon as his feet hit the ground.

Davidson watched the man start to go off the rails then nearly jumped when a huge, hairy arm dropped from the sky and literally plucked him from the ground by his head. "Oh my god…they're on the roof!"

A guard at the far end of the RV tossed a carbine to Davidson and he pointed it straight up. He flipped the lever to full auto and emptied the magazine into the ceiling of the MCC, spraying the technicians with spent brass. "I'm out!"

He extended his arm and the guard tossed him another magazine as he fired his pistol into the ceiling. Davidson charged the carbine again then jumped out of the open door, rolling as he hit the ground. He intended to put himself out of reach of the monster on the roof and give himself a sight line to the attackers.

As he came up beside the logistics building, he caught sight of the creature swaying, one hand pressed to its mud-covered chest and the other cupping the family jewels. He brought the rifle up again and took aim on the creature's head. One round fired and the monster folded, sliding off the roof of the RV and landing in a crumpled mess beside the driver's window.

Davidson approached slowly and noted that the monster's crotch was a bloody mess. He could only assume the rounds fired through the ceiling had entered one of the few vulnerable areas and liquefied organs as it traveled upward.

"I'll take it."

He nearly jumped when Ford appeared beside him. "I brought a spare." He slung the extra carbine over his shoulder and the two men began marching through the camp, weapons shouldered.

"Aim for their heads," Davidson yelled over the noise of war.

Ford chuckled to himself. "You killed that one shooting him in the balls."

"Yeah—from below." Davidson checked left and fired at one of the creatures attempting to climb the rear of the MCC. "No mud covering his dick."

"Make sense. It would be hard to piss through a cement cup." Ford ticked slight right and fired three rounds at a charging 'squatch. "Fucking Mozambique drills. It's hard to break myself."

"As long as it works." Davidson gripped his arm and pointed with the barrel of his carbine. "Look."

Ford glanced to the left and relaxed his grip as he watched the hairy beasts suddenly break and run for the trees again. "What gives? They had us dead to rights."

Davidson lowered his weapon and felt his hand shake as the adrenaline began to burn off. "I don't know, and I honestly don't care." His knees started to weaken and he slowly lowered himself to a kneeling position, his eyes glued to the retreating forms disappearing back into the shadows.

Ford pressed a hand to his temple again and felt his mouth watering. "They must be calling a retreat, but…" he spat to the side and squinted toward the trees. "But why?"

Davidson squeezed his eyes shut and cupped his middle. "I think I'm going to puke."

"Yeah, they do that to ya." Ford turned and fought the urge to puke again. "I wish Bodie was here to lob another grenade and make them stop." He moaned as he lowered himself to one knee. "Yeah, I'm fixing to hurl."

"Do what you gotta do." Davidson spat to the side and continued to stare at the tree line, watching as the last of the creatures disappeared into the forest. "—I think I'll join you."

As suddenly as the infrasound began, it ended and Ford collapsed to the ground, clutching his bandaged wound. "I hate those fucking things."

"I'm no fan, myself." Davidson took a deep breath, feeling the cold night air hit his lungs. "They got West."

Ford bent his legs and splayed his arms on the cold, hard ground. "Okay…so now what?"

Davidson slowly shook his head. "I guess they have another in their chain of command who will step up." He glanced around the ruined remains of the camp and sighed. "If there's anybody left."

Ford groaned and rolled to his side, struggling to stand. "Fuck…. Bodie."

"Your friend?"

Ford came up onto all fours and nodded. "I gotta see if he survived."

Davidson stood on shaky legs and extended a hand, helping Ford to his feet. "I'll help you search."

The two men stood in the middle of the bullpen and stared into the darkness. "You hear that?" Ford asked.

Davidson strained to listen then slowly shook his head. "I don't hear anything."

Ford ground his teeth. "Exactly." He glanced at his boss and raised a brow. "I would expect to hear men yelling or…hell, just moaning if they survived."

Davidson felt the weight of defeat as it settled over his shoulders. "Damn it."

28

FOB Dog Town

Ford sat across from Bodie as the medic rewrapped his wound. "Cracked ribs, eh?" He winced as the medic began wrapping an ace bandage across his middle.

Bodie nodded slightly as his own middle was wrapped. "All things considered, I got off light. It was my last grenade." He struggled to suck in air. "I threw it and the damned thing swatted it from the air like it was a mosquito." He winced as the medic tugged the wrap tighter and used the aluminum toothed clamps to lock it in place. "I just knew I was dead. The damn thing hit the dirt not fifteen feet from me."

Davidson hiked a brow. "How did you…?"

Bodie chuckled then instantly regretted it. "The 'squatch never slowed. Marched right over it and was reaching for me when it blew." He sucked in air and glanced at the two men. "Grenade killed it. It was between me and the blast, protected me from the shrapnel, but it fell right on top of me."

"Hence the cracked ribs," Davidson stated the obvious.

"Now when somebody mentions an eight hundred pound gorilla, I'll have a good reference."

The men all turned as the sounds of rotors slicing the air approached. "Talk about a day late and a dollar short," Ford grumbled as he pulled his BDU blouse back on and buttoned it.

Director Davidson turned for the door and both men fell into step behind him. They emerged into the first licks of sunlight creeping over the eastern horizon and the roar of two Bell AH-1 Cobras gently setting down outside of camp.

They waited as the engines powered down and the side doors opened with gunners stepping out before approaching. "We sure could have used your help about an hour ago." Davidson held his hand out in greeting as the men ignored him, their eyes scanning the destruction of the base camp.

"Where's Commander West?" Davidson turned to see the pilot exiting the craft, clearly perturbed.

He lowered his eyes momentarily and shook his head. "I'm afraid he didn't survive this last altercation."

The pilot glanced at the two gunners, who gave a barely perceptible nod before turning back for the helicopter. Bodie caught the interchange and stepped forward, gripping the pilot's arm. "What the hell?"

The pilot glared at him then at the hand holding his arm. "We were called by West. If his mission has failed this soon then the op is over." He tugged his arm free and slowly removed his sunglasses. "Your orders are to procure the salvageable equipment and personnel and return to HQ." The pilot's face was stoic. "That's from the CEO himself."

Bodie couldn't hide his surprise. "Garrett said that? Because West screwed the pooch, we're supposed to pull up stakes? Do you have any idea how many people we've lost out here?"

The pilot gave him a blank look. "Orders are orders, Captain. Rally your people, collect your equipment and return to HQ." He turned and tugged open the door of the helicopter as his men entered the rear and pulled the door closed behind them.

"What's going on?" Ford asked quietly.

Bodie shrugged. "I don't know but I intend to find out." He jerked open the door of the chopper and quietly spoke to the pilot. A moment later he stepped away with a satellite phone in his hand. He paced a slow circle as he spoke into the phone then his head dropped, gently nodding, before handing the pilot back the device.

"Bad news, I take it," Davidson muttered as Bodie stepped closer.

Bodie shot Ford a solemn look. "The pilot wasn't kidding. The resources lost on this op have been…" he trailed off. He cleared his throat as he glanced back at the helicopter beginning its engine start up. "It all came down to numbers."

Ford's mouth fell open. "So Haze Gray is just pulling up stakes?"

Bodie sighed heavily and shrugged. "Garret is all about the numbers. They have some kind of contract with the Bureau that covers certain aspects of the operation just for showing up. As things stand now, the amount of loss surpassed the possible returns, so they're pulling out."

"Son of a bitch." Davidson's anger grew as realization took root. "I'm going to have to speak to whoever handles these contractors and discuss the terms of these agreements."

Ford felt his chest tighten. "So I guess you're leaving."

The three men stepped away as the rotors began to turn, stirring up the dust in the air and deafening them with their noise. Bodie basically pushed them toward the logistics building and turned his back to the helicopters as they continued revving, preparing to leave the site.

Bodie glanced around the destroyed camp and slowly shook his head. "Technically my orders are to gather my people and the equipment that wasn't destroyed and then leave." He shot a glance over his shoulder as the choppers rose from the ground and began to back away before banking. "I suppose I could drag my feet a bit on those orders. Give you and your people a chance to make your way out of the woods so you can either resupply and return or…" he shrugged.

Ford shot Davidson a knowing look. "We know what we're up against now. We could bring more armaments and men and—"

Davidson held a hand up, cutting him off. "Every time we've thought of something new, these creatures have found a work around."

"The gas worked," Ford offered.

"Did it, though?" Bodie shot him a questioning look. "I mean, yeah, it was effective, but only against the women and children…I mean, females and…" he trailed off again.

"I know what you mean, I'm just saying that it worked."

"Technology isn't the answer here." Davidson wiped a heavy hand over his face. "The drones showed us that. The gas bombs struck the wrong demographic and our attempts at boobytrapping the woods didn't work." He scoffed and shot them both a tight-lipped smile. "We had a helicopter gunship and they brought it down with a fucking spear."

Bodie nodded and hung his head. "The other gunships might have worked if they had an element of surprise, but now?"

Ford glanced around the remains of the camp and the number of wounded personnel hobbling to and fro. "The real question is, would the 'squatches even let us leave?" He turned back to Davidson and shrugged. "They attacked the heavy trucks departing with our dead on it. Totally disabled one of them and killed the drivers. What makes us think they'll let us go?"

Davidson sighed and tried to take in the damage of the camp. "You may be right."

"So we leave as a convoy," Bodie offered. "The Bureau gathers their personnel and equipment while we do the same and we get every vehicle that might possibly run and provide armed escort for each other."

"Maybe they'll let us leave if they know we're all going?" Ford asked.

Davidson sighed heavily and closed his eyes. "Either way, this op is over. Providing cover for each other would be the smart thing to do." He squared his shoulders and turned for the med tent. "I need an accurate headcount and an idea of the number of wounded. You two drag your feet packing up the gear.

We might not be able to go as soon as our bosses would like."

"Copy that." Ford turned to Bodie and raised a brow. "Any ideas?"

Bodie slowly shook his head. "I know we barely have enough people left to call it a skeleton crew. I think I'll hit the MCC and try to get a current status of our situation." He started for the RV with Ford in tow.

"I believe our current status is 'screwed,' but that might not be the technical term for it."

"I'd guesstimate that's an accurate description." He pulled open the RV door and found the techs inside already in action, shutting down equipment and preparing to mobilize the MCC. "Who gave the order?" Bodie asked, already knowing the answer.

The lead tech turned and gave an animated sigh. "Word came down from HQ. Garret pulled the plug." He scoffed as he turned and began removing cords and dropping them into the Pelican cases.

One of the techs leaned away from his monitor and nodded to Agent Ford. "We were preparing the last data blast to the city. You have any last minute reports to add?"

Ford stared at the man for a moment then slowly nodded. "Yeah, actually I think there's some things I could add to it."

The tech pushed away from his station and stood, allowing Ford access to the computers. Ford stepped into the MCC then turned to Bodie. "If you would, start spreading the word amongst the men and let any Bureau personnel know to start packing up."

"You got it." Bodie turned and left leaving Ford to his work.

Agent Ford sat gingerly behind the keyboard and stared at the readout. The tech leaned over his shoulder and pointed to an icon on the screen. "Just click that when you're done and it will transmit the data burst."

"Got it." He offered the man a crooked smile. "Thanks." He turned his attention to the data files and scanned through them. Information on the entire operation was contained in the data burst, including the initial Gamboa incident. Ford looked at the receiving address and smiled to himself. *It's just an email address.*

He reached for his wallet and withdrew a single business card. A quick glance around the MCC showed that the techs were too busy with their own work to pay him any attention. He added a blind CC to the receiving email list then closed the screen quickly as he hit the "send" button.

Coming to his feet, Ford tugged his BDU blouse down then exited the MCC, leaving the techs to their duties.

New York City

Patricia Murphy sat down at the desk of her cramped cubicle in the Daily Informer offices. She reflexively wiggled the mouse on her computer, waking the device, as she dropped her purse to the floor and her leather satchel to the only cleared surface of her desk.

The chime alerted her to the missed emails and she sipped at her vanilla latte as the screen came to life. She scanned the incoming messages and paused when her eyes caught the sender of her most current message. “What the hell?”

She leaned forward and reread the subject line. “Johnny, did you send this by mistake?” she mumbled as she clicked the email.

The attachments were huge and encrypted, but the file names had her more than intrigued.

She reached for her cell and tried to call her brother. She waited while it rang then ground her teeth when it went to voicemail. “Johnny, call me when you get this. I think you sent me something I wasn’t supposed to see.” She paused for a moment as a smile crossed her lips. “Unless it’s something juicy that I can report on, in which case, I’ll need the file encryption you used. See ya, Squirt.”

“What’s that?” She turned and saw Hector Ramirez holding a half-eaten doughnut and smiling at her. “You get something from your brother?”

“Just because you cover the cop beat doesn’t mean you have to eat like one.” She raised a brow at him, staring at the doughnut in his hand, then his expanding waistline. “You know there’s a reason cops rarely live past forty.”

“Yeah,” he replied, taking a bite of the doughnut. “They get shot at by bad people.” He leaned on the edge of her cubicle while he chewed. “Your brother is kind of a cop. If he sent you something, you should really share it with me.” He wagged his brows at her teasingly.

“Right.” She shoved her cell phone back into her purse and exited from her email. “Whatever he sent is encrypted, so I can’t read it. Yet.”

Hector stood upright and looked down at her. "How big was the file?"

"Huge." She crossed her arms and stared at him stoically.

Hector swallowed the bite, his face unreadable. "How huge?"

"Like, 'I shouldn't have even received it' huge. I'm shocked it made it past our server."

Hector's features went stern. "If it's encrypted, I might know somebody who could help." He set his doughnut on the edge of her cubicle and reached for his cellphone.

"Remove your fat pill, please. I don't want sticky stuff all over my office walls, thank you."

"Hold on." He flipped through the names in his cell phone then smiled. "I got him right here."

"So?" She shrugged, her eyes darting back to the doughnut.

"So…share your intel with me and I'll get it unencrypted. And remove the doughnut. We both win."

"Not hardly." She waved him away with her hand. "I like a big scoop as much as the next reporter, but if Johnny sent that to me by accident, I'm not going to cost him his job. He worked too hard to get where he is for me to screw it up for him."

Hector shrugged. "Hey, maybe he wanted you to get that information." He picked up his doughnut and popped the last of it into his mouth and leaned on the cubicle again. "I mean, why else would he 'accidentally' send it to his sister, who just happens to be a reporter in one of the most widely read newspapers in the city?" He chewed slowly, his eyes studying her reaction. "He's a

Fed, right? They don't usually make mistakes like that on accident, do they?"

Patricia considered his point for a moment then reached for her cell phone again. "I'm going to try him one more time."

"Then you'll send me the files so we can work together and report on this…great big whatever it is?"

She listened to the call go to voicemail again then hung up. She nervously tapped a nail against her front teeth while she thought.

"Come on, Pat. There's gotta be a reason he sent that to you." He took a long drink of his coffee and wiped his hands on his pants leg, removing the remnants of the doughnut. "Work with me here. I got the contacts and the resources…" He wagged his brows at her once more. "You know you want to know what that stuff says."

Patricia ground her teeth then rolled her eyes. "How long would it take your guy to get us the data?"

"Probably before lunch." He smiled broadly at her.

"Fine," she groaned. "But I reserve the right to look at the data first. If I think he sent it to me on purpose and we can use it, *then* I'll share with you."

"Deal."

29

FOB Dog Town

Agent Ford inspected each rifle before handing it to another bureau man who would then stuff it into the foam cutouts in an oversized Pelican crate. Damaged weapons were boxed in a separate crate to be disassembled for usable parts back at HQ.

"Them mountain monkeys sure did a number on these, didn't they?"

Ford barely glanced at the man. "Too bad our people took a worse beating." He handed him another serviceable weapon. "I'd gladly trade every piece of gear we have for our people back."

The other agent stammered a moment. "I-I didn't mean it like that. I was just—"

"I know what you meant." He winced slightly as he stretched for a rifle on the other side of the table. "Any idea if we got all the weapons back?"

The other agent nodded solemnly. "All but two. One

of our sniper's weapons and the one that was assigned to Palmer." He pulled the crate lid over and latched it before setting it aside and opening another empty one. "We assume that it was lost when the chopper went down." He gave Ford a curious look. "I don't suppose you saw anything out there?"

He shook his head absently. "To be honest, his weapon was the last thing on my mind." He paused and stared off, his brow furrowing. "But now that you mention it, I don't think it was in the chopper."

The other agent shrugged. "I doubt we'd get many volunteers to trek out there and take another look."

Ford took a deep breath and let it out slowly. "Eighty percent loss rate. That's totally unacceptable."

The other agent nodded. "And we're pulling out, letting the monkeys win."

Ford scoffed. "We didn't *let* them do anything. They beat us, that's all. They were a lot smarter than we gave them credit for."

"Still, it just doesn't feel right. Pulling out the way we are? We're surrendering to them." He chuckled to himself. "I mean, we conquered fire thousands of years ago and have all sorts of technology. How the hell did they level the battle field?"

"It's their backyard." He tossed another non serviceable weapon aside. "Look at Afghanistan. They held off the Russians for decades while living in caves. Then we went in there hunting terrorists and they were able to stay hidden until we finally pulled out." He glanced at the other agent. "It's called 'home field advantage.' And anybody who tells you there isn't such a thing has never been in a fire fight."

The armory door opened and Gil Bodie stuck his head in. "You about done?"

Ford did a quick mental count of the remaining weapons and nodded. "Just about. What's up?"

"One of my guys wants to strip some parts from one of your heavies, but I can't find Davidson anywhere. Can you authorize it?"

Ford handed the weapon in his hand to the other agent and stepped outside with Bodie. "Which truck do they want to cannibalize?"

"The blue one with all the flat tires." Bodie pointed to a modified two ton truck with a canvas cover over the back. "He said there were some parts that he could make work. It will help us get both of our big trucks out."

Ford rubbed at his jaw and glanced at the men meandering about the camp. "Will there still be room for all of our people?"

Bodie gave him a flat look. "With plenty of room to spare."

Ford nodded slightly. "Do what you have to. We need to salvage as many vehicles as we can."

"Speaking of…" Bodie raised a brow at him. "What about your other heavy truck that the 'squatches stopped? The one that was carrying your dead out."

"What of it?"

"Is it salvageable?"

Ford shrugged. "I was told it wouldn't turn over." He leaned closer and lowered his voice. "I was also told that inside the cab was covered in blood, so…"

"Possible biohazard. Got it." Bodie seemed deep in thought for a moment. "I wonder if it's worth the risk to check it for usable parts?"

"If I recall, the tires were up. Maybe we strip it down and get this one running."

Bodie gave him a knowing look. "How long would we be exposed out there?"

Ford sighed. "Good point. But we're going to have to move it to get the RV out. It's blocking the trail."

Bodie nodded to himself. "Tell ya what. I'll grab a couple of batteries and some of my guys. We can use the last Tahoe to shoot out there and try to start it. If it starts, we bring it back and strip it. We'll help you swap the tires out so you can get your heavy running."

Ford reached for his radio. "Gather your guys and I'll contact Davidson and let him know the plan."

As the dust-covered black Tahoe bounced over the rough terrain, the men inside constantly scanned their surroundings, waiting for an ambush. The driver came to a stop just yards from the target vehicle and shut off the engine.

All four men strained to listen to the surrounding woods and after a long moment, Gil Bodie opened his door and stepped out. "I think we're good."

"For the moment." Ford gently shut his door, being careful not to slam it. "I'll grab the plastic if your guys will install the batteries."

Bodie nodded to the two men and took up a defensive position next to the front bumper as his guys carefully opened the hood on the old converted GMC box truck.

Ford opened the driver's door and made a sour face at all the splattered brown patches of dried blood. He quickly opened the clear plastic and spread it out over the bench, tucking it behind the seatback and letting it fall to the floor. A quick glance at the steering wheel and dash made him reach for his gloves. "This is beyond nasty in here."

Bodie shot him a sideways grin. "Be happy the window was left down. It's had plenty of time to air out."

"No meat scraps that I can see." He raised a brow at Bodie. "Does dried blood rot and stink?"

"If there's enough of it." Bodie stepped around the corner of the truck and continued to scan the tree line. "Step it up fellas. I feel like I'm out here with my pecker swinging free."

His men finished tightening the battery cables and reached for the hood to close it, slowly pulling it down until they could see Ford behind the steering wheel. "Give it a go."

Ford twisted the gore covered key and held his breath as the diesel engine turned over then roared to a start. "Let's go!"

The man slammed the hood and ran back to the Tahoe, pulling the door open and falling into the seat. Ford watched as Bodie made a tactical retreat, scanning the trees with his rifle before getting in on the passenger side, his rifle pointed out the window.

Ford put the truck into gear and eased on the accelerator, pulling the truck closer as the Tahoe made a quick turn around and started back to camp. He'd finally allowed himself the opportunity to breathe when the first rock impacted the side of the truck.

"Dammit," he cursed. He pulled his radio and keyed the mic, "They're on us!"

He watched as rocks bounced off the top of the Tahoe and a large diameter spear sliced through the rear window of the SUV, jamming itself in the middle of the truck.

"They're turning us into shish kabob here!" Bodie yelled over the air. "We gotta move!"

Ford watched the Tahoe accelerate and put more space between them. He pushed the truck harder but had to slow again when the trail began to bounce him closer into the trees, threatening to end his drive quickly.

"I gotta slow down," he called out over the radio. "This trail is going to beat the truck to death."

"Keep it going or the apes will beat you to death!" Bodie called back.

Ford watched Bodie pull himself up and sit in the open window of the Tahoe, firing into the woods alongside the box truck. His attention was pulled upward and he began to fire into the tree tops, spraying the canopy as the two trucks did their best to vacate the area.

Once the vehicles entered a small clearing; Bodie scanned the trees ahead. "I'm not seeing anything, but stay on your toes."

Ford slowed the truck as a sharp turn came up on them and could feel the top of the box lean precariously over. "Come on you top-heavy bitch…" he growled as he fought the steering wheel.

Just as the truck righted itself, he stood on the brakes, sliding up to the rear of the black Tahoe. "What gives?" he barked into the radio.

"Roadblock," Bodie quietly responded.

Ford sat up in the seat and couldn't see ahead of the

Tahoe. He watched as the passenger door opened and Bodie stepped out, rifle instantly at the ready and aiming downfield.

"What's going on?" Ford muttered to himself as he opened his own door. He stood up in the cab and peered over the top of the black SUV. A very large Genoskwa stood in the middle of the trail, a menacing spear in his hand. "Oh, shit."

Bodie stepped away from the SUV and kept the creature in his sights. "I don't want to have to shoot you," he lied as he bumped the door shut with his hip. "We just want to get out of here, bud. We need these trucks to load our people and leave." He slowly lowered the barrel of his weapon and held his hands out, showing them empty.

"What are you doing?" Ford quietly asked over the radio.

Bodie held a finger up, silently telling him to hold on. He took a tentative step forward, his eyes locked with the hairy giant blocking their path. "I don't know about you, but I'm tired of all the killing. We just want to pack up and leave your woods." He nodded slowly, smiling as he spoke. "We want to leave you and yours alone to live your lives however you see fit."

He stopped just ahead of the Tahoe and continued to stare at the creature. "What do you say? Wanna let us slip by you so we can grab our stuff and get it out of your territory?"

The creature's heavy breathing could be heard inside the SUV, and the driver leaned his head out of the window. "Cap, I think you should get back inside."

Bodie slowly shook his head. "He could shish kabob

us both before we could get around him and he knows it. Inside ain't no safer than right here."

The massive reddish brown male eyed the driver then Bodie again. It exhaled forcefully then pounded its chest with its free hand, its eyes narrowing at the man daring to stand before him.

"Yeah, I've seen gorillas do that but I never realized just how intimidating it really is until now." He slowly backed towards the Tahoe again and reached gently for the door handle. "We're just going to leave now, if it's all the same to you." He offered a weak smile before he broke eye contact to look for the door handle.

The moment Bodie broke eye contact, the creature hefted the spear and launched it. The driver tried to yell a warning but it came too late as Bodie found himself knocked to the ground, the giant spear pinning him beside the truck.

"Dammit!" Ford screamed as he floored the accelerator, hoping he could get past the Tahoe and run over the giant hominid.

The driver mashed the gas pedal to the floor and made a quick swerve around the alpha male in the road, spraying double rooster tails of loose dirt and rock behind the SUV as he raced back to the camp.

"You mother fucking son of a bitch!" Ford screamed as he aimed the truck for the creature still standing in a cloud of dust. He was actually shocked when there was no sound of impact and even more shocked when he drove through the dust cloud and was still on the road.

He craned his neck to look in the rear view mirror but the monster was lost in the haze. He felt his grip tighten on the steering wheel and ground his teeth. "This ain't over. It will *never* be over."

FORD HUNG his head and continually clenched his hands into fists. Director Davidson stood over him, his arms crossed, trying to take in the facts as Ford had given them. "Why in God's name would he step out of the vehicle?"

Ford slowly shook his head. "Desperation. Nothing's worked yet, but it was obviously the wrong move." He looked up at him through reddened eyes and gave him a tight-lipped smile. "I want their heads, sir."

"I know you do." Davidson sighed and ran a hand over his face. "We both do. Unfortunately, we simply don't have the resources."

Ford shook his head adamantly. "I'll stay behind. Mark me as MIA."

"And do what, exactly?" The disapproval in Davidson's voice wasn't missed.

"All I need is a few MRE's, my rifle and some ammunition." He looked up at him, his face stoic. "I don't need to kill them all, just that big one."

"I can't authorize that. Besides, you're still wounded." He raised a brow at him. "These things can probably smell the blood in your dressing."

"I don't care." Ford came to his feet, not feeling the pain of his wound. "These things took my team. They took Murphy. They took Gil." He clenched his teeth so hard he feared his molars would crack. "They've killed eighty percent of our people, sir."

Davidson's voice had an edge that Ford had never heard before. "Believe me, I am acutely aware of exactly what this little expedition has cost us."

Ford felt his jaw quiver as he searched for the words. "Just let me stay behind."

"I can't do that." Davidson took a deep cleansing breath and let it out slowly. "But once you're healed up, if you still want to return…and if I still have a job, then maybe the two of us will plan a 'camping trip.' Maybe even one here in the Catskills."

"Sir, I'm afraid that if I don't strike now, I might actually cool down and second guess that decision."

Davidson clapped his shoulder. "Then maybe that's exactly what we should do." He probed the other man's eyes. "Maybe we need to step back and take a deep breath and actually think about what we want to do. What we *can* do."

Ford gently shook his head. "I can't, sir."

"You have to." Davidson squared his shoulders. "That's an order."

"But—"

"But nothing." He glanced down at Ford's middle. "You still got a lot of healing to do."

Ford hung his head and sighed. "Sir, I need this."

"You and every other man left standing out there. We've all lost friends." He turned for the exit of the tent then paused. "Who knows? Maybe we'll all decide to go camping out here."

Ford lifted his face in time to see him walk away and fought the urge to scream.

30

New York City

Patricia Murphy paced slowly as Hector spoke with his "encryption guy." She would pause long enough to offer a heavy sigh then resume her pacing. Eventually both men turned and gave her a frustrated look. "I told you this might take a bit," he said "The Feds use a lot of different encryption algorithms and we need to find the right one."

She replied with yet another heavy sigh then resumed her pacing.

After what seemed entirely too long, the printer fired up and began spewing out sheet after sheet from the numerous files. She stepped over by the machine and tried to glance at the documents as they stacked loosely atop one another. "Wait a second—"

She plucked one of the sheets from the list and held it up close, her finger running down a long list of personnel. "Oh, no."

"What's wrong?" Hector asked.

She felt her hand begin to shake and her jaw quivered as she handed him the paper. He scanned it quickly then saw what had her so upset. He lowered the sheet and sighed, his hand reaching for her shoulder. "Pat, I'm so sorry."

"Wait a minute." She turned and faced him, her eyes hopeful. "How could Johnny have sent that to me if he was killed in action?"

Hector slowly shook his head. "I don't...if he was..." He shrugged. "Would somebody else have sent this to you? I mean, who would risk their career over this?"

She continued to stare at him, her mind racing. She had a quick realization moment and could feel the tears start to well in her eyes again. "His boss." She collapsed into the chair near the printer and fought back sobs. "His team leader would have, if he thought the agency was in the wrong."

Hector scoffed. "Ain't a bureau man out there ever thinks the agency is in the wrong."

She looked at him with a tight-lipped smile. "David would." She sniffed back the tears and forced herself to stand, her eyes turning to the large stack of papers accumulating in the printer. "Do you have enough paper?"

"I got cases of it." Hector's friend crossed his arms and raised a brow at her. "Of course, nothing is free these days."

Patricia glanced at Hector, who reached instinctively for his wallet. He glanced at his friend and narrowed his gaze. "I'll need a receipt for this so I can turn it in on my expense report."

"Yeah, yeah." The man rolled his eyes. "Force me to report it to the IRS, why don't ya."

FOB Dog Town

Ford watched the men load their gear into the trucks silently. A dark cloud of loss had fallen on everyone in the camp, and none were too excited to write off the deaths of their friends without giving the wood apes one more round.

Director Davidson marched through the camp with one of the logistics technicians. The two did their best to account for what was being loaded against the manifest of what had been brought out with them. Neither man truly seemed to be paying attention to the details as they went about their duties.

"What happens now?"

Ford turned to see the contractor, Larry Davis standing at his side. He shrugged as he spoke, "No idea. I guess we go back to whatever our lives were before this fuckin' fiasco."

Larry watched as the men went about their work and sighed. "For what it's worth, your friend Bodie seemed like a real stand up fella."

"He was." Ford squinted in the bright of the day as the sun made its lazy arc over the sky. "Then again, so was Murphy. And Walker. And Corbit. And Wilkins and Langford. And McCoy and Palmer and…" he trailed off as his throat squeezed tight. "Okay, maybe not Walker so much. He was a bit of a prick, but the other guys were all solid."

"I'm so sorry, agent Ford."

He took a deep breath and let it out slowly. "We knew what we were signing on for when we joined the Bureau." He turned and glanced out to the trees. "Even then, there's no way I ever would have guessed we'd face something like…these things."

Larry nodded to himself. "Amazing though, isn't it? What were essentially a bunch of cavemen beating us at our own game?" He sucked at his teeth. "Incredible really, when you think about it."

"Yeah, I'm gonna try not to."

Davis cleared his throat nervously. "You know, I used to watch all the documentaries on sasquatch. I think I always believed they were real, but since the sightings were so seldom and over broad distances, I never thought they would be so high in numbers."

Ford turned and scoffed. "Your point?"

Davis shrugged. "I just found it fascinating that they could increase their numbers so quickly. I mean, that would imply that they are a lot more pervasive in nature than I originally suspected."

Ford started to walk away. "I really don't care."

"You should," Davis called out. He watched Ford pause and turn slightly. "I mean, I've known people like you my whole adult life. Most were special operators. Tier-one guys. But, like you, they were all made of the same stuff."

"Blood and bones?"

Davis chuckled. "Yes, but I meant grit." He stepped closer and lowered his voice. "The men I've known wouldn't let the monkeys win. They would find a way to return and finish the job." He searched Ford's eyes for the truth. "Much as, I assume, you plan to do the moment you can."

"I don't know what you're talking about."

"Yes, agent Ford, you do." Davis stepped closer and glanced around to ensure they were alone. "And while you convalesce and regain your strength, I plan to go through every line of code in the AI of my drones."

"Good for you." Ford turned to leave again when Davis grasped his arm.

"I would appreciate it if you would contact me before you embark on your next adventure in these woods." He raised a brow at him and handed him a card. "Hopefully by the time you're ready to finish what you started here, I'll have worked out all of the bugs in my little flying friends."

Ford narrowed his gaze at the man. "What are you saying?"

"What I'm saying, agent Ford, is that I would appreciate the opportunity to do some real world testing with my creations. And I can't think of a better place to do it than out here in the quiet solitude of the Catskills." The smile he offered didn't reach his eyes and Ford knew exactly what he was offering.

"Once you've worked out the bugs."

"I won't allow them back into the field until I can guarantee that what happened here can never happen again."

Ford accepted the card and slipped it into his blouse pocket. "I'll call you." He turned to leave then turned back. "Work fast, Davis."

Larry smiled broadly. "Oh, I intend to."

"I WANT every man capable of pulling a trigger armed and ready to protect this convoy." Director Davidson addressed the men before they loaded into the transports. He glanced at the logistics building and the remnants of the tents still standing and being left behind. "I realize we're bugging out with little more than the clothes on our backs, our computers and the weapons we hauled in, but circumstances have changed. If we want to leave these mountains under our own power, we need to hustle." He glanced at his watch and shook his head. "We have barely three hours until sundown. You know the condition of the road we used to come in here. It's not made for moving quickly, but that's exactly what we're going to have to do." He glanced at Ford and nodded.

David stepped forward and cleared his throat. "Earlier today, Captain Gil Bodie and I took two of his men and retrieved one of our heavies that the Genoskwa had intercepted. We brought it back so that we could transport our dead home and give them a proper burial." He paused for a moment and took a deep breath. "That action cost us the life of Captain Bodie. He had the strange notion that he could reason with the…that he could communicate—" he broke off and closed his eyes. "It doesn't matter. What does matter is this. We have to make a four hour drive through these woods in less than three. The trucks are loaded and those who are able have weapons to defend this convoy." He glanced at the Haze Gray personnel listening in. "We have a six vehicle convoy and the whole train can only move as fast as the slowest car. This won't be easy and it definitely will not be fun. Stay diligent and don't hesitate to shoot if the opportunity presents itself."

"Sir?" a voice in the rear asked. "Why don't we wait and leave at daybreak?"

Ford scoffed. "After what happened here over the last few days, do you really think the wood apes are going to sit back and let us do our thing tonight?" He bit back the epithets that threatened to flower his language. "We won't survive another night in these woods. I think every man here already knows that." He squared his shoulders and nodded to the men. "Load up and let's move out."

He stood back and watched as the men climbed into their vehicles and was actually happy to see the number of rifle barrels pointing out of the sides of the larger trucks. "I think we're ready, Director."

"Load up."

Ford gave him a curt nod and climbed into the passenger seat of the box truck they had retrieved for hauling out the dead. As he slammed the door the driver glanced at him and offered a weak smile. "Feels weird, doesn't it, sir?"

"What's that?"

"Driving a truck this big that's full of the dead."

Ford tried to ignore the visual that popped into his mind. "Lucky for us, they were stored in the chiller. They should stay frozen until we get a lot closer to civilization."

"I certainly hope so, sir." The man turned the key and started the truck, putting it into gear and falling in behind the those in front.

Ford triple checked his rifle and loaded the chamber before bringing the barrel up and extending it out the window. "Just try to keep the same distance with the truck in front of you and we'll be just fine."

"Yes, sir."

Ford tried not to second guess the things left behind and couldn't imagine that the monsters would find any use for any of it with the exception of some of the food still in the mess tent. He wondered if their acute sense of smell could discern that there was food inside the heavy plastic of the MRE pouches. He chuckled at himself and pushed the thoughts of the creatures from his mind.

"No sense in letting them live rent free in my head."

"Sir?"

He glanced at the driver and waved him off. "Just thinking aloud." He offered him a crooked smile. "When you get my age, you'll be lucky if all you do is talk to yourself."

"Understood, sir." The driver turned his attention back to the road and tried to anticipate the condition of the trail based on the swerve and bounce of the truck ahead.

The drive seemed almost uneventful, and for a brief moment, Ford hoped that the monsters realized they were leaving and would let them pass. That hope was shattered when the truck ahead came to a sliding stop and their own truck nearly rear-ended it.

Ford keyed his radio. "What the hell is going on up there?"

Director Davidson replied, "There's a huge sasquatch standing in the road."

Ford felt his blood turn cold as he keyed his mic. “Shoot that motherfucker in the head!” He glanced at his driver and watched as the young man’s face went pale. “Do it now! It’s a trap!”

31

New York City

Patricia Murphy sifted through the different papers, attempting to recreate the digital files into their appropriate folders. "Are you reading this?"

Hector sat in the floor of her apartment and leaned back on the couch, piles of papers stacked in front of him. "I would almost think that someone was pulling an elaborate hoax on you." He looked up at her and shrugged. "Bigfoot?"

She rubbed at her eyes and sighed, pushing away from the multiple stacks of papers. "I know. Weird." She stood and stretched her lower back. "I mean, it's one thing for the government to admit to itself that they knew they were real, but going to war with an *animal*?" She shook her head and reached for the wine bottle. "Want more?"

Hector waved her off. "I'm more of a beer and pretzel kind of guy."

"Of course you are." She emptied the bottle into her glass then walked the empty to the trash. She opened the fridge and pulled out a bottle of Miller Genuine Draft. "My brother used to come over to watch hockey games and he always brought MGD." She handed him the beer. "It's this or chardonnay."

Hector twisted the cap off and tilted it back. "Your brother may not have the best taste in beer, but at least he was man enough to drink it." He set the bottle aside then stiffened, forgetting that the loss of her kin was so fresh. He glanced at her and found her with her eyes closed and a smile forming. "Sorry. I didn't mean to…"

"It's okay." She opened her eyes and offered a wan smile. "I was just remembering some of the bets he'd offer during the games." She chuckled and set her glass down. "Like I follow hockey."

"Nothing wrong with futball though." Hector looked up and his face went stoic. "Sorry. You white people call it soccer."

"Piss off, Hector." She slid into the floor and picked up one of the stacks of papers. "These files are so complete. Logistics, supplies, communication logs, personnel, weapons, ammunition…. Everything we could have ever hoped for."

"Did they really need a helicopter to scare away a bigfoot though?" He shrugged as he set down the digital logbook for the craft. "Everything I've ever heard about bigfoot, he avoids people. I don't think I've ever heard of one being aggressive."

Patricia snapped her fingers then twisted, looking for something specific. "Aha. Here." She handed him a short stack of papers. "The Iroquois called them 'Genoskwa,' and they're supposed to be really super aggressive." Her features twisted. "Says here they would twist people's heads off."

"Joy." Hector scanned the documents. "Sounds like a real hit. I wonder if they do birthday parties."

She picked up her wine glass again and cradled it in her hands. "Agent Red Moon really believed that's what they were facing out there."

"Okay." Hector set the files down and rubbed at his eyes. "We have about three reams of paper here, and most of it's ready to be manila foldered." He glanced at her. "How are we supposed to tell this story?"

She laughed and set her wine down. "Oh, we don't." She motioned to the stacks of papers. "We can't. We can't verify any of this. Like you said before, it could be one hell of a hoax somebody is pulling on us."

Hector slumped against the couch. "So, what do we do with all of this? Stash it away until somebody from the *X-Files* wants a new story line?"

Patricia took a deep breath and let it out slowly. "We verify it."

Hector stared at her as if she had grown a second head. "Say what?"

"We verify it."

Hector loosed a belly roll laugh. "There's no way the FBI is going to verify any of this. They'd laugh us right out of their office."

Patricia nodded. "Agreed." She picked up her wine and took a long drink, her eyes locked to Hector's.

"Wait…what are you saying?"

She set the empty glass down and smiled at him. "When was the last time you went camping?"

"The hell you say!" Hector scrambled to his feet, nearly knocking over his beer. "If any of this is real, there's no way in hell either of us are going into those woods."

Patricia gripped the arm of the couch and pulled herself to a standing position. "We have one of the biggest stories of our lifetimes right here. Not only do they admit bigfoot is real, the government knew the danger and didn't bother to tell anyone." She cocked her head to the side. "Why not? What harm would come from people knowing that there is a…a…wood ape running around in the mountains?" She shook her head. "Absolutely no reason not to let that information out."

"Maybe they were afraid people wouldn't go the parks anymore?" Hector shrugged.

"Most of these things are like you said. Docile. They avoid humans at all costs." She shook her head. "Imagine how many hikers are lost every year. How many of them could have come home if they'd only been made aware of these things?"

Hector groaned and slowly sat on the couch. "So, the government lied to the people again. What day of the week is this?"

"Exactly." She planted her hands on her hips and raised a brow at him. "But not only did they lie about it, they sent highly trained federal agents out to kill these things. If they're so rare, shouldn't they be on the endangered species list? Instead, we're going out there to exterminate them?"

Hector shrugged again. "Maybe they taste like bald eagle and the Illuminati wanted a feast."

"Stop it." She waved him off. "Now you sound like Chuck in the Lifestyle section." She huffed as she rifled through the files. "How do they plan to explain the loss of life? Training exercises in the woods? In New York? The fucking Catskills? Please."

Hector ran a hand over his face. "So you want to verify it by going out to where all of these trained special agents of the Federal Bureau of Investigation and their SWAT teams were *killed*? By bigfoot?"

She nodded, her eyes locked to his. "WE are going to verify."

"Me?" He scoffed. "Oh, hell no. I'm keeping my fat ass right here in the city where it's safe. I'd rather risk being mugged or shot by a gang banger than go into the woods on purpose and confront one of these things."

"You're going." She bent and picked up her wine glass. "And you're going to watch my back while I dig around."

"Dig around for what? They're not going to just leave FBI guy's bodies lying around for you to find."

"Somebody always leaves something. Gun casings, food wrappers…something."

"So you find where some asshole went camping and didn't pack out his trash. That doesn't prove anything!"

"Hello? Did you not hear me say gun casings? I mean, bullets get shot, the brass gets flung all over the place. Surely they can't pick it all up."

"You're loco. Certifiable crazy." Hector stood and tilted back the last of his beer. "I'm leaving before you try to use your feminine wiles on me."

Patricia laughed then covered her mouth. "I don't have to resort to such lewd behavior, Hector. And you know why?"

His face fell and he dropped the beer bottle in the trash. "No…tell me."

"Because you want to break this story just as much

as I do, and we both know what we got to do to be able to do that."

Hector hung his head and sighed heavily. "Great. When do we leave?"

Deep in the Catskills

Ford felt his stomach drop when the woods erupted into a cacophony of noise. War whoops, barks, grunts, hoots and screams echoed through the dark and dense woods until his hair stood on end.

"Sir?" the driver asked nervously, his eyes darting from side to side. "What the hell? It's still daylight!"

Ford ground his teeth as he reached for the door handle.

"What the hell are you doing?" the driver screeched.

"I need to be able to cover a wider area." Ford turned and met his worried gaze. "Lock your door. Stay here. Do not try to leave the truck!"

"But…" he trailed off as Ford kicked open the door and dropped to the ground, the rifle at the ready.

"Incoming!" a voice shouted over the radio.

Ford pressed his back to the side of the box truck and ducked as rocks and tree limbs impacted the sides. He hunkered lower and could feel the bottom edge of the cargo box slide across his shoulders. Instinctively, he dropped down and slipped under the truck, seeking refuge from the incoming missiles while continually scanning the shadows for movement.

"Aw, fuck this," he growled as he rolled out from under the truck again and began firing into the woods. A moment later and the other armed men began firing into the trees as well.

Ford took a moment to slam a fresh magazine into the belly of his carbine and bent under the cargo box again. He craned his neck and peered high into the trees and finally caught movement. "Son of a bitch," he growled as he pressed his shoulders to the rear tires and aimed the barrel up into the canopy. "I got you now." He opened fire at the shadowy shapes above and actually whooped when one of the creatures screamed and fell from the trees, landing with a satisfying thud next to the truck.

The creature's face was turned to him as the spark left its eyes and for the briefest moment, David felt like he had killed another human.

A huge rock crashed into the tires behind him a moment later, breaking the spell, and he turned his attention back to his attackers. He continued to scan the shadows in the woods and cursed as the evening sky began to darken.

"No…it's too soon." He rolled out from under the truck and slid along the cargo box to the rear of the truck. There he caught a glimpse of others standing outside of their trucks, firing into the trees.

Ford gripped the nearest man by the shoulder. "How ya doing on ammo?"

"Four more mags!" He scanned the trees, firing blindly into the shadows.

"Make 'em last!" he shouted back over the din.

Ford began moving towards the front of the truck again, ducking the larger rocks and tree limbs being launched at the convoy. He was almost halfway along the cargo box when a large limb—or small tree—was slammed into the side of the truck, cutting off his path. Thinking quickly he dove under the truck and duck-walked toward the front, bypassing the largest obstacles between him and the cab.

As he rounded the top of the tree limb and was about to emerge from under the truck, it suddenly lurched and rolled forward. Dave instinctively lay down and rolled toward the edge. He watched in horror as the dual rear tires crushed the smaller limbs and continued toward him.

Mere feet from his legs, the front of the truck impacted the rear of the truck ahead and Dave felt his body go weak. "Too fuckin' close," he mumbled as he scrambled out from under the chassis.

Just as he came to his feet, he heard the distinct sound of something very heavy impacting the top of the cargo box. He spun and brought his rifle to bear on a large male standing just behind the cab of the truck, its arms extended and ready to catch another boulder tossed down to it from the treetops.

Dave brought his rifle up and fired three rounds into the beast. One ripped through its neck and the other exploded its nasal bone before exiting the rear of its skull. The creature began to crumple just as the thrown rock hit the edge of the cargo box and ricocheted onto the top of the cab.

The creature fell back and Dave glanced at the driver splayed across the steering wheel, his face a bloody pulp. He could only imagine that one of the beasts had connected with a rock through the driver's window. He spun back amidst the din of war cries, gunfire, and human screams to continue scanning the trees. "Come on you bastards! It ain't ending like this!"

Director Davidson eased down the driver's side of the truck and emerged on the opposite side of Ford's position. "We're pinned down!"

"Have the drivers push on! Drive over them!" Ford yelled.

Davidson shook his head animatedly. "They felled a tree across the path. We can't get over it. We'll have to back our way out!"

Ford glanced behind him and had to step to the side to peer past the line of vehicles. He could plainly see a thick tree trunk, its root ball visible along the edge of the path. "They've penned us in. The rear is blocked, too!"

Davidson waved Ford down the side of the truck and the two met at the rear of the cargo box. "I'm almost out of ammunition." Davidson ejected his last magazine then reached for his pistol. "I've got two mags left."

Ford patted his vest and cringed. "I've got one mag."

Davidson's face fell for a moment then he broke into a toothy grin. "It's been a pleasure, Agent Ford." He held his hand out and Ford gripped it tightly.

"It's not over yet, boss."

Davidson took a quick look around then nodded. "No, but it's damned close."

Ford pressed his back to the rear of the cargo truck and actually listened. The war cries had all but died down and the screams of men had now fallen silent. An occasional pop of gunfire would echo but the shots were erratic…sporadic. Dying.

Ford turned to Davidson and offered a wan smile. "You're right, boss. It has been a pleasure."

Davidson's features suddenly sobered. "If I had it all

to do over again, I would have forced your sorry ass to leave when you were first wounded. At least one of my men would have survived this."

Ford offered him a weak smile. "One did." He gave him a knowing look. "We just chose to ignore his advice and stay the hell out of the woods."

Davidson nodded, refusing to second guess his command decisions. "'Til Valhalla, my friend." He spun and began marching up along the side of the trucks, firing at the creatures that were just now starting to emerge from the trees.

Ford heard the unmistakable howl of pain from one of the creatures and smiled to himself. "Give 'em hell, boss."

He spun and came up behind Davidson, leveling his carbine on anything with hair that happened to move. He watched as a huge arm appeared between the front of the trucks and literally plucked Director Davidson from the ground and hurled him into a nearby tree. The sickening thud of his body impacting the immovable tree trunk told Ford everything he needed to know.

Ford stumbled to a stop and turned a slow circle, his eyes taking in the army of movement around him. The area had grown eerily silent and only the sound of dirt and gravel crunching under his boots sounded in his ears.

His eyes searched the sea of hairy creatures for one in particular. The large reddish-brown male that had killed Bodie. He looked past the enemy slowly advancing toward him and spun a slow circle.

He brought his rifle up to the ready position and peered through the red dot. "Come on you big bastard. I know you're still out there."

Ford continued to turn, taking in all the monsters slowly encompassing his position. Suddenly Bodie's assassin stepped out from the shadows, seeming to square his shoulders as he stared down at the puny human.

Ford smiled inwardly. “My final act.” He brought the red dot back up to his eye and planted it directly between the creature’s eyes. “Sayonara, asshole.”

EPILOGUE

PATRICIA MURPHY DOUBLE CHECKED HER NOTES BEFORE reaching for the car door handle. She opened it cautiously and stepped out, looking for oncoming traffic. Just as she shut her door, her cell phone rang.

Answering it, she wasn't surprised to hear Hector on the other end. "Well?"

"Not yet. I just got here."

"Are you sure you have the right address?" His voice sounded even more nervous than she felt.

"My sources are rarely ever wrong." She swallowed hard as she looked across the street at the unassuming house. "Wish me luck."

"Call me back as soon as you're done."

"I promise." She pressed the end call button and slipped the phone into her raincoat pocket. The light mist of drizzle wetted her shoulders as she crossed the street and pushed open the tidy picket fence gate.

The creak of the hinges made her stiffen, afraid that announcing her arrival would somehow jinx her ability to do what needed to be done.

She trotted up the short sidewalk to the house, her heels clacking on the cement path. She ducked under the cover of the porch and did her best to screw up her nerve.

She stepped forward and pressed the doorbell before stepping back. She waited nervously for somebody to answer then pressed the button again. Straining to listen, she didn't hear a chime from within, so she resorted to knocking.

Her gloved hand muffled the sound somewhat, but a moment later she noticed shadows moving inside.

She stepped back from the door and squared her shoulders, clearing her throat as the locks inside turned. She planted her best smile as the door cracked then opened.

A weary-eyed gentleman stood inside, wiping at his mouth with a paper towel. "Can I help you with something?"

She cleared her throat again and held her hand out. "My name is Patricia Murphy." The man stared at her hand then looked up at her, his brow raised.

"So?"

She slowly lowered her hand and licked her lips nervously. "Are you, by chance, FBI Special Agent Dale Archer?"

FROM THE DESK OF HEATH STALLCUP

A personal note-

Thank you so much for investing your time in reading my story. If you enjoyed it, please take a moment and leave a review. I realize that it may be an inconvenience, but reviews mean the world to authors.

Also, I love hearing from my readers. You can reach me at my blog:

http://heathstallcup.com/

or via email at heathstallcup@gmail.com

Feel free to check out my Facebook page for information on upcoming releases:

https://www.facebook.com/heathstallcup

find me on Twitter at @HeathStallcup, Goodreads or via my

Author Page at Amazon.

ABOUT THE AUTHOR

Heath Stallcup was born in Salinas, California and relocated to Tupelo, Oklahoma in his tween years. He joined the US Navy and was stationed in Charleston, SC and Bangor, WA shortly after junior college. After his second tour he attended East Central University where he obtained BS degrees in Biology and Chemistry. He then served ten years with the State of Oklahoma as a Compliance and Enforcement Officer while moonlighting nights and weekends with his local Sheriff's Office. He still lives in the small township of Tupelo, Oklahoma with his wife. He steals time to write between household duties, going to ballgames, being a grandfather and the pet of numerous animals that have taken over his home. Visit him at heathstallcup.com or Facebook.com for news of his upcoming releases.

GENOSKWA THE SERIES

GENOSKWA
SURVIVAL
3
HEATH
STALLCUP

ALSO BY HEATH STALLCUP

Caldera The Series

Monster Squad The Series

Hunter The Series

Nocturna The Series

Whispers Trilogy

Bobbie Bridger series

Genoskwa Series

Ain't No St. Nick

Sinful

Forneus Corson The Idea Man

Mind Trip

ALSO FROM DEVILDOG PRESS

www.devildogpress.com

Zombie Fallout Series By Mark Tufo

Caldera Book 1 By Heath Stallcup

All That Remain By Travis Tufo

From The Ash by Dave Heron

Heart Of Jet By Sheila Shedd

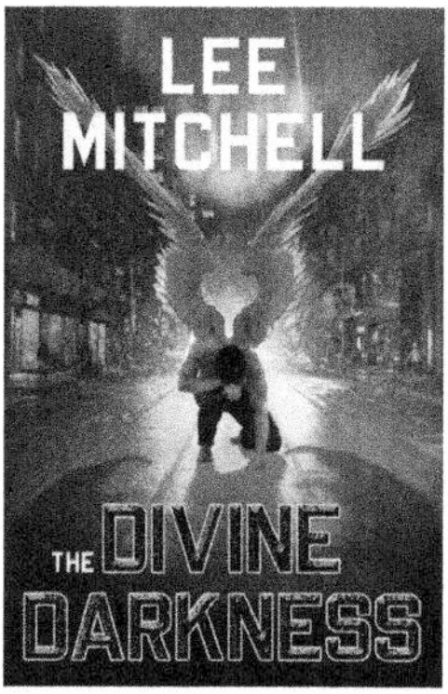

The Devine Darkness by Lee Mitchell

Shifters: A Samantha Reece Mystery Book 1 by Jaime Johnesee

CUSTOMERS ALSO PURCHASED

Printed in Great Britain
by Amazon

62976470R00190